Van

Eight

Luna,
Hope you enjoy!

George Kramer

George Kramer

Other books by George Kramer:
YA Fantasy:
Arcadis Prophecy
Arcadis War
Arcadis Special Edition (Books one and two plus a short story)
Arcadis Decimation
Arcadis Emperor of all, Emperor on None
Arcadis Convergence
Arcadis To walk among the Gods
Arcadis Days of Reckoning
Arcadis Crucial Choices
Arcadis Nothing is as it Seems

Murder/Mystery:
To Some It's Just A Rose

Medical Horror:
Blind to Blood
Blind to Blood 2 The Endgame

Collection of short stories:
Shattered Lives

Poetry:
Pondering Existence
What then is the written word for?

Non-fiction:
Conversations with Caris

Supernatural:
Vampires Of The Eight

Graphic novel:
Arcadis Prophecy's Origin

(Only available through me. Use my email below)

If you want to read more about my books, please go to:
www.amazon.com/author/georgekramer

If you enjoyed my book(s) and would like to email me, go to:
georgekramerauthor@gmail.com

Dedication

I want to thank Ray Wininger for his usual support while I am writing a new book. To Bryan Evans, who always provides me with a "sciencey" response that has merit. Chris Maksymczak was instrumental in helping me find a solution to a struggle I had at the beginning of the story.

To my beta readers, Michelle Sargent and Ginger Cook, I thank you!

To my wife and daughter, as always, give me the freedom to write, especially when I am in my writing zone.

A special heartfelt thanks and shout out to my friend and editor Kelly Lopez Dillion! She did a fantastic job!

And to the people that enjoy my books, thank you!

BLOOD TYPE COMPATIBILITY CHART

Can <u>Receive</u> From or <u>Take</u> Blood From

BLOOD TYPES	O-	O+	B-	B+	A-	A+	AB-	AB+
AB+	X	X	X	X	X	X	X	X
AB-	X		X		X		X	
A+	X	X			X	X		
A-	X				X			
B+	X	X	X	X				
B-	X		X					
O+	X	X						
O-	X							

*This is **not** a **donation** chart. Instead, it's a **receiving** chart. Nor does it contain plasma criteria. For example, an O negative person can **donate** to any other blood type, but can only **receive** O negative blood. **Being able to take blood** is the focus of my book.

List of blood types and their rulers:

O Positive	Sol Rastin, Ray Greenwell
A Positive	Octavus, the Brooder
B Positive	Silvia, the Hopeful
AB Positive	Clayton Cole, the Archetype
O Negative	Maryl Rosser, the Seeker
A Negative	Salvatore, the Great
B Negative	Trevor, the Giant
AB Negative	Platov, the Compromiser

Chapter One

Present Day, May 3rd

Clayton Cole was leisurely strolling along the worn-out path on his estate when he sniffed the air, stopped, and trembled with delight. His well-toned six-foot frame stiffened as he determined the origin of the delicious aroma. His long brown hair twisted in all directions in the summer's swift breeze.

His ultra-keen vision found his potential prey sixty yards to the north. With unmatched stealth, Clayton silently sped to the brink of the tree line. He stole a gaze from the edge of the thick tree trunk. There was a clearing with a large meadow where Clayton saw a human woman who was humming an unfamiliar tune. The woman was picking flowers and herbs and placing them in her woven basket.

The tall green grass went well past her thighs as she leaned over to smell a flower. As she stood upright, the woman smiled as a warm breeze skirted through, which made her long blond hair fall in her face. She gazed down, picked a flower, stood up, and swatted flies away with her basket.

"Shoo, you pesky buggers!"

Clayton could see her blood throbbing and pumping throughout her soft, delicate body.

Clayton silently gauged how much longer the woman had to live when he unconsciously placed his hand on the tree. He saw the ancient language made from dried blood that remained engraved in it from his finger a hundred years ago. The blood was much brighter than he remembered. Clayton slowly traced the old and familiar tongue when he realized he was at the perimeter where he wouldn't step beyond. If he didn't want to break the treaty with the other blood types, Clayton would remain where he was.

He was hungry, but he would not cross the boundary line. "Damn!" He cursed silently to himself. The human woman was his blood type too!

Clayton took one last look at his lost meal and was turning when something caught his attention. He went back to the enormous tree trunk and could smell predators that were eyeing *his* abandoned prey. Then a thought surfaced. If Clayton could breathe in their scent, it was more than likely the other intruders could smell him too.

Curious, Clayton let his presence be known and walked to the opening between his treeline and the vast field that stretched for miles. He watched as the other raiders quickly overtook the woman. The woman's woven basket flew in the air while all the plants and herbs scattered on the ground. Before they attempted to devour the precious ingredient of life, the vampires looked straight at Clayton and smiled.

Clayton came to the edge of the perimeter and stared at the three vampires as he put his hands behind his back. He was not afraid of them or of them crossing the boundary line.

"Nice try," Clayton called to them.

The biggest of the three vampires, who wore a hunter green tee shirt and jeans, spoke first. "What do you mean?" he demanded.

Clayton sniffed the air. He let a few seconds go by before responding. "I could smell the three of you." He pointed to one of them. "You, the big guy, are O positive blood type. The other two are O negative. You know what that means?" he said with a smile.

They remained silent. The human woman was frantically trying to escape the clutches of the men.

Clayton looked at the taller of the three vampires and exhaled deeply. Why must he have to explain to the younger vampires the rules of their existence? They should know. "Then let me refresh your young memory. O positive vampires can only take blood from O positive or O negative humans." He turned his head to the other two and pointed. "And both of you are O negatives, which means you can only obtain blood from O negative humans. So stop pretending you're going to suck her blood because she is AB positive. (1) Unless, of course, you want to so I can witness your slow and agonizing deaths."

The shortest of the three took hold of the crying human woman. He sniffed the air as his eyes turned dark. "And I know *you're* an AB positive, which means you want her blood, don't you mister?" He took a finger and sliced a deep thin line across her throat. The human started to gurgle. Fear and incomprehension fell upon her face. "You want some of her? Come here and get some while she's still warm."

Clayton felt the familiar stirring from the crimson fluid even though he knew it was a trap. The three of them had to be relatively new vampires to think he was stupid enough to cross the boundary line. "Doesn't matter," Clayton stated casually even as his hunger intensified as he saw the sweet red nectar gently oozing downward from her creamy throat.

"Oh, it doesn't matter?" The shortest vampire challenged. "Then, this won't matter…" He took the woman's head and snapped it as if it were a twig. The woman fell to the ground, unmoving. Her brown eyes looked vacantly up to the sky. The flowers and herbs, now free, were dancing with the wind in a circular motion.

Clayton refused to show emotion at the useless waste of a good meal.

The vampires smirked as they slowly walked to the borderline.

Clayton walked to his side of the boundary until they were a couple of feet away from each other. The wind picked up and caused Clayton's long hair to sway at the wind's discretion.

"Looks like you won't be having a meal anytime soon."

"Look like it," Clayton stated casually. He smiled and turned around. He walked a few feet before one of the vampires commented.

"Your time is coming!" one of them yelled.

Clayton gave a slight pause before walking further away.

"Did you hear me?"

With sudden ferociousness, Clayton zipped back to his borderline. "Do tell."

The sudden appearance of Clayton startled them for a second.

"You don't scare us!" The bigger one boasted.

"I shouldn't scare you; after all, there are three of you and only one of me," Clayton said with slight amusement. He brushed his hair back in place with his long fingers.

The taller vampire sniffed the air in contempt. "Maybe you'll have more luck on your side of the border."

"Maybe," Clayton said, taking a few steps backward, facing them in the event they tried to cross his borderline. He continued taking steps back, thinking the conversation was over.

"That's right, go ahead and retreat!" the shortest vampire taunted.

Clayton held his laughter in check as he stopped in his tracks. "How old are the three of you?"

The tallest one said, "I am the oldest of these parts. I turned twelve years ago. The middle guy, Steven, turned eight years ago, and Jerry, the smallest one of us, had only recently turned five years ago."

Jerry's bald head grew red, and his teeth clenched. "Davey, you just told the Stranger our names!"

"Really? Ah, to be young again! Do you have any idea how old I am, and who I am?" Clayton asked in a whispered tone.

Jerry, the shortest vampire, looked at him with contempt. "No, and we don't care, you're an AB type. It doesn't matter if it's negative or positive. The AB's have had their time!"

"Quiet!" admonished Davey, the big one.

"Really, and why is that?" Clayton asked with curiosity.

"Remember the Great Yeomen Purge of 1751?" Jerry boasted.

Clayton hid his anguish and suppressed a shudder. "You know of the Purge? Did they teach you that in school?

"Just answer my question, mister!" Jerry said with rising anger. "Do you remember the Great Yeomen Purge of 1751?"

Clayton sighed. "Yes, of course, *because I was there*. And?"

"You, you were there?" Jerry asked in awe.

"Yes," Clayton stated.

"Shut up!" the other vampires said in unison.

Jerry regained his composure. "No, I will not shut up! For far too long, the AB tribe have thought themselves the top of the vampire food chain. Remember, history tends to repeat itself!"

Clayton walked in anger until his feet were at the cusp of the boundary. His body stiffened to the point of being rigid. "*A great deal of my family perished in the great yeomen purge of 1751*," Clayton said between clenched teeth. "So, before I break the treaty and break all of your necks, let me tell you something about myself. My name is Clayton Cole of the Cole tribe, and spare me your useless scare tactics. It will not work on me. In a few days, I will be celebrating my thousandth birthday. And the three of you combined are only twenty-five years old, just two and a half percent of my age!"

Clayton knew *his* scare tactic worked because their stance shifted to a fighting posture. Clayton waited for them to try something foolish despite knowing they wouldn't dare. They knew who he was now; he saw not only fear in their eyes but recognition too.

Without another word, the three of them retraced their steps and left. Clayton stood in place for a few minutes. While the three vampires retreated, he contemplated what one of them had said. Was there a strife or war brewing among the different blood types of vampires? And if so, why wasn't he aware of it? In a few short weeks, it would not matter. His well thought out plan would come to fruition.

He walked back to the tall, thick tree. So much had changed within the centuries he had been alive. With gentleness, he placed his hand on the ancient tree, closed his eyes, and remembered the day it all began when he ascended to vampire-hood almost a thousand years ago. Quiet tears found their way out of his eye ducts as they gently strolled down his face.

Chapter Two
1020 AD Year of Clayton's Ascension

Clayton paused before entering the dark, dank, and foreboding underground cave. He peered at his mother with anxiety. "What's going to happen to me?"

His mother, Tabatha, looked at her son. "You know I can't tell you much, Clayton. The only thing you need to know is it's your thirteenth birthday, and you will ascend to vampire-hood just like the rest of our tribe."

Clayton nodded and, at his mother's insistence, began to move forward.

"Why couldn't I just be born a vampire? Why do I have to ascend at thirteen?" Clayton asked. He could feel his heart race and his palms were sweaty.

Tabatha took a few deep breaths as she prodded her son to move forward. "When we are born, we are called in-betweeners. While we can take nourishment from the blood sack when we're in our mother's womb, our bodies can't handle the power when we are given human blood as babies. Children, even babies, have gone insane, and if you think puberty in humans can be rough, imagine times that by ten thousand with our culture." Tabatha sighed. "Generations ago, our ancestors decided the transformation was too difficult and brutal on babies, kids, and of course, the parents. Our tribe met and decided to enact a law forbidding anyone to transform before the age of thirteen."

"Why?"

Tabatha put out her hand. "Come, Clayton. There's no time for more questions."

Clayton looked ahead. "It's dark at the end of the tunnel, mother."

"Yes, and it needs to be so. There are candles further down to light your way," his mother said with a composure that she did not feel.

Clayton walked several more yards and stopped. His body shook and quivered. "I don't know if I am ready for my ascension, mother!"

Tabatha went to her knee and knelt beside Clayton. She placed her steady hands on his trembling shoulders. "Look at me, Clayton! Get hold of yourself! You are going to ascend today. Everyone in our tribe does. You *have* to push through your fears just like the rest of us had to."

Clayton bit his lower lip. "But I am nervous, mother! Suppose I die?"

"Don't be silly. No one has ever died in the ascension to vampire-hood."

"But I am both a non-vampire and a vampire. I am an in-betweener until I ascend. I can be hurt!"

"True, but you are far tougher and stronger than a human." Tabatha looked at her young son.

His dark hair came down to his nose. Tabatha combed his hair with her fingers and straightened his posture. She looked at her son and smiled warmly.

"I will let you in on a well-kept secret, Clayton. Vampires are not the undead creatures described in the oral history of humans. We have all of the *same* body parts as a typical human. Our hearts pump and beat like them. We can cry; we have hunger pains, and women give birth. But how we differ from humans is our skin is impenetrable, meaning nothing can get through it. A wooden stake will not kill us, nor will sunlight. Garlic and holy water do not affect us, nor does anything in folklore. We have superhuman strength, hyper hearing, and hyper seeing abilities. We are *nearly* immortal, yet you're afraid of some silly ritual?" She seized Clayton's innocent face. *"Think of the power that will course throughout your body once you ascend, Clayton!"*

"What can kill us?" Clayton asked his mother to stall for time.

Tabatha stood up and looked down at her son. "The only thing known that can kill us is by another vampire. Only we have the strength to penetrate each other's skin."

"Huh? You told me we couldn't be hurt because we have skin that no one can pierce."

Tabatha looked at the darkened cave and held her hand out to Clayton. "All the other smeller vampires are strong enough. We don't have time to talk about this topic. You will ascend. You *must* ascend!"

"What are other smeller vampires?"

Tabatha ignored his question. The ceremony will provide the answers he sought.

They walked several yards. The darkness surrounded them.

"Where are we going, mother? I can't see."

"When you gain your powers, you will be able to see much better in the dark. We have to make a right turn soon."

"I thought you said there were candles."

"There are Clayton. It will start to get lighter soon. Don't worry; I will guide you. We placed the candles much further in to avoid any nosey and curious humans."

They turned right and walked for some time. Clayton tried to listen for any sounds or signs to tell him they were close. He heard a chorus of voices in his language. Strange, thought Clayton. He could discern a human man nearby, and the man was yelling and screaming in the human tongue.

The further along they went, the brighter it became. Clayton and his mother made another right and came to a large clearing. He noticed that his relatives were sitting side by side. He looked up at the ceiling; it towered over himself and his mother.

Clayton saw a thick chain descending from the high ceiling that went down, which kept the yelling human bound. The man was on his knees, with the chain behind his back that held his arms and legs secure. He was not wearing any cloth skins or sandals.

Clayton looked back down and saw his family gathered around the inner circle, and several outer groups surrounded them with members of his and other tribes. They were chanting a familiar tune used in the ancient ritual.

Clayton waved to his younger sister and brother, and they eagerly waved back.

Clayton's father, Tarson, rose. As he stood erect, the chanting halted. His eyes grew dark, and he lifted his hands to the towering ceiling as he addressed the tribes.

"Fellow tribesman, we stand before you today, as we have for generations, to welcome my son, Clayton Cole, to ascend to his vampire-hood!"

Cheers echoed over the steep canyon.

Tarson looked around and beamed with pride as he gazed upon his son for a moment. His attention turned back to the tribes. "All of you who are standing here today have bore witness to our other tribesmen in celebrating their ascension. I only wish my great-grandfather and father were alive to see!"

Tarson thought of the battle with the other smellers that killed some of his lineages. He shook the memory away. It took him a few seconds to regain his composure.

"Now, in accordance with the bylaws that have been handed down orally since my grandfather, we will start the ceremony!" Tarson roared.

Tabatha squirmed where she stood. She hoped Clayton would go through the ceremony without complaint. Her son questioned everything.

Tabatha noticed a distant relative look at her, but couldn't remember her name. Tabatha politely smiled despite the trepidation she felt inside.

She shivered. The next part of the ceremony was vital.

"As you know, my tribe has difficulty bearing children. To have three children was a gift from the gods!"

Praises reverberated from the walls of the vast room.

"As per part of the ceremony, I must ask, does anyone object to my son's ascension?" Tarson asked coldly. Tarson expected no resistance, and none spoke up. No one dared to. No vampire in their right mind would deny his son ascension. Being an archetype had its perks, Tarson mused to himself.

Tabatha sighed with relief. She had heard the rumors circling the tribes of Clayton not fitting in the vampire's world and hoped no one would question her son's ascension. Tabatha knew, with certainty, Clayton needed to ascend because he was a thinker and not a being that would play by the rules. Changes were coming, she knew, and Clayton was the vampire that could make the necessary changes. Her younger son, Milas, and her youngest daughter, Beatrice, would not. They were followers, not leaders. She came out of her daydream when she heard her husband speak again.

"Clayton, come to me!" Tarson demanded.

Clayton's long dark hair bounced up and down as he sprinted to his father. The tribesmen let him pass as he stood next to his father.

"As in the oral traditions of the past, I will ask you only *once*; Clayton, my eldest son, do you agree to ascend to vampire-hood and forsake your former life as an in-betweener?"

Clayton felt a sense of pride as he scanned the room. He could *feel* the electrifying atmosphere. "I do! I so swear it!" He gazed around and witnessed the joy coming from his mother and father.

Tabatha's apprehension vanished when the clapping of her tribesmen's fists into their palms rose in chorus.

Tarson acknowledged his tribe's reaction by smiling for a moment. Then a change came over him. His eyes grew even darker, and his posture stiffened.

"It is time to talk about the rules of our tribe, Clayton! These rules apply to everyone, and they will ensure our survival." He looked at Clayton to make sure he had his attention.

"First off, you are never allowed to kill one of your own types, but if threatened, you may kill other types of vampires."

"I don't understand, father," Clayton said in earnest.

Tarson looked at his son with seriousness. "The rules are clear, Clayton."

"I understand that, father. What I don't understand are the other types of vampires you mentioned."

A sudden understanding came over Tarson. "Ah, the different types. When you feed, you can not only feed on a human with sweet-smelling blood but any other smelling human."

"Sweet-smelling blood?"

"Yes. There is sweeter smelling blood, while some are saltier, and still, others are sour. One type had a bitter taste."

"Isn't sour and bitter the same thing, father?"

"No. Sour is like some yellow fruits, while bitter is similar to the broths your mother makes. But don't worry. Once you attain vampire-hood, you'll be able to smell the different types of blood."

"How could you tell unless you drank their blood?"

"Once you become a vampire, your senses will emerge much more robust and potent than humans! You will be able to smell which kind of blood the other vampires have and, more importantly, what type the humans have."

"What happens if a salt smeller, a bitter smeller, or a sour smeller took our sweeter blood?"

Tarson looked at the crowd. "My son is asking important questions before his ascension! To those that will eventually ascend, take notice!" He returned his attention to Clayton. "They would die a painful death because the types of blood are mismatched. Even though our tribe is small, we can take blood from *any* human, and because of that, we are far stronger than the other tribes. That's why the other vampires have hunted us throughout the ages. However, we are at our strongest when we feed upon the sweet-smelling humans."

"Honey, enough questions for your father. We have a ceremony to perform," Tabatha said in frustration.

Tarson put up a hand. "It's no bother, wife. He is learning. Other tribesmen have had similar questions in times past. Clayton's questions must be answered before the ceremony continues." He looked at Clayton. "Any more questions, son?"

"Yes, father. Don't some humans become vampires?"

His father's eyes grew tighter. "Yes, although we sweet smellers, do *not* partake."

"Why not?"

"Because it decreases the purity of our tribe!" Tarson spat.

The tribe acknowledged Tarson's statement by the robust clapping of fists to their palms.

Clayton had to wait for the clapping to finish to resume. "How come I don't possess a thirst for blood?"

"Because, at this point, you still eat human food because you're still an in-betweener. Food suppresses the urge for blood."

"After I ascend, will I still be able to eat human food?"

"Yes, if you wanted to suppress your vampire-hood. The only reason you would need to suppress your blood thirst is if there is a shortage of humans to feed upon."

"Okay. One more question, father, if I may?"

Tarson nodded. "As I've stated, there are other children here that will eventually ascend that need to hear your questions, Clayton."

"How, and when, did several types of smellers become different?"

Tarson's face hardened. That was the most challenging question to answer.

"The lineage of our family of vampires started with my great-grandfather a millennia ago. The oral history tells us of a tall lone woman who roamed the lands where we dwell. It was said the Stranger came to the farm my great-grandfather owned, begging for food. However, as the story goes, the Stranger wanted food of a different kind. She sought blood. The beggar promised our ancestor goods equal to and above gold if the Stranger could have some of his pregnant wife's blood. The hobo promised eternal life."

"And she produced all types of smelling vampires, father?"

"Yes," Tarson stated simply.

"We are the sweet-smelling blood you have told me about, father. How did we get the other types?" Clayton asked.

"Back then, when my great-grandfather agreed to the conditions set forth by the Stranger, he learned the same vagabond made agreements with seven other pregnant women in the area after his. Each family member, once bitten, discovered they smelled differently."

"Who was the Stranger?"

"No one knows."

Tarson turned to his audience. His voice boomed over the whimpering human who was attempting to break his chains. "And every hundred years, the Stranger comes back and promises other expectant families the same arrangement!" Tarson put up his index finger. "Lest all of you remember! My family, the Cole Tribe, is the oldest member of our Tribes, for they were bitten first!"

Thunderous applause erupted through the enormous room. Palms to fist reverberated across the vast room. When the praise ended, Clayton looked at his father.

"Has anyone ever turned the woman down with her request?" Clayton asked with concern.

"Not to my knowledge," Tarson said impatiently.

Clayton nodded.

"Now, for the final part of the ceremony!" He turned to his son. "Clayton, you *must* now drink the blood of the chained human for the transformation to take place!"

A chanting rose from the gathered. "*Drink! Drink! Drink!*" The chorus became deafening as Clayton deliberately slowed his pace to the shackled human.

Tabatha smiled in pride as her eldest son approached the worthless puny human.

The human's eyes enlarged with fear when Clayton was upon him. He struggled to break the thick restraints.

"See how he cowers in fear of you, Clayton? Yet he is unaware his sacrifice will continue to allow our bloodline to survive!" Tarson yelled to his flock.

Clayton's body shuddered, but this time it was not from fear. No, Clayton had surpassed that emotion. It was a new feeling that emerged. It now became a sense of supremacy that he, Clayton Cole, felt knowing he would be welcomed and accepted into his and the other tribes.

Clayton stood beside the human, bent down, and forced the man up for all those to see.

"With my family and tribes before me, I now become a vampire!"

"Get your filthy fangs off me!" the man screamed.

"Clayton, as you drink the human's blood, you will feel unbelievable power course through your body! Your strength, eyesight, bone thickness, and unbreakable skin will increase to a level you never dreamt about!" Tarson shouted above the human's whimpering.

Clayton took hold of the human's head and moved it to the left to make his throat exposed.

"Son, there are two places to suck the blood out. Since you're new, feel his throat and go for the thinner place where blood flows slower!" Tarson warned.

He turned from the human. "Why?" demanded Clayton? By now, the anticipation was overwhelming.

"If you suck blood from the thicker blood flow, the blood comes out much faster, and the change comes over you much quicker! Sometimes the rush of energy is too much for an in-betweener."

Clayton turned back to the human and felt for the thicker blood flow, ignoring his father's request. He could see and feel the crimson fluid pumping. He felt a rush like no other overcome his senses! Like a beast that was starving, Clayton bit into the center of the thicker stream that coursed through the human that would provide him with life-altering energy and nourishment.

As he drank the dark fluid that was gushing into his mouth, Clayton soaked in the potent blood at such a rapid pace; he couldn't stop himself!

After a few seconds, Tabatha grew concerned. "That's enough, Clayton!"

Clayton heard his mother, but it was more like a voice from a distant dream. The sheer rush of energy and power made him ignore his mother's command as he continued to soak up the blood that flew freely from the human's throbbing neck.

He was slowly being pushed away from his meal. Someone was trying to thwart his ascension, and he would have none of it! How dare they!

"That's enough, son!" Tarson ordered.

He heard his father's command but ignored it. He was so close to draining the life from his food supply, couldn't they see that?

Clayton was facing the human, draining the life-juice out of the man until Tarson grabbed his shoulders and threw him across the room. "I said that was enough!"

Clayton swiftly scurried on all fours to a nearby corner. His vision became sharper, as did his hearing. He put his fists into the air and shouted in unbelievable joy at the unparalleled power he felt coursing through his body!

The different tribes, which were all offshoots of the Cole tribe, stood up in unison and sang praise for the ascension of Clayton Cole.

Clayton Cole was now officially a vampire.

Chapter Three
The Council Square 1522

The birth of the twins Grady and Markus Cole was a cause for celebration. It had been over five hundred years since the childbirth of a sweet blood vampire had been born in the Cole tribe. The difficulty with the sweet smellers and the continuation of their kind weighed heavily on Clayton's mind.

After the three-day celebration in which he got to see his family once again, Clayton was in his small kitchen having dinner, while Ada Cole was feeding the twins in their bedroom.

Ada walked in and sat down beside Clayton. He was contemplative as Ada studied him. His long brown hair parted in the middle gave him a look of a holy man. Clayton had the bluest eyes she had ever seen. He had a thin, but a muscular body that astounded Ada with his feats of strength. Clayton was over five hundred years old, and she was only two hundred and forty-one, which was a young woman by their standards.

"What are you thinking about, husband?"

He looked at Ada, his wife of thirty-seven years. Her brown eyes were rare in this part of England. Her robust frame only enhanced her beauty. Ada's long blond hair fell until it reached her lower back.

"I think there are far too few humans around these parts. I think we should move."

Ada was taken aback. "Move? Move where?"

"Somewhere there are more sweet-smelling humans," Clayton said cautiously.

"Why can't we suck the blood from animals? They run around unchecked as if they're daring us to suck nourishment from them!" Ada said in exasperation. Ever since she could remember, she was forbidden to take blood from animals.

"Other vampires have tried and died horribly. I imagine it has something to do with our blood not being able to recognize theirs." Clayton pondered for a moment. "I don't want to keep eating human food; while it sustains our existence, it suppresses our vampirism. If other types of smelling vampires sense any kind of weakness, our sweet-smelling kind will be in trouble!"

"But Clayton, we have family and friends here! Where will we go?"

He looked at Ada. He hesitated before speaking. "I was in private talks with a boatsman this past week. The boatsman knows of land across the pond that is big and vast."

"Does he even know if humans live there?" Ada asked with concern.

"The man claims he has seen native people, tribes just like us."

"I don't know, Clayton," Ada said reluctantly. "Even if we do decide to move, we would need permission from the council."

"I am the head of the council, Ada," Clayton said with a touch of annoyance.

"I know that, Clayton! But, if we don't seek and get their approval, especially from your mother, we will be banished for life. Think of our children!"

Clayton stood up and pounded his fist on the oak table. "Dammit, Ada! I am thinking of them. I am thinking of us and our very survival too! Do you think we're the only ones in this predicament?"

"So, you've been talking to other sweet smellers about moving away from our tribes without my knowledge?"

"Consider yourself told," Clayton said a little too forcibly.

He looked at Ada, sat back down, and put his hands over hers. "I am sorry, Ada. But honey, we have to do *something*. I haven't taken blood from a human in a while. Is there anything you can suggest that I didn't think of that could help?"

Ada thought for a moment. Her eyes darted back and forth. "How about if our entire tribe moved with us? There's strength in numbers. No other vampires are going there that you know about, right?"

"Yes, none that I know about. Your point does have merit. It would take some convincing from the other council members."

"And what about your mother? Do you think she will go along with your scheme? After all, she is on the council too. She's rooted in the affairs of our tribe. You do not care about the day to day activities; therefore, she holds more sway than even you."

"We shall see," Clayton said as they heard loud banging on the door.

"Who could it be this late in the evening? The festivities are complete," Ada complained.

Clayton took a whiff of the scent outside. "It's one of our sweet smellers."

He opened the door. His neighbor, Pierre, fell on top of him.

Clayton carried him to the couch, propped up a giant fluffy pillow, which he knew was a sign of affluence many of his neighbors did not have. Clayton made him rest while he retrieved water from the well outside.

After Pierre took several sips of water, he managed to sit upright. He glanced at the expensive pillow but said nothing.

"Pierre, what was so urgent that you banged on my door at this hour?" Clayton asked with compassion.

"The sour smellers attacked us!"

"What? Are you sure?" Ada asked with skepticism.

"Of course, I'm sure, Ada! I barely made it out alive!"

"How many of them are there, and are they still here?" Clayton asked as anger built up inside him.

Pierre took a quick gulp of water before answering. "At least a half dozen of them. And they are still here because they were looking for you! You need to go out there and save our families! They want you to meet them at the Council Square now, Clayton."

Clayton was out the door in less than a second, followed by Ada. It took them less than five seconds to get to the Council Square.

The Council Square was in the middle of the town. The square itself was made of wood from the abundance of trees that surrounded outside their village of crops. The square wasn't square but built round to accommodate a circle so every council member could face each other.

Clayton walked up the steps and smelled five male sour smellers and one female. He looked at Ada, and she knew that she would have to take care of the woman vampire despite being in a weakened state. She nodded.

Six vampires came out from behind one of the houses from the right side of the large wooden deck where the council met. Each of the sour smellers had a sweet-smelling vampire as hostages.

Only he and Ada were at the Council Square ready to do battle, but he could smell his vampires, and he could smell their fear despite being stronger than the enemy.

"I am called Eli, and I am the one in charge here!" Eli was taller than Clayton, but not by much. Eli did have thirty or forty pounds on Clayton, which didn't concern him. What bothered him was he had been eating human food for the past two weeks. He didn't know how much strength he had left against them.

"You're in charge? I don't think so," Clayton said with contempt.

"Where are all your friends? You and your Maid going to fight the six of us?"

Clayton chuckled. "Maid? That was funny, Eli. Tell you what, since you made me laugh, I will let you and your friends go without killing you."

"My, my, aren't you the confident one? See, here's where I tell you the bad news. We've been doing some scouting." Eli pointed his finger all around the village.

"You haven't had much to drink or eat for two weeks or so."

Carefully concealing his shock, Clayton said, "It doesn't matter. If I have to, I will die to save my friends."

Eli brought the captured vampire close to him, closed his eyes, and took a whiff. "You'd die for these sweet-smelling folks?"

Clayton had enough as he stepped down from the square. He and Ada took several steps toward them.

"That's far enough, mister!" one of Eli's friends said as he placed both hands on Pierre's wife.

Without warning, the sour-smelling woman vampire rushed to Ada and punched her in her chest. Ada went sailing into a nearby house and was rendered unconscious.

Clayton ran at top speed, grabbed the woman vampire by the head, and snapped her neck, instantly killing her. He looked down at her and spat.

"You just killed my wife!" Eli yelled.

"Shame. Call it justification!" He pointed around the village. "This is my land, not yours! And I will fight for it with my dying breath!" Clayton said with conviction.

"Your place? Not for long!" Eli said with supreme confidence.

Clayton put his hands around his back. "I'll make a deal with you, Eli."

Eli's blue eyes lit up with excitement. "What kind of deal are we talking about?"

"Release all of my friends, and I will single handedly fight the six... sorry, your wife is dead, make that five of you, I will fight."

Eli did not like Clayton's comment. He and the others took a few steps toward Clayton.

Instead of backing away, Clayton walked toward them. Eli seemed confused Clayton did not fear them.

"You know you cannot hope to win against the five of us, right?"

Clayton shrugged his shoulders.

"Think you're pretty tough, Clayton?"

"Are you going to accept my deal, or are you going to talk me to death?"

Eli looked at Clayton, then looked at his friends. All of them nodded in agreement.

"Okay, we accept your offer!"

They quickly surrounded Clayton. He knew at his current level of strength from not sucking blood for so long; he could take two, maybe three of them, but not all five. But he would not, could not back down in front of his tribe. Clayton was hoping one of his tribesmen would help him because he knew he would not win the fight. And that meant certain death.

Clayton had to make the first move, or his death would be quick. He sped toward Eli's friend and snapped his neck, but less than a second later, he felt a kick in his back, which made him fall. He was far weaker than he realized.

"Not up to your usual strength level, are you, Clayton?" Eli said tauntingly.

The four vampires rushed to Clayton. They started kicking him and beating him to a pulp. Clayton was helpless as Eli lifted him harshly by his throat. Eli addressed the vampires that refused to come out of their homes.

"There's a new breed of vampires here today! We shall take over your lands and kill every one of you, sweet-smellers!" Eli said in triumph.

While Eli was bragging, Clayton took a whiff, whirled around, and managed to get loose.

Eli saw the two newcomers entering the area. "And who are you?"

"I am Clayton's father, Tarson, and this is my wife, Tabatha, and we have come to aid Clayton."

Eli looked at Tarson and Tabatha, shook his head, and scorned. "You can't do that; it's against the engagement rules. Clayton agreed to fight alone and without help."

"I am not planning on giving my son any *physical* help," Tabatha stated simply.

"Then how are you to aid him?" Eli asked in confusion.

"By doing this!" Tabatha removed a cup and threw it in the air.

Clayton sprang into action as he leaped in the air, caught the cup, and landed with the cup still in his hand. He drank greedily from it. Unbridled power surged through him quickly! In no time, Clayton was upon the sour smellers. He rushed to each vampire and, one by one with breathtaking speed broke the necks of all of them except Eli.

"I'm pretty sure that was against the rules," Eli remarked in protest.

"You took advantage of a bad situation. I made sure to even the odds," Tarson said with hatred.

"How did you know about Eli?" Clayton asked his parents as he grabbed Eli's throat and squeezed.

"We were out on patrol when we spotted them hurrying toward here. We knew we hadn't been at our best. Your mother and I went to several towns trying to find a human who had the same blood as we do to make you stronger than if you had other smelling human blood."

The bruising of Clayton's ribs and his face were slowly disappearing. He felt whole again.

Clayton walked to where Ada was sitting up and leaning against a house. Eli fought to release himself from Clayton's iron grip.

"Let me go, Clayton! Now that you're at full vamp power, I won't be able to go anywhere!"

Clayton released him and gave him a stern glance.

"Your parents arrived just in time, husband!"

"Yes, they sure did. How are you feeling?" Clayton asked in concern as he helped her up.

"I've been better. I wish they had more blood for us."

"Me too, Ada. It is getting harder and harder for us to find *any* type of smelling humans to nourish ourselves."

"At least we were able to help you, Clayton," Tabatha said as she pointed at Eli. "What are you going to do with him?"

"He knew of our lack of nourishment."

"What? How?" Tarson asked in surprise.

"He told me other vampires have been scouting us," Clayton said with concern.

"Impossible!" Tabatha said in surprise.

"There's only one way to find out," Clayton said as he pushed Eli away from the Council Square.

"What are you planning on doing to him to extract the information?" Ada asked as she walked next to Clayton and Eli.

"What do you think I am going to do with him? I am going to torture him until he tells me what else he's learned of his secret surveillance."

Tabatha looked at Eli. "Do you eat human food too?"

"That is none of your business, Madame," Eli said softly.

"Son, bring him to the prison shack, and let's give him some human food. If we can stomach it, they should be able to do so as well. If not," she shrugged as if she didn't care.

"There are slight differences between the different species of vampires, Tabatha. Perhaps we should be careful," Ada said carefully.

Tarson looked sternly at Ada. "They were going to kill all of us, *our entire tribe*, and you want to show them *mercy*? Did I hear that correctly, Ada?"

Clayton looked at his wife in disbelief. "I agree with my father, Ada." He turned to Tabatha. "Mother, after I take Eli to the shack and give him human food, I am calling for a special council session immediately. Please summon the others."

Tabatha nodded. "It is your right."

Clayton took Eli by the scruff of Eli's neck. "Let's get you something to eat."

Tarson waited until Clayton left to speak to Ada. "Ada, your show of leniency disturbs me."

"Why is that? Because I think all of the vampires should be treated fairly?" Ada said quietly.

"I have heard talk from other vampires in our area with that same nonsense! You sound like one of them! Are you a vampire, or are you a sympathizer?" Tarson shouted.

"I am a vampire!" Ada said with confidence.

"Good! It better stay that way!" Tarson glared at her. "It's best if you kept your opinions to yourself about our treatment of other vampires! Do I make myself clear?"

Ada nodded. "Of course, sir."

"Good. I expect you will go to the council session as an observer *only*."

Ada nodded. "I will do as you commanded, sir."

"I am going to summon the council now. Remember my husband's warning, Ada!" Tabatha said as she glared at Ada for a few seconds before speeding away.

Clayton walked with Eli just outside of the village.

"Tell me something, Clayton. Why is it that you're the leader of the Cole tribe, yet Tarson, your father, still lives? Shouldn't he be the ruler?"

"He would rather lead our territorial army then deal with the tribal policies, so I put him in charge. Why?" Clayton said suspiciously.

"Because I fear *him* far more than I fear *you*."

"You should fear both of us!" Clayton said as they came upon a small shack that stood right before the crops started.

Eli saw there was only one window, and it was small, with metal bars. Eli was surprised the hut was made from bricks.

"Nice accommodations, Clayton." He sniffed the air. "Why does it smell like urine and feces?"

Clayton shrugged his shoulders. "It's from the previous prisoners. The former occupants had to relieve themselves somewhere. We've had both vampires and humans held here."

"You don't have to give me human food, Clayton. We can make some sort of arrangement."

Clayton scoffed. "Why would I do that when you had every intention of killing me and my entire village?"

Eli frowned. "Our species has always sought blood and conflict. It has always been like that. And don't tell me your sweet-smelling kind hasn't done the same thing!"

"Not interested," Clayton said as he took a key from a small bag tied to his pants. He unlocked the door and threw Eli inside. "Don't go anywhere. I'll be back."

Eli put his hands on the metal bars. "Wouldn't dream of it." He tested the metal bars. "Has anyone ever escaped the shack?"

"No."

Eli tested the metal bars again. "They seem flimsy to me."

Clayton looked at him and smirked. "You could probably escape. Usually, there are several guards to prevent that from happening. I wish you would try so I can kill you myself."

"You had the opportunity."

"Don't make me regret that decision. If you aren't here when I come back, I will hunt you down, and I don't care who I have to go through!"

A few minutes later, Clayton came back with bread and water.

"Is that the best you can do, Clayton? Bread and water?"

"For prisoners, yes."

"I am not going to eat that," Eli said with mounting dread.

"Yes, you are. If you don't, I will force you to eat it."

Clayton opened the door carefully with one hand.

Eli cringed and walked unsteadily to the back of the tiny shack. "Get that disgusting food away from me!"

Clayton closed the shack door. The putrid smell coming from the dirt floor engulfed both their nostrils. "I will not force you to eat the food if you tell me what you learned about us."

Clayton came closer to Eli, set the water down, but kept the bread in his hand. "Tell me!"

"The fact that there are a lot more different smelling vampires than your precious sweet ones is not my fault!"

"No, it's not. But the extinction of my tribe is—last chance."

"Other than finding out you've been eating human food for some time, nothing, Clayton! I swear it! Anyone with half of a brain knows our sense of smell is significantly better than humans. We travel, we walk, we talk, we observe!"

Clayton shoved the bread under Eli's nose. He noticed red lines starting to form on his face. "So, what you're saying is that everyone knows?"

Eli's eyes watered. "Yes! How could we not? The difference between my kind of smellers and your kind of sweet-smelling vampires is significant!"

"You tried to exploit our weakness!" Clayton took a small piece of bread and stuffed it in one of Eli's nose holes.

Eli coughed, and the red lines were all over his face and starting to go down his neck and throat.

Clayton didn't want to kill Eli, at least not right away. He removed the bread from Eli's nose and put it on the floor near the door. Within a few seconds, Eli returned to normal.

"We will always exploit your weaknesses! And the other kinds of vampires will too rest assured!" Eli yelled.

"I am debating whether or not to kill you right now."

"If you let me live, I will tell the others to leave you and your tribes alone."

Clayton held his stomach while he gave a deep belly laugh. "Right, and I am just supposed to believe you?"

Eli switched tactics. "What would you want to trade my life for?"

Clayton went within inches to Eli's face. "I don't know. What do you have to offer?"

Eli moved back as far as he could. "Sorry, but your sweet-smelling blood sickens me in such close proximity."

Clayton pulled back. "What could you possibly offer me that I would spare your life?"

Eli put his arms across his chest. "What if I told you a secret?"

"It would have to be a big one for me to let you go and explain why to the other council members."

"Will you let me go?"

"Will I live to regret it?"

"Probably."

"At least you're honest, Eli." Clayton stared hard at Eli and debated. "Tell you what, why don't you tell me your secret, and if I think it is worth the pushback I will get from the tribe, I will let you go?"

"How about you promise first?"

"Eli, I just feasted from a sweet-smelling human. I am feeling mighty strong right now; give me another reason to kill you."

Eli knew he had no options left if he wanted to live to see another day. "Fine! The secret is all the tribes are restless. We are tired of England and the king's taxes."

"And your point? All the vampires and humans are too." Clayton walked closer to Eli and did not care if his sweet-smelling blood repulsed him. " I am getting tired of listening to you ramble on."

Eli looked at Clayton. He had to tell him the truth. "My point is they want to migrate to another place."

Clayton folded his arms across his chest. "Another place? Really? Where exactly would that be?"

Eli's eyes darted back and forth. "There are a few boatsmen that we are conversing with that will take us to another faraway land."

"Are they the ones docked not far from here?"

"Yes, there are a handful of boats. They think we're humans and peddling goods."

"How many boats will you need?"

Eli's face grew tense. "That does not concern you, Clayton, nor is that knowledge part of our deal!"

Clayton looked at him for a moment, lost in thought. "Okay, then tell me this, Eli. Did they tell you there are other tribes like yours?"

Eli's eyes squinted. "Yes, why? Were you planning on doing the same thing?"

"Not anymore. You're free to go. And go quickly, before I change my mind."

Clayton opened the door, and Eli fled. Clayton walked to the Council Square and saw the other council members sitting in the center of the wooden deck huddled in a small circle.

"I can't smell the sour smelling prisoner anymore. You let him go?" his mother fumed.

"Yes," Clayton said as he walked up the steps and faced the elder tribal leaders.

"And why did you think it necessary to let him go when it's the council's decision and not yours alone?" another council member demanded.

"I did what I did because I am the leader of this council. I traded his life for a secret."

"What secret was worth sparing his miserable existence, Clayton?" Tabatha demanded.

"He provided me with information that warrants all of your attention."

"Spit it out, son! What did he tell you?"

He looked over the council members and sighed. He hoped the information he gave them would suffice. "The sour smeller, Eli, told me the other tribes had made secret deals with some of the boatsmen to leave England and go across the pond to the vast, mostly unexplored world far away."

"Why would they want to do that?" asked Tabatha.

"For two reasons, the boatsmen claimed there are other tribes there too. I doubt they are our kind of tribe, but they wouldn't have to fight for land."

"And the second reason?" Tabatha inquired.

"The King is demanding more and more payments from all of us. He's probably planning another war. I know we don't have much money left, but I am unsure about the other smeller's wealth."

Tabatha stood up and addressed the council members. "Good! Let them go! More food for us!"

Everyone nodded except Clayton.

Tabatha looked at her son with disapproval. "It seems you don't approve, Clayton."

"No, I do not, mother. We may get more food, but the king's taxes will increase if the others leave. He has to get revenue from somewhere."

"You've been quiet, husband. What do you say?" Tabatha said to Tarson.

Tarson looked around the circle. "I don't typically come to the council meetings, but I felt it important this one time." He peered at Clayton. "When, and if the other smellers go, we will deal with the king," Tarson argued.

"Father, I urge you and the other council members to reconsider. I feel it prudent we leave too!" Clayton remarked coldly.

Tarson looked at his son. "Now is not the time for cowardice, Clayton."

"Cowardice? By wanting our tribe to have better meals? By expanding our land? Your definition of being spineless is skewed, father!"

Tabatha looked at her son. She kept her temper in check. "While you are the head of the council, the members agree with *my* decision. However, you may wish to invoke the overrule law if you wish."

"I have no wish to pit council members against each other. You have spoken." Clayton had heard enough. They were not going to leave.

He nodded, looked at Ada, and sped home.

Tabatha looked at Ada. "I expect you to tell me if Clayton tries anything against our code, Ada."

Ada nodded her agreement.

Tabatha's face softened. "How are my grandchildren?"

"They are doing wonderful. The two of them are little sucklings! Thank goodness our type can handle cow milk."

"I'm in complete agreement! Who is watching them now?"

"No one. I can smell them and hear them as if they were right beside me."

"Good! I will come over tomorrow and visit."

"Of course. May I go home to my husband now?"

"Yes, but remember what I told you."

Ada gave a slight bow and sped home.

When Ada got home, Clayton was packing his clothes in a burlap bag.

"What do you think you are doing, Clayton?"

"I am leaving this accursed place!"

"The council forbids such actions, and so do I!"

"Don't you see the pointlessness of our situation? Do you think the humans are just going to waltz in here and say, 'We heard there weren't many humans in your area, come take my blood'? No! Of course not! Some other tribes that don't leave will extend their reach! There are a lot more of the other smellers than there are of us!"

Ada took the burlap bag from Clayton's hands and threw it to the ground. "And going to a foreign land will help how?"

Clayton walked to Ada and took her hands. "It will allow us to start fresh. Start new in a new land with different people."

Ada released Clayton's hands. "I forbid you to go! We will not be responsible for creating any factions in our tribe! That is the end of the discussion! Do you hear me, Clayton Cole? Because the twins and I are staying here!"

"I won't leave without my family," Clayton said with certainty.

"Then I suggest you take your clothes out of the bag and come to bed! I will check on the twins, then meet you in the bedroom."

Ada left the room to attend to the twins while Clayton looked at the bag, looked at the receding figure of Ada, and then to the bag again. He nearly left right there, but could not, would not leave his family.

He will wait it out and see what happens. Clayton picked up the bag, looked inside, and sighed. Slowly he took his belongings out of the sac.

Chapter Four
Sequencing Enzymes Institute of Technology

S.E.I.T. Present Day, June 30th

Doctor Shelly Leadstone arrived at the spacious lab an hour early. Her anticipation of extracting a vital enzyme using cutting edge technology that she developed, thrilled her.

She got out of her vehicle and marveled at the superstructure. Less than five years old, the building was the envy of any scientist wanting to make a name for themselves. The all-glass structure towered at fifty stories, which contained various disciplines of science, including her enzyme department on the top floor.

Shelly walked in and greeted the old tall security guard.

"Hi, Lester. How are the grandchildren?"

The older man took off his security hat and brushed his silver hair back a few times. "Well, I'll tell you, Doctor Leadstone…"

Shelly waved her hand. "Lester, please call me Shelly."

"I can't do that. You worked too hard for your position. My grandchildren are fine, thanks for asking, Doctor Leadstone."

Shelly nodded and walked by Lacey at the information desk, waved at her, then walked to the all-glass elevator.

She pressed the elevator button and waited. It always excited Shelly when she entered the elevator, pressed the fiftieth-floor button, and watched through the glass elevator as the outside world grew smaller and smaller when the elevator ascended. The people and their cars became dots when the door finally opened. As she badged into the laboratory, she put on her face mask, face shield, and the rest of her personal protection equipment.

Shelly sat down at her computer terminal and thought as the computer booted up. Spurred by her recent successes, Shelly felt renewed and determined in her purpose. If her experiment today was a success, it would change the course of history. Of course, she wanted a Nobel peace prize, but she would take other accolades.

One such reward was attempting to enter the laboratory. Doctor Stephen Ward was outside the lab trying to find his badge to enter.

Shelly noticed Stephen's habit of pulling on his tie when he got frustrated. Stephen had a large green bag that was hindering him from gaining entry. Shelly smiled. Every day Stephen had the same issue of getting inside. Either his tote bag got in the way, or he couldn't find his badge.

Finally, finding his badge in his back pocket, Stephen swiped and entered. He put on his face mask and his personal protection equipment.

Shelly went to him and gave Stephen a look of love. "Took you long enough, Stephen."

He looked at her green eyes. "Sometimes, I can be forgetful when I look at you and your wonderful mind." He smiled sheepishly. "And among other things…"

"A sign of a true scientist!" Shelly said as she sat back down. She took off a pair of gloves and put on another pair.

Stephen took his green tote bag and put it on his desk. He turned on his computer and looked expectantly at Shelly.

"So, today might be the day, huh?"

She rubbed her gloved hands together. "Let's hope so!"

"It will revolutionize the blood industry, Shelly."

"That's the plan. Shall we proceed?"

He held out his hand. "After you, my dear."

Shelly peered in her microscope. "So, as you know, I created an antigen-slicing enzyme."

"Which is astounding in its implications!" Stephen marveled.

"Yes, it is! The synthetic elimination from the sugar of A- or B-antigens, generates universal O-type blood! Still, we have to be cautious because the immune system is susceptible to blood groups, and even small amounts of residual antigens could generate an immune response." (2)

"So, in essence, if your new enzyme can strip the antigens off the A and B blood group, we can make the O blood type the only universal donor!" Stephen remarked in awe.

"Yes, it will help people with any blood type who needs it. It can also help in trauma situations like car accidents or getting the blood for surgeries," Shelly said enthusiastically.

Stephen reflected a moment. "Still, I see challenges emerging from this new technology."

"Oh? Like what?"

"A person's blood type has been used by attorneys for paternity claims and not to mention crime scenes."

"Meaning?"

Stephen bit his lip. "If everyone is given the serum and then everyone had only the O type of blood, it would be much more difficult to prove someone murdered someone if everyone had the same blood type without any other viable evidence. And it would be a little more challenging to determine who is the rightful parent."

"True, the ethical and legal repercussions will be problematic, but I like to believe we are helping those with afflicted disorders, or those in accidents, those who have had trauma and need for blood, as I've stated earlier."

"This reminds me of our very first conversation last year," Stephen said as he took his gloved hand into hers.

Shelly nodded enthusiastically. "I remember. You were new and looked out of place, so I invited you out for drinks."

"Yup, although I don't know how we got on the subject of blood."

Shelly smiled. "You put your hand on the table and moved it to get your beer. A thick splinter ended up being embedded in your finger. You bled some before I managed to get a bandage from my purse. It was then I asked you what blood type you were. After all, you were assigned to my lab."

"And I asked why you wanted to know my blood type because I didn't even know."

"And the rest of the story culminates right here and now," Shelly said as she looked into Stephen's eyes.

She had fallen hopelessly in love with him. She had told him a couple of months ago. They agreed after the serum was perfected, they would move in together. Right now, Shelly needed her time at home to think.

"Shall we begin, my love?" Stephen asked.

Shelly nodded as she came out of her daydream. She withdrew her hands from Stephen's, put on another pair of sterile gloves. She took several Petri dishes that contained the A & B blood types, along with an AB positive and negative, and placed them side by side.

She made sure the marking was in front of her, so she knew which blood type the newly created enzyme was going in was correct.

Shelly took a pipette and immersed it in the beaker that contained her new enzyme. She extracted the substance until the pipette was full and then carefully placed her patent-pending material in each of the Petri dishes that housed the different A and B blood types.

"Now we wait," Shelly said with excitement. "The A positives and A negatives should convert to O negative."

"What about the AB negative and the AB positive blood types? They haven't changed yet." Stephen asked.

"In theory, they should change too. They seem a little more resilient."

"What generation is this enzyme?" Stephen asked as he peered into one of the Petri dishes.

"I have replicated it and spliced it to its current form over three hundred and seventy-seven generations."

After a short time, Stephen was looking at one of the Petri dishes under the powerful microscope and was amazed. "Wow! The process of stripping away the antigen on the A blood is working!"

"Yes, it is working on the B type as well!" Shelly shouted in excitement.

They waited until all of the Petri dishes had changed to O negative.

"Success!" Stephen shouted. He jumped up and hugged her. "I love you!"

Shelly looked into the eyes of her soulmate and smiled. "My life's work is complete! Now, in time, anyone can get a transfusion and not worry about the blood supply!" Shelly exclaimed proudly. "And eventually, maybe in the next twenty or thirty years, everyone will become O type of blood!"

"That process may take longer, but that's in the future," Stephen said as he took her into his arms. Stephen looked at Shelly and smiled. He gave her a warm, passionate kiss. "So, how much enzyme did you create?"

"A boatload! So much that we can talk to the board of directors who will apply my serum to the Food and Drug Administration for approval and not worry about creating more!"

"I'm so proud of you, Shelly, for the work you've accomplished!"

"You're undying support, love, and belief in me helped me through the rough patches, Stephen."

"That is because I love you so much!" Stephen grew serious. He looked around the vast lab. "We better keep the serum under lock and key. Where did you put all of the enzymes?"

Shelly stood up. "Follow me!" she said with excitement.

They walked hand in hand to the end of the aisle from where they were sitting and came to an enormous refrigerator. There were eight shelves filled with hundreds of small, thin beakers.

Shelly's green eyes glittered, and her pupils dilated. She spread her hand up and down.

"All of these beakers?" Stephen asked incredulously.

"Yes," Shelly beamed at him. "This is the culmination of my life's work!" She gazed into Stephen's eyes. "With this much at our disposal, we won't have to worry about our competitors. We're so far ahead of them!"

Stephen looked at the abundant amount of beakers one more time then turned to Shelly. "Okay, let's make sure there weren't any complications in the Petri dishes!"

"Of course, my love!"

They walked back to their station. Stephen moved the chair back so Shelly could sit down.

"You're such a gentleman! I'm such a lucky woman to have a man like you in my life!"

"No, I am the lucky one who has such an attractive and brilliant woman by my side," Stephen said as he sat down.

Shelly blushed and looked at Stephen. Her attention turned to the Petri dish. "Let's see how they're doing!"

Her eyes adjusted to the magnification of the microscope. Yes, she thought. No complications! Everything is perfect! "Hey, Stephen, want to go out to dinner to celebrate?" She said as she looked up in time to see Stephen smashing his microscope on the back of her head.

Her face fell into the Petri dish. Stephen took a clump of hair from the back of her head and threw her backward onto the floor.

Shelly was reeling in pain. She held her head with her hand. "What the hell, Stephen?"

Stephen smashed the microscope across her jaw, instantly breaking it. "Sorry, dear. I need your serum. All of it."

Shelly was barely able to mutter, "Why?" before Stephen slammed the heavy instrument several more times to her face.

"Don't worry, sweetie. I'm not taking it to a competitor. Oh no, it's far worse than a rival company," Stephen said as he slammed the scope one more time.

He took off his red-stained gown, gloves, and facemask and threw them on a neighboring table.

Stephen took out his phone from his pocket and dialed.

"You have the serum?" a voice boomed at the other end.

"Yes, sir."

"And the good doctor?"

Stephen looked at the inert body of Shelly. "Motionless, dead. Just as we agreed upon."

"How much of the enzyme do you have?"

"Much more than we anticipated, sir. Hundreds of beakers!"

"Excellent. Take all of it, and I will text you where to meet. Good work!"

"Thank you, sir. I will await your text."

"And to make sure I know it's indeed you, what type of carrying case will you have? Our enemies are smart at deception."

"I will be carrying a *green* tote bag, sir." Stephen hung up. He grabbed the green tote bag and hurried to the fridge. Carefully, Stephen took the beakers by the trays they were housed in and placed them in his large carrying case. He went back to the desk and put the gown and anything else that had blood on it, and set it inside the large bag.

He had to hurry. In forty minutes, the building officially opened.

Stephen went back to his work station, put on the jacket he came in with, and delicately put his tote bag across his shoulder.

He pressed the first floor of the elevator and waited patiently. He got out and passed the information booth where Lacey sat talking to another employee.

He went by her and nodded.

Lacey stood up. "Doctor Ward, leaving so early? You barely just got here."

He turned around and noticed Lacey was tall with long brown hair. He had never paid attention. "Yes, family emergency, I'm afraid."

"Oh, I'm sorry to hear that!" Lacey replied with downcast eyes.

"Thank you," he said as he started walking away. He stopped and turned to Lacey. "I almost forgot, Lacey."

Lacey looked at him expectantly. "Yes, Doctor Ward?"

"Doctor Leadstone asked me to tell you she doesn't want any interruptions for the rest of the day. She has a hectic day ahead of her."

"Of course. I will see Doctor Leadstone is not disturbed. Thank you, Doctor Ward. I hope everything works out with your emergency."

Stephen nodded and walked out of the building with a smile on his face.

Chapter Five
The Council of Blood ~
Present Day, July 11th

Clayton shook his shoulders loose and took a few deep breaths before he entered the hotel lobby. He checked his phone and realized he was running late.

His previous meeting with the leaders of the different blood types was a hundred years ago, right after the Stranger bit another eight expecting mothers. At that time, secrecy was essential. Now? He did not care who knew. It was he who had requested the meeting through open channels. Something was brewing, Clayton could sense it.

One troubling event no one was talking about was the Stranger was past due. She had not appeared, nor had any pregnant women been bitten this year. He was positive about that. His spies were widespread. Once families were bitten, they tended to behave differently, or a surge of human killings occurred. He looked at the date on his phone—July the eleventh. Even taken into account the last change of the human calendar in 1752, (3) the date and time were always the same—May the fourth at seven thirty-three in the morning. Clayton had no idea why a specific time or date, but he was certain no one had been bitten and changed.

Another thing troubling him was the statement from a vampire several weeks ago that said his kind was on the way out with the mention of the Great Yeomen Purge of 1751.

It was there where his beloved wife, his twin boys Grady and Markus, his father, mother, his younger brother Milas and his younger sister, Beatrice, died at the hands of the O type vampires did not sit well with him. He shrugged back the horrific memory.

He was the last to enter and sit down. The other seven blood types were already seated. Clayton sensed tension among the factions.

"Sorry, I am late," Clayton remarked. "I wanted to make sure I dined before I got here."

"In case of what?" the O negative leader, Maryl Rosser, the Seeker, asked.

"I like to be at full power when I am in the midst of discussions with the leaders of the other seven blood types."

A person unknown to Clayton rose from his chair. "Since I am the newest member, and many may not know who I am, I am the leader of the O Positive blood type. My name is Ray Greenwell, the Conqueror."

"What happened to Sol, the former leader of your group?" Clayton asked in surprise. Usually, he had intel on the latest changes in the other types.

"Our people age slowly but not nearly as slow as your A & B blood types. I challenged Sol, who was old, and he lost. I defeated him, quite easily I might add," Ray the Conqueror boasted.

"Why are we here, Clayton? Why did you call this meeting?" the leader of the AB negative group, Platov, the Compromiser asked.

Clayton studied the leaders. He needed answers.

He pointed to Ray. "Before we get to the heart of the matter, since Ray the Conqueror is new, why doesn't he provide more information about himself, and then we introduce ourselves to him?"

"I don't want to. I have no need. I know who all of you are, and I despise all of you except Maryl Rosser. I don't care who all of you are," Ray the Conqueror said in defiance.

"*I insist,*" Clayton said with force.

"And I said I don't care!" Ray said as he stood up.

Clayton sighed and got up too. "You will introduce yourself to our group that is probably older than you by centuries, and you will be respectful!"

"Or else?" Ray demanded. His face turned deep red as his blood pumped furiously. He seemed poised to attack.

Clayton rushed to Ray the Conqueror. He had to squelch the new person, or he would look vulnerable. He slammed Ray to the hotel wall with such force Ray was embedded several inches deep.

"*I don't care what blood type leader you are,* you will listen to me, or I will tear your heart out and feed it to the wolves!" Clayton seethed in anger.

No matter how hard Ray tried to pry himself free, Clayton was far stronger than himself. He gave Clayton a slight nod and was let loose. Clayton backed up slowly, never taking his eyes off his opponent.

With sudden ferociousness, Ray the Conqueror sped to Clayton and fully expected to slam him in the wall as Clayton did to him.

Clayton saw the anger and embarrassment in Ray's eyes. He knew he would attack, and Clayton was prepared. As Ray was upon him, Clayton pivoted to the left. With nothing in the way, Ray ran into the wall headfirst. Clayton turned him around, held him steady by the throat with one hand, took his other hand, and started to go inward to Ray's heart.

Ray the Conqueror's screams reverberated across the hotel walls.

"You've made your point, Clayton the Archetype. Release him, please," Silvia the Hopeful insisted.

Clayton took hold of Ray's beating heart and squeezed it a little. It would be nothing for him to extract it. Out in battle, he would have removed it without any remorse. Here, in the Hotel with the other leaders, he complied. He slowly removed his hand from Ray's inside. Ray staggered to the floor, holding his chest.

Clayton sat down. "I apologize to the other council members for my actions. I have serious business to discuss here." He took out a handkerchief and wiped his bloodied hand. He looked at Ray as he attempted to get up three times before succeeding. Then he looked at the other members as he pocketed the stained handkerchief. "And I will not have any interruptions from a new member who doesn't know or doesn't care about the rules of respect."

Clayton waited patiently until Ray was able to make it back to the table to sit down. "We now know Ray the Conqueror is the ruler of the O positive tribes through battle, so he will forfeit his turn. Who is next?"

A large bald man with a long beard stood up. His beard had rubber bands that lead down to a point. Several looped earrings were on both sides of his ears. "I am Octavus the Brooder, leader of the A positive group of vampires. We are a subset of Clayton Coles tribe and proud of it! We will defend our groups until death!"

A woman with long brown hair on one side while shaved bald on the other side stood up. Necklaces and bracelets adorned her neck and wrists. "I am Maryl Rosser, the Seeker, and I am the ruler of the O negative vampires. I have been the ruler for almost as long as Clayton. Had my family been bitten first and not second by the Stranger, my type would be the Archetype."

Clayton Cole stood up and glanced at the bitterness that was on Maryl's face. "I am Clayton Cole, the Archetype, leader of the AB positive tribe of vampires. I am the oldest member here." He looked at Maryl, the Seeker. "I see you've changed your look since the last time we saw each other."

Maryl Rosser smiled mischievously.

A tall, slender woman with jet black hair that went down to her lower back stood up. "I am Silvia the Hopeful, and I am the ruler of the B positive vampires. We vanquish who dare cross our boundary, but never seek conquest."

A towering figure rose who was wearing a black shirt with gold pants. He had jet black hair and bushy eyebrows. "I am Platov, the Compromiser, and I am the supreme ruler of the AB negative vampires. We are the frontline defense for all A and B blood types. We serve Clayton Coles tribe with honor and distinction."

Clayton looked at Platov and bowed in respect.

"I am Salvatore but do not wish to stand for I was in a minor skirmish recently with Maryl Rosser's handiwork!" Salvatore said in anger. "I have healed, but wish to remain seated."

"Of course," Clayton remarked. He noticed a long deep scar that ran across his right side of his face and down his throat. His mustache curled up at both ends of his lips.

"It was a minor misunderstanding, Salvatore," Maryl said without elaborating.

Salvatore glared at her. "How dare you say it was a misunderstanding!"

Maryl shrugged. "Things happen. I deeply apologize."

Salvatore looked at Clayton with unchecked rage. "Are you going to allow this?"

Clayton chose his words carefully. "Yes, but I do not condone her actions! This is a meeting *I* requested. If you want to take this matter up further, you must wait until my docket is complete."

Salvatore sneered at Maryl. "No, I do not want to push this through. However, next time you enter my boundaries without my consent, you will pay!"

"Maryl wanted to see how you responded, and gauge your line of defense," Silvia commented. "She has done the same in my territories."

"This line of conversation can be discussed *later*! We are not done with the introductions," Clayton said in irritation.

Salvatore was not happy but proceeded anyway. "I am Salvatore the Great, leader of the A negative vampires. We do not seek battle, but we do not shy away from it!"

"And finally, I am Trevor, the Giant. As you can see, I am nearly seven feet tall. I rule the B negative vampires with an iron fist. When in battle, surrendering is never an option!"

"Your group of A's and B's seem almost militant in nature, Clayton," Maryl Rosser, the Seeker remarked.

"Given our history of conflict with each other, and being the least of the populated vampires, it is no wonder we have a certain *perspective*," Clayton said with a hint of defiance.

"That is an illusion, Clayton!" Ray said as he continued to rub his chest.

Clayton turned his attention to Ray. "How so?"

"The O type vampires have only O positive and O negative, which comprises about forty-four percent. You have AB positive, AB negative, B positive, B negative, A positive and A negative. You outnumber us with fifty-six percent."

"Maybe with blood types, but there are ten thousand times more O type vampires than there are of all the A's and B's combined," Clayton said with contempt.

"We can't help it if your types have to wait thirteen years to ascend. In that timeframe, we reproduce at a much higher rate," Ray the Conqueror stated.

"Let's not forget the number of vampires you make out of humans!" Clayton yelled.

"While we have done that in the past, Clayton, we rarely, if ever, change a human anymore," Maryl stated calmly.

"Enough of the arguing! The introductions are done as you requested. Why call this meeting, Clayton, The Archetype?" Silvia, the Hopeful, demanded.

Clayton took a minute to calm down and collect his thoughts. Even though he was the one who proposed the council centuries earlier, which led to the boundary lines of the eight different blood types, and an accord that was forged in blood, he couldn't fathom why someone here wanted to jeopardize the goodwill. If anyone did that, it would be himself.

"I have a few things to discuss with the members here," Clayton said as he looked at each vampire sitting at the oval table. "First off, why has no one mentioned that the Stranger has not appeared this past May and changed eight expectant mothers?"

"Is that really high on our priority list, Clayton?" Maryl asked lightheartedly.

"It might not be a concern for the O families, but it is for the others represented here. Reproduction among my species is especially difficult. Very few of us are able to reproduce. We are heavily dependent upon the Stranger to continue with our line of vampires."

"So, your impotence is our problem?" Ray said with laughter.

Clayton rose in anger, followed by all the rulers except Maryl. She remained calm.

"Enough! Ray, sit your ass down!" Maryl scolded.

Ray looked at her in disbelief.

"You heard me. Sit! Think about it, Ray. There are six vampires versus you and me. The odds are *not* in our favor."

Ray looked at Clayton in contempt, then looked at Maryl, who gave a slight nod.

Reluctantly Ray sat back down, grumbling under his breath.

"The Stranger not coming this past May is enough of a cause for alarm to bring it to everyone's attention, Maryl," Clayton said with seriousness.

"Okay, Clayton," Maryl said as she looked around the room. "I propose all of us contact our resources and find out why the Stranger has not returned. All in agreement?"

Everyone raised their hands except Ray. Clayton was annoyed, but being the leader of his particular blood type, it was his right.

"Okay, that agenda has been addressed. What else do you have on the docket, Clayton?" Trevor, the giant, leader of the B negatives, asked with respect.

"I want to discuss something that was said to me weeks ago by both O positive and O negative vampires near the boundary line at my property."

"Oh? And what was said?" Maryl asked.

"One O positive and two O negatives came to the edge of the boundary at my property. They dared me to cross the line. Obviously, I refused."

"And what were their names, Clayton?" Maryl asked as she leaned in and put her elbows on the table.

"Their names are inconsequential because I only got their first names. What they said to me was important."

"Proceed," Maryl said.

"One of them said, 'my time was coming,' along with 'you're an AB type. It does not matter if it's negative or positive. The AB's have had their time,' and 'Remember the Great Yeomen Purge of 1751?' What is bothersome to me is the last part. 'For far too long, the AB tribe have thought themselves the top of the food chain. Remember, history tends to repeat itself!'"

"Interesting," Maryl quipped.

Clayton laid his hands upon the table. "Now, I ask both you, Maryl and you Ray, what are you planning? Another war? Something more devious?"

"I assure you, Clayton, I am not planning anything," Maryl said in earnest.

Clayton looked at Ray. "And what of you? You seem to be filled with conquest and evidently have hatred for me."

"If I planned on attacking your blood type, would I be stupid enough to let other vampires know outside of my top elite army generals?" Ray said defiantly.

He had a point, thought Clayton.

"What else did you want to talk about, Clayton?" Platov, the Compromiser, asked as he looked at the wall clock.

"Two weeks ago, a prominent scientist, Doctor Shelly Leadstone, was killed at the Sequencing Enzymes Institute of Technology on the fiftieth floor."

"Tragic," Ray Greenwell said sarcastically.

"It *is* tragic because she was able to produce an incredibly powerful enzyme in her lab that can shred the antigens off the surface of all A and B blood types to develop an O type blood that would be universal. Sadly, it was stolen from her lab. Clearly, I can't let that serum get into the wrong hands. I will not allow it!"

"And you think *we* had something to do with it?" Ray demanded to know.

Clayton raised his shoulders in a shrug. "I don't know. That's why I requested this meeting."

The murmurs turned to accusations to shouting. Clayton slapped his hand against the solid oak table. "Enough! I called this meeting to talk and not bicker."

"Personally, I think it's a great idea because you A and B types can finally come down from your high horse, and everyone can become just one group of vampires," Maryl said as she leaned back in her chair.

"Maryl, I respect your opinion, but when the Stranger came to our ancestor's houses nearly two thousand years ago, she purposely created the variations of the blood types. She had a reason for it. Was it to stir discord and to fight endless battles? Maybe. Or, did she deliver the different blood types to see if we would one day reach this point and try to dilute the blood types? Again, I don't know."

"Dilute? *Dilute*?" Ray yelled. "How dare you insinuate our blood types are somehow inferior to yours!"

Clayton put out his hands. "I apologize, Ray, the Conqueror. I was out of line and meant no disrespect."

Ray looked at Clayton, and a smile emerged. It was a small victory for his blood types.

Clayton looked around the room before he spoke again. "There was another scientist with Doctor Leadstone. His name is Doctor Stephen Ward. His credentials were falsified to allow him access to a highly restricted building. I believe his goal was to get close to Doctor Leadstone, get the serum, and leave without a trace."

"You have his name, let's go find him!" Platov shouted.

"He has fled. At this point, we cannot locate him. The woman at the information booth, Lacey Donovan, described Stephen Ward to the police who called in an artist that drew the sketch, but his face is not in any of the databases I've searched."

"Send us the picture, and we will search within our boundaries as a sign of good faith," Maryl suggested.

"Thank you," Clayton said as he stood up, put his head down in thought, and placed his hands on the top of the chair.

"Something else on your mind, Clayton?" Maryl asked. She remained seated while the others rose from their chairs.

"Yes," he said as he looked up at the other leaders. "I want the boundaries that separate the different blood types eliminated for good."

"What? That's preposterous!" Ray bellowed.

"*You* were the one that fought for the boundary lines in the first place!" Maryl said in bafflement. "Even your blood cousins were against it!"

Clayton put up a hand. "Hear me out! Even the A positives and negatives, along with B positives and negatives, have different lands, and we cannot cross without permission, except with the infrequent exception of helping in battles."

"You wanted the separation, Clayton! As I recall, you claimed it was best for all groups," Maryl said somberly.

He looked at her. "That was in the past. Look at us right now, right here! All eight blood groups together in neutral territory."

"This isn't about food supply, is it?" suggested Ray.

"No. We have plenty of humans to consume for nourishment. I think the time is right for us. It's the twenty-first century!"

"So, what? Would we be able to cross into your lands to nourish ourselves?" Ray Greenwell asked in contempt.

"What is the real reason you want the border lines gone, Clayton?" Trevor, the Giant, asked.

"If you must know, I want unrestricted access to all the borders so I can conduct my own investigation with regards to the serum. This is a matter I take very seriously!"

"Granted, I think it's a huge problem but only for the A's and B's and not to the O's," Ray said without sarcasm.

Clayton drummed his fingers on the top of the chair. He closed his eyes for a second. When he opened them, they were as black as night. "*I need to be able to pass the lands and oceans if need be without being hindered. I* would prefer everyone's permission; that's why I am asking nicely."

"Oh, I see. You'll do it regardless if we say no," Ray said matter-of-factly. He turned to Maryl. "When did this become a dictatorship and not a council?"

"Ray is correct, Clayton. We cannot allow one vampire to rule above all else. My answer is no." She turned to Ray. "What does the ruler of the O positive blood say?"

"Absolutely not! You may *not* cross our boundaries. Cross them at your own peril, Clayton!" Ray said with conviction.

"Fools! You're not looking at the bigger picture!" Clayton yelled.

"Did you really expect us to say yes? And then what? Become chummy? Become friends? Have all of us over for human dinner that we can't consume? Oh, wait! Maybe we can have human hunting parties together?" Ray shouted in disgust.

"I agree with my counterpart, Clayton. The A's and B's have always maintained they are superior to the O types. The boundaries are what keep you from overrunning our territories," Maryl said with bitterness.

Clayton stood up and shook his head in disgust. "I can see this meeting was pointless. I call for this meeting to be adjourned. Anyone second the motion?"

"I second the motion," Platov the Compromiser said quickly.

Clayton watched as six of the seven rulers walked out of the conference room.

Maryl Rosser, the seeker, stayed seated.

Intrigued, Clayton sat beside Maryl. "Why did you stay? And I noticed something. How are you able to retain your youth, yet Sol did not?"

Maryl looked at Clayton. "You're sitting in my other half's seat."

Clayton could not tell if she was kidding or not. He got up and went back to his original seat.

"Better?"

"Yes. Your sweet scent does not bode well with my acute sense of smell."

"Answer my questions, Maryl Rosser."

"As my name implies, I am a seeker. In this case, the seeker of truth and other things."

"I too am a seeker of the truth, Maryl," Clayton said in a deliberately measured tone.

"Really? Come off your high and mighty horse, Clayton! You've been spinning half-truths and innuendos for centuries. I know you're up to something."

"I want to make sure we're not going to have another purge, and all I want to do is to investigate the missing serum. Nothing more, nothing less."

"I don't believe you, Clayton. What are you really up to?"

"Careful of your accusations, Maryl."

"Why? Are you going to kill me? Will one of your tribe members happen to find me in some ditch on an A or B territory to make me look guilty by trespassing upon *your* boundaries?"

Clayton's face grew tense. "Careful where you're treading! Let's not forget the great yeomen purge, Maryl Rosser! Sol, before he lost to Ray in combat, and *you* were chiefly responsible for my family's death!"

Maryl lowered her eyes to the table. She played with her youthful hands for a moment.

She looked up. "I am sorry about that mishap, Clayton. It has weighed on my mind for over three hundred years."

"I don't believe you. And you still possess the treaty we all signed in blood! Because of that, we all had to comply with the boundaries!" Clayton said with ferociousness.

"At first, I was against it, but when I went into your home and found it, I knew I would need it someday. However, I find it interesting you seek to threaten the peace by not abiding by it any longer."

Clayton's face grew cold as the memories resurfaced. The murder of his family forever changed him. He trembled for a minute before regaining some measure of calmness. "Nothing you can do or say will bring them back, Maryl. Are we done here?" he said with a touch of building anger.

Maryl rose with dignity. "Clayton Cole, you're hiding something, and I will make it my job to find out what it is."

Clayton got up in one smooth motion and stood before Maryl. "I am not hiding anything. I want the serum destroyed. If the antigens on the surface of the A and B blood type were stripped away, and every human was an O blood type, it would weaken my blood type. I will not allow that." He stood even closer to her. "And I don't care if you don't like my sweet smell. I am not particularly fond of your sour smell either. Just remember something, Maryl. I can suck *your* blood while you can't take mine!"

"*You wouldn't dare!*" Maryl said with apprehension.

"Try me, Maryl Rosser! And let's not forget your exceptionally potent gray mist that rendered and killed my blood families by vomiting up their blood and bleeding from their orifices!"

Maryl looked at Clayton with pity. "So I have a weapon against you? Big deal. Your tribes are far stronger than ours, and because of that, we will not be pushed around any longer. That is my failsafe deterrent. And if the serum can produce just O type blood, poor Clayton and the rest of the A and B tribes will only be as strong as the O's. I am weeping for your blood types."

"I hope you don't have anything to do with the disappearance of the enzyme Maryl, or the consequences might be war!"

"Are those your parting words, Clayton? If so, I am disappointed."

"You seem awfully confident, Maryl. What are *you* hiding?"

"I am withholding nothing from you, but I can't say the same thing about you."

Clayton's eyes squeezed to the point of closing. He contemplated draining her blood right there in the conference room. He barely made room for her to pass through as he watched her leave and head down the long corridor.

"She's up to something. I can feel it," Clayton said out loud as he left the conference room.

Chapter Six
Doctor Stephen Ward
One week prior

The bus station in downtown Indianapolis was packed with wall to wall commuter traffic. People lined up as far as the eye could see.

Stephen chose neutral color clothing to make him blend in, in case the police or the dreaded A and B vampires were looking for him.

While he waited for the bus to arrive, Stephen daydreamed and rejoiced in the fact that soon the mass population of humanity will go through a genetic metamorphosis, unlike any other within the last ten thousand years, and Stephen could not wait. And if the government refused the enhanced serum, the O types had a contingency plan for that as well!

The bus stopped a couple of feet in front of Stephen. He rushed on as the door opened. He grabbed a seat in the front while looking in all directions as he adjusted his sunglasses. He pretended to look at his phone despite taking out the battery. His tote bag that carried the future of humankind was on his lap with his coat covering it. Every once in a while, Stephen would glance around to see if anyone had followed him.

He lifted his shirt sleeve and snuck a glance at his left wrist. He traced the small tattoo of two fangs a half-inch apart from one another with four tiny droplets of red blood just underneath one of the pearly white fangs. Despite being the grandson of the founder, he still had to go through the challenging rituals to take over one day.

"The fellowship of the fangs," he whispered with reverence. No five words ever sounded so beautiful and horrific at the same time. Stephen's induction, and the subsequent tattoo of the secret society, were worth every breach of moral injustices he had committed, including the permanent removal of Doctor Shelly Leadstone.

The fellowship provided Stephen a way to work alongside Shelly, but it was up to him to study up on the work she was involved with at the institute. Stephen smiled. It had not been that difficult with his vast medical background in immunology. Enzymology was an emerging field, and all the sub-disciplines were in their infancy. Shelly had been instrumental in propelling her field of study forward by a decade. That much he admired about her. The other parts, Stephen discarded mentally. He had to look at the bigger picture. The fellowship had to make sure the serum was placed in the right hands.

The bus's air brakes screeched to a halt. The hissing made Stephen look up as passengers departed, and more came on board. He looked out the window to see where he was and how much further he needed to go. "One more stop," Stephen whispered softly. He patted the tote bag for assurance.

The short ride to the next stop filled Stephen with anxiety. He would finally get to meet the caller from one of the higher members of an O blood type who had first told him about the serum and its implications. He was told it would be the next step in his advancement in the fellowship of the fangs! How he dreamt of the impending mutation of the human race! Everyone would be equal with O blood type, so those damned A and B vampires wouldn't be the top of the food chain! And once he got up the ladder in the fellowship, he was promised to be turned into one too! He didn't care whether or not his blood would become O positive or O negative. He wanted to be as strong as the AB's once the serum was administered worldwide.

Sweat dripped from his brows and fell onto his shirt. Stephen practically jumped up, put his jacket on, and hoisted the tote bag over his shoulder as the bus pulled over. Checking to make sure he wasn't followed, Stephen walked with purpose to the house a block away. He was happy the area chosen for the meet was on neutral ground. Everyone in the fellowship was given access to all the neutral sites. That way, Stephen knew where he would be safe from the arrogant A and B blood tribes. And if any O type of vampire would try to attack him, all Stephen had to do was show them the fellowship tattoo, and he would be left alone.

Stephen strolled down the road as the afternoon sun descended upon the landscape. Flowers of all colors and sizes bloomed, gardens abounded with fresh herbs and vegetation. He could hear lawnmowers nearby slice down the tall grass blades that permeated the neighborhood.

He took out a small piece of paper from his pants pocket and noted the address on the paper matched the mailbox number. He nodded to himself, straightened his large bulging tote bag, and walked up the cracked driveway. Stephen noticed the house was an older model that had been somewhat unkempt. The lawn had patches of yellow flowers that the bees were taking advantage of with relish. A sprinkler was feeding the hungry grass, and a large oak tree on the other side of the property was providing shade to a couple of rabbits and their offspring.

Perhaps the ordinary house was a way of the fellowship blending in like himself. At the same time, they were doing invaluable work to shed the world of the elitist vampires that comprised a fraction of the O blood type tribe's population.

But, he thought as a smile formed on his lips, it won't be that way for much longer!

Stephen knocked two times, waited five seconds, and then knocked four more times to indicate he was a member.

The door creaked open, and the sound made Stephen think the front door wasn't used much. A beautiful African-American woman slid the door open. She was on the tall side and wearing a crisp Orange jacket that barely passed her knees. Her white shorts barely went lower than the coat as she stood with her hands folded in front of her. Stephen waited for the woman to introduce herself. She did not.

Stephen extended his hand. "Hi, I'm Stephen Ward. I have an appointment to see 'Max.'"

The woman did not return the gesture but motioned for Stephen to follow her. When they got to the first room, the woman stopped and turned to him.

"I need to frisk you," she said with a commanding voice.

Stephen took off his tote bag and set it down. He lifted his arms.

The woman took notice of Stephen's watch and removed it.

"No watches, jewelry, or phones."

"It's just a watch," Stephen stated with a hint of apprehension. Surely most, if not all, of the higher echelon of O type blood vampires knew of the watch's purpose.

The woman put the watch in her pocket.

"Hey! You can't do that! That watch belongs to me! Your kind gave it to me!"

"And you will get it back once the meeting is concluded," the woman said in a manner where there was no room for discussion.

Stephen allowed himself to be thoroughly frisked. "Satisfied?"

The woman ignored him. They walked straight through a sparsely decorated room. Stephen noticed there wasn't a sofa, no chairs, just a beige carpet, and some abstract art that celebrated a different era. They walked in silence as they went down a long hallway and came to a room with the door closed.

The woman straightened herself erect, pulled on her jacket, and did the same knock as Stephen did at the front door. She looked at Stephen and then walked away.

Stephen looked at the receding figure. "Nice to meet you, too," he murmured with sarcasm.

"Come!" a voice boomed from inside.

Stephen repositioned the tote bag across his shoulder and walked in.

A well-built man sat at a mahogany desk that spoke of money. Ironic since the neighborhood suggested otherwise, thought Stephen.

The man stood up and outstretched a hand. Stephen took it. "Mister Ward, glad we finally meet! I am Max."

Stephen looked at the man. "You don't seem familiar to me, Max. Are you a member of the Fellowship of the Fangs?" He said as a test.

Max smiled. "No. I work for one of the higher echelons of the O positive group that wants to remain anonymous."

Stephen took a seat in front of the desk. "Okay, I looked you up and found you legit. But before we begin, Max, I feel it wise to tell you that my grandfather was *the* founding member."

"Yes, I believe I knew that. Your father was at a lecture at Stanford University in 1912, wasn't he?"

"Yes, he was Stanley Pearson's assistant."

Max let the conversation die down. He did not care about Stephen's ancestry even though he attended the lecture.

"I trust the serum is in your bag?" Max stated simply as his gaze fell upon it.

"That is correct."

"I would like to see it," Max said with eagerness.

"In a moment. I want to make sure we are clear on something. When I hand this to you, what assurances do I have that you will use this in the way it was intended? I went through a thorough process to learn all about enzymes, not necessarily on parr with Doctor Leadstone, but enough to convince her I knew more than the basics. And then had to befriend her, and at your request, kill her."

Max eased forward in his chair. "Why wouldn't I have the best interest of the O blood types? All the A and B's deserve to feed on just the O's, blood, and by the serum stripping off the antigens from the red blood cells, we will make it happen!"

"And my tattoo? Will I get another blood droplet under a fang, like promised? Because I am not handing the serum over unless I get a guarantee!"

"Of course. You have my word."

Max's assistant walked in and came around the desk. She whispered something for a few moments that made Max nod several times.

"Thank you." His assistant left without looking at Stephen.

Stephen looked at the closed door, then at Max. "Tell me, Max, why did your friend take my watch away?"

Clayton shrugged his shoulders. "It's a standard security protocol."

"But this is neutral ground. It should not matter," Stephen argued.

"It is especially prudent on neutral ground," Max said with conviction.

"Why?"

"Are we here to talk about your watch or the serum?"

"The watch first. It's important to me. I need some sort of basis for trusting you."

Max sighed. "Very well. We don't allow any devices of any kind. Cell phones, USB sticks, tablets, laptops, you get my drift. We do not allow them on neutral ground in case an incident should occur. If there was a recording of secret talks, or if a fight erupted here, then there would be no need for a place for all blood type vampires to meet without the risk of war."

Stephen shrugged. "A laptop is a laptop. A phone is a phone. A watch is a watch."

"A laptop, USB, or phone, and a watch may contain listening devices or cameras."

Stephen leaned forward. "It's just a watch."

"If it's *just a watch*, then it should not matter if you don't get it back until after our meeting is over."

Stephen leaned forward and peered at Max. "Tell me, Max, do you even know the significance of the watch?"

"Yes, of course."

"Perhaps you could let me know? That way, I would feel I can trust you a lot more than I do right now."

"Sure, I'd be happy to," Max said as he put his arms around his head and leaned back in his chair. "The watch is a blood type indicator. You scan the person with the watch, by waving it up and down, or side by side, and it automatically displays your blood type regardless if you are human or vampire. As an added feature, it can tell if you're a vampire of a certain type or if you are human."

"And the reason for such a device?" Stephen inquired.

"To differentiate between humans and vampires," Max replied.

"How can they tell humans and vampires apart?"

"Vampires have thicker bone density and almost impenetrable skin, which the watch scans and identifies. Satisfied?"

"Why would we need to know that, Max?"

"To gauge if they are friend or foe."

Stephen smiled and stood up. "I think our business here is concluded." He got up and handed Max the tote bag.

Max grabbed the bag and led him to the door. "I will contact you when your tattoo ceremony is ready."

Stephen nodded eagerly, shook hands, and walked out the door.

Max's friend was waiting for him. She handed back Stephen his watch and led him to a nearby door.

Stephen looked around in annoyance. "This is a different door than I came through."

"This is the back door exit. Please proceed."

As Stephen passed her, the woman grabbed Stephen from behind and snapped his neck. Stephen was dead before he hit the floor.

"Humans," she said as he bent down and took the watch off Stephen's wrist.

She walked back to Max's office and handed him the watch.

"Good job, Desiree."

"Thank you, sir."

"How did the Fellowship of the Fangs get their hands on such technology?" Max asked as he looked over the silver watch.

Desiree looked at him. "Sir, I have been your bodyguard for three centuries, and in that timeframe, I have never seen the O blood types display any sort of technological advantage over the other blood types."

"I disagree, Desiree."

"What do you mean?"

"Firstly, Maryl had the capability to produce a great deal of the fine grey misty powder that killed most of my family. And that was *over three hundred years ago*."

"I remember, sir. I was there."

"Of course, Desiree. You saved mine and other A and B vampires that gruesome day."

Desiree nodded.

"Secondly, Maryl Rosser hasn't seemed to have aged as quickly as Sol or even Ray. How?"

Desiree shrugged her powerful shoulders.

"Fourth, Stephen Ward was able to penetrate a top-secret institute which took a clearance level even I couldn't get."

He went to the window behind his desk and put his hands behind his back. "And lastly, Stephen's alliance with the Fellowship of the Fangs who have the technology and skill to read and project blood types from humans and vampires, all from a simple watch!"

"Sir, may I be blunt?"

Max came around the desk and stood inches from Desiree. "Of course. You of all people should know I respect your opinions."

"With what you just told me, there is a secret war that has been going on behind your back, and I think you're losing. You have always depended upon your brute strength for countless eons. The O's are fighting back.

After all, the O's comprise only two of the eight blood types."

"But they outnumber us at least a thousand to one. Shouldn't the strength in numbers be enough for them?"

"No, I don't think so. I think it runs deeper than that."

"Explain yourself, Desiree."

"I think they aren't just content with outnumbering you. I believe they, the O types, feel it's their right to exterminate your types."

Clayton looked at Desiree, his most trusted ally. "Do you feel any tension or hatred from me since you are an O negative and aren't in my blood type family?"

"No, sir. You've never given me a reason to."

Clayton nodded. He retrieved the tote bag and handed it to Desiree. "I need you to take this over to our lab in McCordsville, Indiana. I want our technicians to take the serum and modify it to the way we discussed it. Please do this right away. My blood type's very survival depends upon it!"

"Right away, sir," Desiree said as she quickly departed the room.

After Desiree left, Clayton went to his desk, sat down, and contemplated his next move. He looked on the floor to his right. He picked up the green tote bag that had Doctor Leadstone's serum. Desiree had made a foolish blunder. She should have taken more time coming into his office to tell him about the watch. She knew all about the various functions and had explained it to him in great detail while Stephen was waiting. Only someone high up in the O type blood vampires would have access to that knowledge. So,

Desiree Maholmes was exploiting their friendship and reporting everything to Maryl Rosser, the seeker?

When he initially asked Stephen what kind of bag he was going to put the serum in, Clayton bought two green tote bags as a precaution. Never in his wildest dream did he think Desiree would be a traitor, especially since he was fond of her.

He wondered what other valuable information Desiree had told Maryl for the past three hundred years. Clayton sighed as he waited for the call he expected.

A half an hour later, his cellphone rang.

"Hello, Maryl."

"When did you find out?"

"That Desiree Maholmes was a traitor? Not until half an hour ago. She knew way too much about the functions of the watch Stephen Ward was wearing. I couldn't dismiss such an obvious mistake. And let's not forget about you! You're outstanding at deception, Maryl Rosser."

"And so are you, Clayton, by getting Stephen Ward to do your dirty work right under my nose, something I will speak to Desiree about. And let's not forget stealing the serum from Doctor Leadstone and making up the façade of being Max. Brilliant. I imagine Stephen Ward is dead?"

"Yes, I had Desiree do it. What do you want, Maryl Rosser?"

"I need the serum. What you plan on doing with the serum is wrong! Surely, you must understand the plight of being an O negative in a world…"

"Maryl, spare me your sermon!"

"Then I will get to the point. Look outside your window where you are presently standing."

Curious, Clayton went to the window and slightly parted the blinds.

"You realize Desiree told me what you are truly planning on doing with the serum. I can't allow that."

Clayton scanned fifteen O negative vampires, including Desiree, who did not seem pleased she was duped. However, he sniffed five more in the back of the safehouse.

"I am on neutral territory, Maryl. You can't touch me," Clayton said as he approached the nearest closet door.

"Your vile quest to steal the serum trumps the neutral territories. They are no more!" Maryl said in anger.

"Be reasonable, Maryl!"

"I am. I could have sent many more vampires. You could take maybe five or six of them, but not all of them," Maryl said confidently.

"This is a breach of our alliance, which constitutes war, Maryl Rosser! Is that what you want?" Clayton demanded. He walked to the closet door and opened it. He pushed a small coat hook downward. A darkened slender walkway loomed ahead. He closed the closet door and rushed down the small passageway.

Maryl started to say something, but Clayton ended the call.

He scanned the perimeter as he heard the horde of vampires trying to break inside the safehouse. Despite the dwelling made from thick hardened oak wood, he knew it wouldn't take them long to break in and trace his unique AB positive blood.

The narrow corridor gave way to a widened area. Clayton ran to a large workstation that had a computer and several servers that monitored all of the neutral sectors in a three hundred-mile radius. He pressed several keys on the keyboard, found the pre-loaded virus, and hit the enter button. He heard them up above. They were less than a minute away.

He rushed to a nearby covered vehicle. He quickly threw off the blue tarp, jumped in, turned on the ignition, and peeled away as the door broke from the hinges.

Clayton slammed on the accelerator and watched the vampires recede. He pressed a button on the steering wheel, and a large opening in the wall allowed him passage.

As Clayton drove, he thought about Maryl Rosser's continued interference. Her intrusion didn't start recently. Oh, no. It began with the great yeomen purge of 1751, where most of his family were exterminated.

Chapter Seven
The Great Yeomen Purge of 1751
Part One

Clayton was fed up with London and England as a whole. He had made a promise to the council over two hundred years ago to stay in England for his family's sake, and he regrettably abided by that decision.

But how London had changed in the ensuing two centuries! The city was filthy and filled with poor sickly people. Beggars loitered at every street corner. Garbage littered the streets, and the citizenry urinated into the roads as the horses trotted idly by.

There was so much horse dung in the streets it looked like mud, thought Clayton. His hyper eyesight caught the sight of several beautiful large homes in the outskirts that were in stark contrast to the living conditions nearby.

The street vendors were the only thing Clayton looked forward to after tilling the acreage his tribes owned on the fringes of the city. He bought salt, along with some goat filled pastries and some hot pea soup. While London was filled with potential food, most notably humans, they stayed clear from the outer reaches of the city.

It was lucky his blood types could handle human food, he thought as he roamed the slushy roads of London.

Clayton gathered up the food he had bought and quickly walked down the dirt road. He was ready for a meal, no matter if it was human food or a human.

He hadn't walked several paces when a man blocked his path. He was bulky, or it seemed to Clayton since the soiled sweater was too large for him. The bloke wore a cap that once appeared to be yellow, but now only traces of the yellow appeared between the excess of stains.

Clayton was feeling generous, so he moved out of the gentleman's way. The man walked to the same side, effectively blocking him.

The man sniffed the air. "You're one of them sweet smellers, ain't ya?"

"And you smell sour, what of it? Are you going to let me pass, or do I have to go through you?"

"I just wanted to relay a message to you, Clayton Cole of the Cole Tribe," the man said with a tinge of humor.

Clayton hid his surprise. No one in the city knew who he was. To the humans, he was just a farmer. "I can't wait to hear it. What's the message?"

"The Yeomen class, which your tribes are, are going to lose your lands that you've labored for so long."

"But why? I am neither rich nor poor and don't own much land."

"That's what the Yeomen class means, you humbug."

"Hey, now! There's no reason for cuss words," (4) Clayton said with a touch of anger.

"Anyways, that's all I came here for. You can go back to your land before it's taken from ya."

"Who dispatched you to find me?"

The man smiled. He only had three teeth on the top of his mouth and two teeth on the bottom. "Sol Rastin, the mediator, and Maryl Rosser, the Seeker sent me."

The man got out of his way, tipped his hat in Clayton's direction, and walked down the dirt path while whistling a tune.

Clayton hurried his pace, and when he was out of range of the marketplace, he used his vampire speed to race home, eager to learn what was going on with his land.

When he got home, his twin sons, Markus and Grady, were eating human food. Clayton placed the items he had purchased on the kitchen table and looked at them.

"Where is your mother?"

Grady, the husky of the two, replied, "She is at the council. They had an emergency meeting."

"Why was I not summoned?" demanded Clayton.

"Mom told us to let you be, that she would take care of the meeting," Markus said in a soft-spoken manner.

"Come with me, both of you!"

Clayton raced out of the house with his sons right behind him.

When they got to the circular wooden area, all of the spots were taken. Clayton walked to the edge of the wooden deck. A chorus of chatter resounded all around him.

"What is the meaning of this session? Clayton yelled.

The talking stopped, and everyone's eyes turned to him. Ada walked down the steps from the entrance, took hold of Clayton, and guided him to the center stage.

"We are glad you are here, husband!"

Murmurs of approval sprung up and threatened to halt Clayton's questions.

"Everyone, calm down, and tell me what is going on!" Clayton demanded.

"King George, the second, has declared our land Yeomen class and aims to take it away!" Ada in a state of panic.

"Why would he do such a thing?" Clayton asked no one in particular.

"Landowners have crops and animals, both typically make money, according to the decree that was posted on our front door. It was placed soon after you left to go to the marketplace, father," Markus said plainly.

"And King George wants all of our lands! Either we give him our lands, or he will forcibly take it from us!" Ada cried.

"No one is going to take our land!" Clayton decreed.

"Son, if you don't know, King George's army outnumbers all of our kin of smellers by more than a thousand fold," Tabatha stated firmly.

"But we can't die from their muskets or knives. Our skin is imperious to such stuff," Clayton said with exasperation.

"But we can't fight them, son," Tabatha said with sadness.

"Why not?" Clayton said in disbelief.

"Because then he, and the entire kingdom, will know of our existence!" Ada complained.

"It's true, son. We can't let humans know vampires are living among them."

"Doesn't this tribe, and the others represented here, see what I see? They can't kill us, so what would be the worst thing that could happen? We fight, they eventually lose, and we get to keep our land and have plenty of meals to fill our belly's!"

"While that may be true, Clayton, you need to expand your scope of thought," Tabatha said as she folded her arms.

"Make me see the full scope of the picture, would you please, mother? Because apparently, I am not grasping it."

Tabatha looked around at the council members, then at her son. "If we choose to fight and win, it will allow King George to know the existence of our kind. In the process, he will learn of the other types of vampires and, if he was smart, forge relationships with the other smellers who don't have land, which comprises most of the different types of smellers. With them on the King's side, we could conceivably lose both our land and our lives."

"Then we need to have a peace treaty with the other kinds of vampires," Clayton said with seriousness.

"No, there has to be another way, husband!"

"I am open to suggestions. Let me ask you a question, Ada. Do you want them to take our land away from us?"

"No, of course not."

"Did you want to help fight them off?"

"No."

"Then, I am at a loss of what you want, Ada."

"I, Grady Cole and my twin brother, Markus Cole, will volunteer ourselves to go to the other tribes and ask them for a meeting!"

"No!" Tabatha and Ada said at the same time.

"Why not?" Grady asked.

"They might hurt you or even kill you!" Ada retorted.

"And risk the wrath and fury of our father, the leader of the most powerful vampire tribe? I don't think so!" Grady stated passionately.

Clayton went to Ada and wrapped his hands around her ample waist. "Their idea does hold sway with me, Ada," Clayton whispered.

"But what if something happened to them, Clayton? I could never live with myself!"

"Nothing is going to happen to them! I know their tribe leaders, Sol the mediator, and Maryl Rosser, the seeker."

"Yes, but are they trustworthy?" Ada asked as she looked at the man she knew so well and adored.

Clayton pondered for a moment. "Put it this way, Sol and Maryl will need our help if King George should go after them too."

"But we may be dead by then!" Ada said with fear. "If King George went after Sol and Maryl *first*, they would tell the King of more powerful tribes of vampires. They could conspire with King George the second!"

"That would never happen. We own the farmland, and they don't. And both Maryl and Sol dislike humans." He looked around for a second. "Enough talk. I want this put to a vote right now! Who here favor my sons Markus and Grady to contact the other rulers and ask them to meet at a neutral location to discuss a peace treaty to thwart King George the second?"

All hands rose except Tabatha, Clayton's mother, and Ada.

Clayton looked at his two favorite females. "The council has spoken. And remember, Beatrice and Milas, your two younger children, also voted in favor, mother."

"Both of my children are weak. They will abide by anything *you* say or do, Clayton!" Tabatha spat.

"Mother, how are they to grow strong without encouragement? How are they to learn battle skills and mental preparation by staying here in the safety net of our tribes?"

"I am only concerned with their welfare, Clayton," Tabatha said wearily.

"As I am, mother, but they will have to grow up sooner or later. Both are close to two hundred and fifty years old and never have been in a skirmish or a large-scale battle."

"You are the head of the council. You make the call, son."

Clayton bowed. "Grady! Markus! You may go. Mother, I submit to you. What message would you have your grandchildren say to Sol and Maryl?"

Tabatha's face tightened in a smile. The fact Clayton had directed her to give the message was twofold. He let her create the narration, which was both a privilege and extraordinarily rare for a council leader to do, but it came at a price. Depending upon the information and how it was worded, it could provoke Sol and Maryl into thinking the message was a sign of weakness.

"I am honored, Clayton," Tabatha said with uncertainty.

With the council in full session, it put additional pressure on Tabatha. She had to choose her wording wisely.

"Tell the two leaders we want to meet with them, and if they ask why do *not* tell them. Instead, if asked, tell them you were not told why. Do not put any urgency in your voices. The less said, the better. It might even make them curious enough to come."

"And if they ask where and when grandmother?" Grady asked with respect.

"In one week where the trees yield and bend to the ground. They will know where the trees are located."

Grady and Markus bowed.

Tabatha raised her hand in warning. "You will need to feast upon the humans to gain strength. But make sure the humans aren't discarded where they can be easily seen."

"Of course, grandmother," Grady said as he nodded to Markus. They sped off through the crops that dotted the landscape.

"Do you think they will be okay, Clayton?" Tabatha asked with worry.

"They will be fine."

"What makes you so sure?"

"Because if they dare lay a hand upon my family, they will suffer greatly, and they know that," Clayton said as he watched his sons disappear.

Grady put out a hand to stop Markus. They were in a wooded area that was protected by smellers, but not of their tribes. He looked down at a plant.

"Quickly, grab that plant and smear it on your skin!"

"Why? What plant?"

"I know our smell comes from within, but we can mask the scent of the sweet peas a little to confuse them. This particular variety is called Matucana, and it's very potent."

"How do you know so much about plants and herbs? You're a vampire!" Markus said as he quickly grabbed the purple and blue/green leaves and rubbed them against his skin.

"Be quiet, Markus, or you'll give away our position!"

Markus looked at his brother. "But isn't that the whole point of this venture? We want them to see us so we can have the dialogue."

"I would prefer to consume human blood first before speaking with the tribal leaders."

Markus heard ruffling of the tall grass. He looked up and saw a scouting party of three vampires coming from one direction and three more coming from another direction. "It's too late for that."

Grady had heard it too. Both stood up in the field.

The six vampires surrounded them. Even adequately fed, Grady knew there was no way he and Markus would be able to defeat that many.

A tall rugged-looking female vampire spoke first. "And who might you two be?" She sniffed the air. "Rubbing the Matucana plant to hide your sweet-smelling blood? A good tactic for someone about to attack!"

"We come here to deliver a message to Sol the Mediator and Maryl the Seeker," Markus said hurriedly.

"Then why douse yourself to try to hide your scent?" The tall, rugged vampire inquired with no trace of friendliness.

"We wanted to feed before speaking with your tribal leaders," Markus blurted out.

"Markus, shut up and let me do the talking!" Grady snarled.

"That can be viewed as an act of war between our different tribes," another vampire uttered with contempt.

"No, it's not. My brother Markus Cole and I, Grady Cole, were sent here to deliver a message."

The big, rugged vampire's eyebrows rose. "I am familiar with your family name. Why send the both of you and not Clayton himself or Tabatha?"

"My father opted to send us; we know not why," Grady stated plainly.

"I don't believe you," she said simply.

"It's the truth," Grady said with as much confidence as he could assemble.

"Give us the message, and we will confer with the two leaders," another vampire stated.

"No! We were given specific instructions to speak with only Sol and Maryl."

"I don't trust these two, Ariel! Let's kill them!" a vampire said to the tall, rough one.

Markus met Ariel's eyes and was reasonably confident they would perish.

"You don't want to do that," Grady responded instantly.

Ariel put her hand on Grady's head and started stroking his long dark hair. "Oh? And why is that, Grady of the sweet-smellers?"

"Because we're Clayton's…"

Ariel grabbed a chunk and pulled on Grady's long hair tightly. "I said, I know who your family is. Give me one good reason why we shouldn't kill you right here and now?"

Grady's head faced the sky as he felt the pull on his hair tighten. "We come in peace and have to speak to Sol and Maryl *only*. Do you really want to feel my father's wrath, along with my entire tribes? Killing Clayton's children and Tabatha's grandchildren is the same as taking your own life!" Grady countered.

Silence engulfed the group.

"He speaks the truth, Ariel! Let them pass, and we will escort them," one of the vampires said with reservation. "I, for one, do not want to risk the ire of the Cole clan."

Ariel put her long arms on her hips and looked at Grady and Markus for several seconds. "Okay, but I will take rear guard in case more of them are nearby, and this is just a ruse for a full-scale incursion."

They were tied up and bound. The ropes dug into their skin. Grady knew as soon as he and Markus consumed some human blood, the rope burns would vanish despite not feeling any pain.

They walked several kilometers through trees, large bushes, and plenty of grasslands. Grady noticed there was a lack of crop fields. He wondered what sort of occupations the other smellers did.

After a clearing, they came upon dwellings that varied in size. They were led to one of the larger homes. Grady could see smoke coming from a chimney nearby.

The whole village of the vampires came out of their abodes and stared.

He sniffed the air and found it repugnant. He almost vomited. Grady looked at Markus, who was throwing up human food.

"Why the sour look, Grady of the Cole Tribe?" The tall woman asked with amusement.

"What are you cooking? It smells disgusting! I thought you other types didn't like human food?"

"We don't. We loathe it. We are not cooking human food. We are making something your blood types don't like."

"Wait... you purposely produced smells that we can't stand? What for?" After his last sentence, Grady felt the need to throw up. He looked around and threw up beside Markus.

"In case we ever had to protect our villages from the likes of your kind!" Ariel sniffed the air and smiled. "I find the smell rather pleasant."

Grady had nothing left to regurgitate. The dry heaves were worse. He wondered if he was at full strength if the stench would cause so much displeasure.

They were led away from the horrendous smell through some trees until one lone house sat in the middle of a field.

"Sol the Mediator and Maryl, the Seeker, are in that house and agreed to see you both. Consider yourselves lucky. This is as far as we are allowed to go. Go to the house and knock," Ariel said before turning around.

"We need to tell our tribes about their new stench smelling weapon they have invented, Grady!" Markus whispered harshly.

"Hush, Markus! They can hear you!"

They walked hesitantly to the house and knocked.

A smaller man answered the door. Despite his diminutive size, he radiated raw power. Grady could see a few strands of grey hair, which surprised him. He was told vampires were immortal.

"Sit down," Sol commanded.

"Don't be so rude to our guests, Sol," Maryl said as she patted the couch next to the chairs she and Sol sat. Her hair was cut short, which emphasized her soft features. Grady doubted there was anything soft about Maryl.

Grady and Markus walked to the sofa with downcast eyes and sat down. Their tentativeness spoke volumes to the rulers.

"What can we do for the emissaries of the Cole tribe?" Maryl asked in amusement.

"We're not emissaries," Markus stated firmly.

"Do you not represent the Cole tribe?" Maryl said with enjoyment.

"Yes, we do," Grady said as he looked at Markus to keep quiet. "His vocabulary is lacking."

"Ah, nothing is better than a good education, save for the art of combat," Sol remarked.

"Why are you here?" Maryl asked simply.

"We have a message from the council of the A and B tribes," Grady said slowly.

Silence followed.

Maryl put her fingers to her lips in contemplation. "And what is the message, young one?"

"We're nearly two hundred and fifty years old!" Markus remarked.

"Markus, would you please shut up so I can deliver the message? They don't care how old we are!"

Markus fumed but did not respond.

"The council members request a meeting with both of you," Grady said with more confidence than he felt.

"Where do they wish us to meet?" Maryl asked as she took a glass of red nourishment and took a sip.

"In a week by the trees that bend to the ground."

"And what is the nature of the meeting?" Sol demanded.

"We do not know because we were not told," Grady said respectfully.

"Why not?" Sol asked with force.

"We are not privy to such information."

"And why aren't you in the know?" Maryl asked with a mounting smile.

Grady looked at Maryl. "Because we are only emissaries, as you stated. We are not on the council. We just do their bidding."

Sol pointed to Grady. "He's the smart one of the two." He looked at Markus. "And you? You are not. So tell me, Markus, do you know the true nature of why the elders seek a meeting?"

"I do not know. I know as much as my brother," Markus said as his lips quivered.

"Yet the sweat that drips from your upper lip tells me otherwise," Sol said mockingly.

Grady regretted bringing his brother. He did not have the spine for these types of discussions. He wished he would have asked the council to go alone.

"I do not know, I so swear it," Markus stated with confidence he did not feel.

Sol went to the couch and knelt on the floor in front of Markus. He placed a firm hand on his knee and squeezed tightly. "You so swear it, huh?"

Moisture dripped from Markus's back down to his pants. "Yes," he said as Sol continued to apply pressure.

Sol looked sternly at Markus for a moment. Suddenly his sternness turned to a smile. He let go of Markus's knee. "I'm just kidding with you, Markus. We would love to go and see what the elders want of us. Isn't that right, Maryl?'

Maryl smiled. "Of course. Give them our best."

"One more thing," Grady said as he rose from the couch.

"So, demanding for someone on the enemy's turf, young one," Sol said with enjoyment.

"What is it, Grady?" Maryl asked politely.

"We need assurances we will not be attacked on our way home."

Maryl and Sol nodded. Grady and Markus left.

"Gather the council, Maryl. We have a lot of work to do before the week's end."

Grady was several kilometers away before he spoke. "Your incompetence is astounding, Markus!"

"I was nervous, Grady!"

"You will be reported to the council about your shortcomings!"

"I thought it would go smoother than it did," Markus said in despair.

Grady was flabbergasted. "We go into enemy territory, demand to see the elders of the tribes, and you thought it would go easy?"

Markus shrugged. "I thought our name would give us more protection."

"All the more reason I am going to report you," Grady snapped. "Don't assume just because we have the Cole's name that vampires will open their doors with open arms! What is wrong with you?"

They came to the A and B's region and sighed with relief.

"I am going to wash up from the well water to get the stench of the flowers and the awful smell coming from their chimney," Markus said as he walked away.

"Good idea," he murmured as he opened the front door.

Clayton, Ada, and Tabatha were sitting on the davenport. He reached the couch and sat down in front of them.

The three of them smelled the air and repulsed in unison.

"What is that awful smell?" Clayton asked.

"We rubbed scented flowers to avoid detection to make sure we consumed blood but were quickly apprehended."

"I recognize the flowery scent, but I am unfamiliar with the other odor," Tabatha said as she put a hand to her nose.

"I wanted you to smell it because the sour-smelling tribes invented the odor as a restraint or possibly a weapon against us," Grady said with a heavy heart.

"Let's go outside before I hurl," Ada said as she got up and fled the house.

The outdoor air helped them breathe better.

"Apparently, our enemies are actively working on ways to overthrow us," Clayton remarked with concern.

"I think our arrogance pushed them to the brink," Ada observed.

"Nonsense Ada!" Tabatha admonished. "We will deal with this setback later." Tabatha turned to Grady. "Right now, the important thing is to find out the answer to our query."

"They agreed to meet the Council in one week at your desired location," Grady replied.

"Good. Hopefully, Sol and Maryl will agree with our proposal."

"Grandmother, I wish to express the lack of judgment and actions from Markus…"

Tabatha brushed him off with a wave of her hand. "We don't have time for that, Grady. We must attend to more pressing matters."

"Such as?" Grady said with impatience.

Tabatha rushed to him. "Don't you dare question my motives, young man! Do you understand?"

Grady hesitated to respond. He wasn't expecting such a reaction from his grandmother. For his grandmother to be so abrupt meant all wasn't well in the Cole tribes or their other related tribes. "I apologize. May I go now?"

"Yes, and see to it you cleanse yourself of that horrid smell!"

Grady nodded before leaving.

"I think we should schedule another council meeting, mother."

Tabatha bowed. "As you wish, son." She was about to walk away when she turned to Clayton. "We should have told Grady and Markus the bad news," Tabatha remarked sadly.

"Would it matter if they knew the King's army was on the way here to take our lands? Would they have remained calm if they learned his army would be here about the same time as the elders from the other tribes? It would make them worry."

"They will find out when they see their cousins and friends," Ada said quietly.

"Let it be so," Clayton said.

Ada started walking away.

"Where are you going, Ada?"

"I am going to pray," she said sadly.

"For what?"

"Our tribe's survival," she said with gloom.

"You're being dramatic, wife," Clayton said with seriousness.

"No, I am not. Think about the three fronts that are almost upon us."

"I am, but I am confident we will prevail. We always have."

Ada shook her head. "We have the King's army coming, the elders coming at the same time, and we aren't sure if they will help us, and now we learned of a weapon the other tribes have developed to use against us! Take a moment and think about this fact. What have we done in the meantime? Nothing! For centuries we have done nothing! And why is that? Because we have been arrogant and relied incorrectly on our more potent blood, that's what Clayton!"

Clayton took Ada's hands. There was a grain of truth in her logic, thought Clayton. "After King George's army is demolished, we will revisit this conversation, Ada."

Ada removed herself from Clayton's grasp. "Let's hope we survive the ordeal."

Chapter Eight
The Great Yeomen Purge of 1751
Part Two

The fire in the large circular pit burned bright against the cloudless sky. The pale moon helped with the mood, coupled with the crackling of the wood, mesmerized the onlookers into silence. Each member of all the tribes in the nearby areas was represented. They were seated along the long expanse of the circle.

The tip of the fire reached new heights as Clayton placed more firewood on top of the previous ones.

Each of the eight representatives was seated close together. The outer banks of the circle were housed by the oldest to the youngest.

"Thank you for meeting with us," Clayton said to Maryl and Sol.

"We were happy to meet with all of you and thank you for allowing our members to this significant meeting," Sol said solemnly. He looked around. "I don't see your father, Tarson, Clayton."

"He is here but is inside. He did not like you being on our soil."

Sol looked at Clayton but said nothing.

Maryl dipped a thick stick into the fire and moved wood around. Ashes erupted around the perimeter. "Sol and I are incredibly curious about this meeting. Grady and Markus said they did not know what the topic was."

Some ashes flicked on Clayton's pants. He absently brushed them away. "We appreciate you coming. We have some important business to discuss."

"Always to the point, aren't you, Clayton? Can't we relax and let the fire's ember restore the unbalanced vibes I am getting from you?" Maryl said as she smiled her even white teeth.

"I am balanced. My sense of urgency is not made up."

"All right, Clayton. What is so important?" Maryl said as she put down the stick and looked his way.

Clayton looked at Sol and Maryl, trying to gauge how they would react. "I will come to the point. My six tribes are in trouble, and we need the help of both Sol's tribe and your tribe, Maryl."

Maryl and Sol looked at each other. Maryl gave a sly smile. "That surprises me, Clayton. Your six tribes have ruled the lands for quite some time now. The potent bloodline you all have inherited have never needed our small band of bloodsuckers help before, excuse the pun."

"Times change and opportunities present themselves, even to our rivals," Tabatha remarked calmly.

"Poor word choice, Tabatha!" Maryl said with uprising anger. "We were never *rivals*! We always had to submit to your ways, your rules, just because some of your kind can consume blood from every human, and ours cannot!"

"We know the potency of our blood has made some of you hate us," Clayton said carefully. "But I want to make amends."

"How and why, after all these centuries?" Sol demanded.

Clayton had not talked with the other tribe leaders about his proposal so desperate he was, but he knew the King's army was not far. "I propose boundary lines for each of our kind so we can live in peace."

"What?" Tabatha said out loud. Other tribe leaders followed suit.

Maryl looked around the fire pit. "I take it you did not put forth this proposal with the leaders of the other clans, Clayton?" she said humorously.

"No, but I want to show you the importance and respect I have for your two tribes."

"You can't just impose new laws without the other council members agreement!" Tabatha yelled.

"I can, and I will. It is my right as the leader of all the tribes."

"You are invoking the *primacy* law? In a thousand plus years, it has never been used!" Platov said incredulously.

"This is getting interesting," Sol remarked. "You're giving away concession after concession."

"I say we hear him out," said Eli. "After all, he could have killed me over two hundred years ago. He let me live when I and some of our brethren attacked his village."

"Despite Eli not being an elder, I respect his opinion. I will hear Clayton out," Maryl intoned.

Clayton could see the open anger on the elders and the rest of his tribes, but he knew they would never rule against him nor retaliate against him.

"I offer lines being drawn all across Great Britain and beyond."

"How would we know where one boundary ends, and one begins?" Maryl asked.

"We would mark the trees, the lands themselves, and other structures with our blood. No matter how old the blood becomes, we would always be able to smell it. And we can smell over great distances."

"And what of centuries to be?" Sol asked.

"I don't understand," Clayton said with uncertainty.

"When our respective tribes branch out, and new territories are claimed, even across the pond in the Americas, how are we to discern whose territory is whose?"

"I have with me maps of the Americas and beyond. We can draw the lines in blood right here and right now."

"Why are you so desperate that you would divide the lands of the entire world between the eight of us?" Maryl asked.

"Because we require your help," Clayton responded quickly. Even now, he could hear the army approaching a couple of kilometers away.

"I suggest you tell us what you need from us before we commit to an answer. I simply will not offer any assistance of any kind without knowing what mine and Maryl's tribe's responsibilities are," Sol said sternly.

The two tribes nodded in agreement.

"Fair enough," Clayton said as he looked around the fire—open hostility registered on some of the elders. "King George's army is fastly approaching and plan on attacking us and taking away our land. We need your help in defending us."

"Why? Aren't your type able to easily stop them?" Maryl asked with fake sincerity.

"While we are considerably stronger, there will be too many of them."

A silence followed. The hissing and popping of the firewood were a distant memory as the ramifications of Clayton's appeal sunk in.

"You want us to help fight alongside you against the King?" Maryl asked doubtfully.

"Yes."

"In exchange for boundary lines across the globe, so we needn't fear any attack or acts of aggression?"

"Yes, that's exactly what I mean," Clayton said with renewed hope that all was not lost.

Maryl turned to Sol. "What do you think? Should we help them?"

"I think it's in our best interest and survival if we do," Sol remarked simply.

"Then let's draw blood on the written contract right away! That way, right here and right now, the agreement is binding. No one may alter it," Clayton said.

Clayton took the parchment from his pants pocket and unfolded it. "I will pass this around to the elders of all eight tribes. All of us will take our nail and slice our skin and let the flow drip down on the parchment."

Clayton went first, then Maryl and Sol. Platov and the others did the same, but they showed their displeasure.

When the parchment came back to Clayton, he handed it to Grady. "Put this in the cupboard in the kitchen for safekeeping."

Grady sped to their house.

"Now what?" Maryl asked.

"Now, we wait. It won't be too much longer, a couple of minutes at most," Clayton said with relief.

Tabatha hissed in his ear. *"You have no idea what you have just done!"*

"Oh, yes, I do. I saved our tribe," Clayton whispered back.

"Look around you! How many tribal elders would have agreed to your insane proposal?"

"None, that's why I invoked the *primacy* law," Clayton hissed back.

"You better know what you're doing, Clayton. Our continued existence depends on it."

Clayton got up. "It's time. Prepare for an attack. Remember something when we fight today! We will not cave into tyranny! We are proud and able-bodied!"

Everyone rose. Clayton took a quick headcount. He estimated over two thousand vampires. Clayton closed his eyes and put his hyper hearing to use. He counted several thousand heartbeats of soldiers. For the first time in over seven hundred years, he was afraid.

The first soldiers entered the area where the firepit still burned. The king's soldiers looked around while the vampires had scattered before their arrival.

The red uniforms of King George's army made them stand out. Easy targets, thought Clayton as he snuck up behind one. He fed on the man's blood to gain much-needed strength. He noted the other vampires did as well.

Since they could smell the blood, Clayton wasn't worried anyone would die from sucking on the wrong blood type.

After fifteen minutes of fighting, with the mounting bodies of King George's army sprawled over the ground, Clayton thought of something that never entered his mind until now.

If King George did not know about vampires, why was Clayton seeing a bunch of dead vampires on the ground too? The rifles should not be able to penetrate their skin. It was something else Clayton thought as he sniffed a deceased vampire.

And that's when he knew he had been betrayed.

Heartbeats were heartbeats. There was no distinction between humans and vampires when it came to the beating of hearts, except in rare cases when there was a medical condition such as heart murmurs, a fast or slow heartbeat, or if someone had a pacemaker. But the smell of the vampires never changed. He had been tricked. He had been duped, but by whom?

Clayton sped to the edge of his house. He crept beside his home until he was at the front door. Detecting no heartbeats within a twenty-yard range outside, he sped in his house and looked around.

He saw several deceased vampires lying next to his father. Clayton checked for a heartbeat. His father, the mighty Tarson, lay still. Anger swept through him from the loss of his father. He looked around when he realized his sons Grady and Markus were nowhere to be found.

He sensed several humans behind him. He turned around. The soldiers backed away when they saw Clayton's unchecked anger in his eyes. He raced to them and dispatched them without care.

A roar that came from Clayton's anguish eclipsed the sound of the rifles shooting.

He witnessed several soldiers looting his crops and putting them in large burlap bags. They stopped when they heard his battle cry.

Rifles were targeted at him from all angles as he went into the heat of the ongoing battle. Bullets bounced off him as he swept through the soldiers, slaying them with unchecked rage. His side was losing, which was supposed to be impossible. And then he saw the reason.

Sol was looking around and finally saw Clayton. Sol had Grady and Markus in each hand, holding them by the throat. "These your children?" he said tauntingly.

"Why?" the words escaped Clayton as Sol sliced his kid's throats and sped away before Clayton could get to him.

Panic forced Clayton to yell, "Retreat! We were set up! *Retreat!*"

Out of a few hundred vampires that made up his tribes, Clayton saw less than a hundred survivors. He motioned them toward him as he saw the truth unfold. There stood Maryl, and she was looking defiantly at Clayton.

"Now!" Maryl yelled to her right side. Over a hundred of her vampires jumped high into the air. They had burlap bags too, but they weren't stealing crops.

"Oh no," Clayton said as he realized what was in the bags.

"Dump them!" Maryl hollered.

The weapon Grady had told him about was in the bags! A fine mist of gray powder engulfed the skyline and fell steadily to the ground.

Not long before the mist touched the ground, he started to cough up blood. What manner of weaponry did they possess that could penetrate their impenetrable skin without affecting their own?

Before she sped away, he saw Maryl. She smiled fearlessly while she showed him the contract they had all just signed in blood, not an hour ago.

Clayton knelt and threw up. "Had I known you were in cahoots with King George, and not in my weakened state right now, I would kill you!" he said in-between nausea and retching.

Maryl smiled and then raced away.

Clayton staggered to the ground. His eyes burned, and his throat was on fire. He was losing consciousness when a tall African American woman appeared before him.

"Am I dreaming?"

"No, I am Desiree, and I am here to help you, your brothers and sisters."

"Why aren't you sick?"

"Because I am not of your sweet-smelling blood."

"You would help someone, not of your type? Why?"

"Everyone deserves life," Desiree stated simply.

Desiree took Clayton by his shoulders and hoisted him on her back. Her sudden acceleration made his nausea worse. She carefully placed Clayton on the ground well beyond the influence of the mist.

Desiree was swift as she rounded up as many as she could and laid them near Clayton.

Several minutes later, Clayton was able to sit up. He perched himself against a tree as Desiree sat beside him.

"That was a courageous thing to do, Desiree."

"What do you mean?"

"Saving some of my tribes and me. You'll be an outcast with the other smellers like yourself."

"I never really fit in any classification."

"By definition, you have to fit into one of the different smelling groups."

"I base vampires on their actions and not what smell comes from them."

Clayton peered at her youthful appearance. "I find that I am swiftly growing fond of you, Desiree."

"Thank you."

"My name is Clayton of the Cole Tribe."

"I know who you are. Now stand up. We need to get you and your sweet smellers out of here."

Desiree led Clayton several feet further when he fell to the ground. "You're much weaker than you know, Clayton."

"What sort of weaponry did I just witness?" Clayton asked in stark terror.

"I don't know. I am not privy to such information."

"Take me to the nearest town. I have friends there that can help my remaining comrades and me."

"Of course," Desiree said as she zipped away.

As his home grew in the distance, Clayton swore he would avenge his family. He didn't care how long it took.

Chapter Nine
The Inception of the Fellowship of the Fangs
Stanford University, Assembly Hall
1912

Stanley Pearson was behind the curtains and looked at the full upside-down U shaped assembly hall with a measure of delight and unease. His packed audience of affluent and educated people gave him hope he would be taken seriously in California as opposed to his other ridiculed misfortunes across the United States.

He looked at the large poster board and his poster, but the massive clouds of smoke from people's cigarettes threatened to cloak the arena. Pearson saw his new assistant and pulled him aside. "Mister Ward open the curtains and then the windows! I need the assembly hall smoke free for me to proceed!"

"Yes, sir," Marty Ward said and hurriedly walked away.

Marty whisked people from their duties and assigned them the arduous task of opening the massive red curtains and using long poles to unlatch the window locks and open them.

Only after Marty was satisfied most of the smoke was gone did he go to Stanley Pearson.

Stanley Pearson was sitting at a lone desk when Marty whispered, "Ahem."

"Yes, what is it, Marty? Can't you see I'm going over my notes?"

"Of course. I am here to let you know the cigarette smoke has dissipated. You're free to give your lecture, sir."

"Excellent!" Stanley said as he slapped Marty on the back. "I knew I could count on you!"

"Thank you, sir. I just wanted to say I have been following your exploits..."

"Yes, yes, of course, you have," Stanley said absentmindedly as he took a few deep breaths, walked to the curtain, waited a few more seconds, and then, in a dramatic display of showmanship, swung both curtains open wide.

The applause was a bit more unenthusiastic as he had hoped. He refused to let that affect his speech.

Stanley looked around his audience for a few seconds for effect. "Ladies and gentlemen, right now, sitting across from you, or perhaps several rows from you could lurk a species that has gone unnoticed for eons!" The crowd echoed with surprise. Stanley took that as a good sign.

He pointed to the gathering as he walked across the stage. "You see, I've been researching a phenomenon for the past decade! And I am here to tell you in no uncertain terms, that vampires do indeed exist!" He stopped walking and faced the crowded arena.

The laughter was immediate, as Stanley expected. It always was. But this assemblage was going to be different from his other lectures.

A crowd member from the back row rose. "Absurd!"

Another man stood up. "Preposterous!"

Stanley put up his hands. "Gentlemen, let me finish! Please, take a seat!"

Both wives took their husbands by the hand and forced them to sit. Chuckles rippled through the crowd.

"On May the 26^{th,} in 1897, an author published a book about a vampire. The book was loosely based on Vlad the Impaler. I say to my audience that I have credible evidence he based his book about a species of humans that have largely been ignored...."

A person stood up and was rigid in his defiance. "Oh come off it, sir! You expect us to believe this nonsense?"

Stanley looked at the person with assurance. "Of course, I do! You spent your money to come to listen, so why doesn't everyone stop complaining and actually listen to what I have to say?"

All across the vast land of the United States, Stanley Pearson had to listen to people's bellyaching when he lectured about the topic. He was fed up. This time if people left the assembly hall, Stanley would feel he had stuck up for himself.

"I have heard complaints similar to yours all across our great nation. Please, just listen to me for a few moments, and then all of you can go on your merry way. That's all I ask."

Nods of assent swept through the crowd. Finally!

"The author based his book on Transylvania in Romania, but he never went there. However, it was in Eastern Europe, where I researched the topic further!"

"Who funded your research?" a man to Stanley's left asked.

"I belong to the Fellowship of the Fangs. They sponsored me. While I do travel across the globe, when I am in town, we have a meeting every Friday night at the library if anyone is interested."

"What do you do at the meetings?" someone asked.

"We discuss ways of exploring other parts of the world using new and improved technology. We seek to find abnormalities of any kind. Some of the members are scientists!"

He took a handkerchief from his shirt pocket and dabbed his forehead.

Stanley looked at his audience and continued.

"For a millennium or more, in Eastern Europe, there were people of nobility and royalty who had a disorder. Nay! I daresay they had a blood disorder! And what is this blood disorder called? It is called Porphyria! (4) Yes, folks, there are people from times past and evident today that display characteristics like a vampire!"

"What sort of characteristics?" a stout man in the middle aisle stood up and asked mockingly.

"You, sir, are a clever person for asking such an insightful question!" Stanley let the sentence die for maximum effect.

"Let us list the traits, shall we?" Stanley bellowed to the audience as he lifted his left hand and put up his index finger. "Firstly, they exhibit hypersensitivity to light! Just like a vampire does!"

The gallery of people quieted down a little.

Stanley put up another finger. "Secondly, people with Porphyria tend to have repeated attacks from the disorder.

That disease folks, cause the gums of the mouth to recede, which explains their fangs!"

A strange hush fell among the crowd of people. No one moved.

Another one of Stanley's fingers rose steadily. "Thirdly, the urine from people with that particular disease causes their liquid discharge to turn red!"

Gasps echoed through the audience.

Stanley nodded sagely. "Yes, blood-red, folks!"

Stanley let that sink in before continuing. He put up the fourth finger. "Everyone knows vampires don't like garlic. For these people that have the affliction, they have an aversion to garlic! Maybe it's the smell; perhaps it's from a component of garlic like sulfur or something. I will have to do more research. I do know they are in unbearable pain when exposed to garlic! I kid you not folks!"

The crowd shifted uncomfortably in their seats. Each neighbor looked at the other in controlled fear.

"There are more symptoms, but I wanted you to understand the nature of the beast involved!" He looked around his hushed audience. "Ladies and gentlemen, vampires do indeed exist!" Stanley lowered his eyes to the floor.

A gentleman from the front row lifted himself slowly. "My name is Clayton Cole, and I want to know…do you have any proof, sir?"

Stanley gradually raised his head and nodded gravely. "That I do, sir." He peered to his right and moved his head slightly, then looked back at Clayton. "That I do."

A moment later, a small metal cage on wheels pushed by Marty Ward went onstage. Not a peep was heard except the squeaking noise of the wheels turning slowly and reverberated across the quieted stage. *Squeak... squeak... squeak.* Intakes of breath and moans vibrated through the assembly. Several women fainted by the sight of the human inside.

Stanley gazed at the audience's expected reaction at his prized possession.

"Ladies and gentlemen, I give you the modern-day vampire!"

The bald man was dressed in a one-piece black gown that went up to his chin. His skin was exceedingly pale, almost a pasty white. His black fingernails protruded out several inches. His eyes were pitch black as he ran from side to side. He lunged at the cage, trying to free himself. When he banged into the metal bar, he hurt himself and opened his mouth in pain. To the audience, he revealed his teeth that resembled fangs.

"Did you see his fangs? I told you!" Stanley yelled to his horrified audience.

The assembly hall patrons recoiled in terror, and that was fine with Stanley. Word will spread about what they've seen today. Stanley was beside himself with the thought of ticket sales increasing for his next show.

He put out his hands to calm the mass of people from exiting the assembly hall. He hit the metal bars with his hands several times. "See? The metal bars keep him at bay, but only barely! I know it's a lot to take in folks. Rest assured, he is a danger to everyone if he were to be set free!

Don't be fooled by his cowardice nature! He seeks only to suck your blood while you're sleeping!" He turned to the man in the cage. "The man is a monster! But don't worry, he is under lock and key twenty-four hours a day and seven days a week for your protection!"

Stanley waited until the crowd simmered down.

"Thank you, ladies and gentlemen, my assistant, Mister Ward, will see everyone out. But beware! May none of you feast your eyes upon such a beast in the bowels of our good city!"

Applause thundered from the excited crowd.

Several men begged Stanley to see the caged vampire. Stanley allowed it for a price.

After the men were allowed to touch the creature, for an additional hefty fee, Stanley felt an incredible feeling of euphoria. Finally, vindication!

"Okay, Marty, roll him backstage. And for god's sake, clean up his poop and piss!"

"Yes, sir," Marty said without complaint.

Stanley was feeling the bulge of money in his pants pocket when a man and woman walked to him.

"Sorry, folks, the show is over."

"I came over from England to see your show, Mister Pearson. I introduced myself earlier. I am Clayton Cole. I just want to talk."

"And your wife? Does she want to talk too?"

Clayton looked at Maryl. "She is *not* my wife."

"And he certainly isn't my husband."

"Do I sense animosity?" Stanley asked in amusement.

"You might say that," Maryl said as she pushed Clayton out of the way. "I wish to see the creature."

"Lady, I told you the show is over! Come back next week."

Maryl turned around."Did he just tell me no, Clayton?"

"That he did, Maryl," he said with amusement.

Maryl pushed Stanley away with ease. He was hoisted several feet back. He ran and ducked under one of the seats in the back row.

Marty Ward was cleaning out the vampire's excrement when he heard a commotion and checked to see what the noise was. He witnessed a woman not much shorter than the man push Stanley out of her way like he was a rag doll.

He ran in the back room where the caged beast was and hid in a corner before they walked in. Marty wasn't far from where the couple stood. They were observing the vampire and talking. Marty kept his breath to a minimum as he heard their exchange.

Clayton had his hands behind his back, looking at the poor human. "Caged like an animal for the world to see."

"Do you think we descended from the likes of them?"

"No, I don't think so."

"How can you be so sure, Clayton?"

"Because once the expectant mothers gave birth, the effect the Stranger had on us was immediate. This pathetic human looks devolved, not evolved like us."

"Shall we kill it to put it out of his misery?" Maryl asked.

"I wouldn't."

"Why?" Maryl asked, puzzled.

"Because if his kind lives, our kind will be under the radar."

"To think humanity thinks we look like this. I'm insulted," Maryl said jokingly.

"I'm leaving. You can stay if you want to, but please don't kill him."

"I got a *please* from the great Clayton? I'm impressed."

"First and last time."

"Okay, I'll leave him be. But what do you want to do with the human that has been listening to our conversation? He now knows real vampires exist."

Clayton sped to Marty and brought him to the cage. "I don't know. He seems harmless. He cleans the cage and does the dirty work for Stanley Pearson."

"Too bad we don't have the power of persuading people with our eyes like some legends say we do."

"Are you going to kill me?" Marty asked in fear.

"Give us a reason not to," Clayton said with menace.

"I'm just a simple janitor. I don't have money to give you."

"We don't want your money. We are deciding whether we want you to be quiet about what you heard or kill you right now," Clayton said matter-of-factly.

Marty snapped his fingers. "I know! How about making me a real honest to goodness vampire!"

"No, I will not turn any human!" Clayton said, raising his voice in disgust.

"Why not?"

"Because it would dilute his kind," Maryl said sarcastically.

"His kind? Is there more than one kind of vampire? Is there a hierarchy? Is one kind of vampire stronger than the other or others?"

"You ask too many questions, Marty. I reverse my earlier statement. I say we kill him, Maryl."

"I don't know. Marty could fill me in on this interesting creature."

"Then you deal with him. I have some matters I have to attend to. Let me know what you decided."

Maryl bowed slightly.

"Before I go, there is a question I wanted to ask you, Maryl. Why did you come to this presentation?"

"Obviously, I had no idea you would be here, but I did smell you in the audience."

"Likewise," Clayton said with a touch of irritation.

"When we recently amended the boundary areas that expanded the neutral zones to include museums, universities, holy ground, and historical sites, I took advantage of it. I often go to lectures."

Clayton looked at her, gave her a slight nod, and then sped away, leaving Maryl alone with Marty.

"Are you going to kill me?"

"I have a better idea, Marty. Let's form an alliance of sorts. I need ground troops, and you would be perfect."

"He isn't allying with your kind; you devil spawned vampire!"

Maryl turned around to see Stanley with a gun in his hand.

"Put that useless toy away!" Maryl snapped.

"I know it would be useless for you, *vampire*! He pointed the gun at Marty. "But for him? He's as good as dead!"

Maryl sighed a split second before she raced to Stanley and took the gun away from him.

"Take a good look at Stanley, Marty. This is a waste of a human being." She looked at Stanley and sniffed the air. "Well, maybe not a total waste." Maryl lunged at Stanley and sucked the blood from his vein. Stanley fell to the ground with a thud as Maryl wiped the crimson fluid from her blood-soaked lips. She bent to the ground and slit his throat to make sure he wouldn't get up since most humans survive vampire bites. Too much blood to consume.

She turned to Marty. "Where were we?"

"Umm, you wanted ground troops. And if I am someday honored to become a vampire, I will do as you say without question or hesitation from here on out!"

"Okay. But you have to solemnly swear to abide by my rules and no one else's."

"Want to make a pact in blood?" Marty asked with a smile.

"Too soon, Marty."

"I just want to serve you," Marty said in a sad tone.

Maryl thought how best she could use Marty to thwart the other blood types. Then a thought occurred to her. "I got it!"

"What is it? Do I get to kill other people?"

She looked at him. "Maybe. But right now, there is a much more subtle way you can help me."

"Just tell me!"

"You can use Stanley Pearson's group to help me."

"Huh? Do you mean that small group of older men? How?"

"I believe Stanley said the group was called Fellowship of the Fangs?"

"Yes, a few older men talk of tales which no one else believes. But they have funded some of Pearson's expeditions. All of them are wealthy."

"I want you to keep the same name because it has a certain ring to it. However, you will need to revamp the group and make it private and exclusive."

"How?"

"Do I have to do all the thinking for you, Marty Ward?"

"Sorry, all this is new to me. What do you want me to do?" Marty asked with an unparalleled eagerness that took Maryl by surprise.

"First off, get some education. Become a doctor, scientist, a tradesman such as a carpenter, welder, electrician, you know, something that will help the legitimacy of your organization when you enlist other members. And to help fund the Fellowship, you would have to have monthly dues."

"What about some sort of initiation rites and steppingstone being rewarded for hardship and training?"

"You want an initiation?" Maryl looked around to aid her in thinking about an induction into the Fellowship. She glared around the room until she spotted the perfect rite of passage.

"Got it! Come here."

She dragged Marty by the sleeve of his shirt and led him to the cage with the vampire that had the blood disorder.

"You're not making me kill him as an initiation rite, are you?"

"On the contrary, he is going to help you."

"How in the world is that *thing* going to help me?"

Maryl ignored him, went to the cage, and walked inside. The beastly man cowered in the corner; fear registered in his eyes. She bent down on one knee and took a firm grasp of his mouth and forced it open. She looked inside and found the tooth that most resembled a fang. She yanked it out and pushed him backward.

"You want me to wear that fang tooth around my neck like a necklace?"

She looked at the fang and shrugged. "If you want to and hand it down to the generations of your kin. But, right now, I have another idea for its use."

"Like what?" Marty asked with uncertainty.

Maryl walked to Marty. "Take your sweater off and pull up your left sleeve."

"Why? And why my left wrist? I am right-handed."

"The vast majority of people are right-handed. You want to have secrecy. So, if you outstretch your right arm to shake hands, people would see the secret tattoo. Understand? And why are you daring to question me right now? That's not part of the rules, remember?"

Marty struggled to take the sweater off quickly. "Yes, of course. I am sorry."

When he pulled up his sleeve, he held out his exposed left wrist. It's a good thing Stanley had the correct blood type because seeing Marty's skin would have made her hungry.

Maryl rubbed the fang until she could see and smell the burning tooth. She deemed it hot when she placed the small fang on one side of his wrist and pushed it deep into Marty's skin. She left it there for several seconds, watching Marty wither in pain. Then she did the same for the other side a half-inch away. After she was done, there were two impressions of the fang on his left wrist.

"You can get it tattooed some other time, Marty. You wanted an initiation; you got one."

Marty admired the tattoo, but something was missing. "Suppose I do something worth the next step, like building an army for you? What then?"

Humans, all they want is recognition, thought Maryl. She shrugged. "I don't know…vampires like blood… how about having a tattoo of a red blood droplet come down from each side?"

"Great idea!"

"But that part you would have to earn. It won't be easy. Now, we need to discuss the specifics of the Fellowship of the Fangs, Marty."

"And I need to know all about the vampires. You had mentioned that there were different types?"

"Yes. You hungry?"

"For blood?"

"No, human. I meant food, human food."

"Yes. Do you eat our food?"

"No, but I need your full attention. I've noticed people with full bellies tend to remember things longer. Better yet, get some paper and a pencil because it's going to be a long night."

Chapter Ten
Clayton's Lab
Present Day, July 13th

Clayton had to avoid the main roads even in once neutral areas. He was not happy that Maryl Rosser had broken the treaty. She would pay for her offenses!

All he wanted was a peaceful transition into other blood types dominion. Now he was pursued by both Ray's tribes and Maryl's.

Clayton had called in favors from his cousin tribes to get him to his lab.

Now that he was there, he would need his staff's knowledge. Clayton called every one of his blood types, who were scientists in all disciplines, and told them to meet him at the lab as soon as possible.

He went to the conference room where he had his staff do a meet and greet. He counted thirteen experts, far less than he had hoped.

"Where are the other scientists?" Clayton asked.

"There were six others, sir, but they were ambushed en route here," said Jack, an immunologist.

"Were any of you followed? Were the vampires that were ambushed killed or taken away to be tortured into giving away our location?" Clayton asked with frustration.

"The thirteen of us are positive; we were not followed. We think there is a high probability they were taken away and tortured. It's only a matter of time before Maryl and Ray can extract our location from our brethren, sir."

"Damn!"

"Yes, we are, sir," Jack, who was one of the scientists, remarked. "And sir, let's not forget your former assistant, Desiree Maholmes, wants a piece of you too. She knows about this place. They might torture them even if Desiree gave them our location."

"Double damn!"

Clayton paced around the conference room. "How close are we to changing the serum, Jack?"

"Not very, sir."

"Triple damn!" Clayton looked around the room in frustration. "Any good news?"

"Yes. We have ample supply of our types of A B and AB blood for both consumption and use for our purposes," Stuart said.

Clayton raised an eyebrow. "How did you obtain so much of those types of blood, Stuart?"

"When you first informed us of the serum, we decided to do some hunting."

"Sir, if I may?" a scientist whose name escaped Clayton asked.

"I may have more good news."

"Good! What is it?"

She looked around the room. Her dark eyes, coupled with her long black hair, made her look like a warrior and not a scientist. "May I be blunt without punishment?"

"Yes, I don't make it a habit of punishing vampires, except if they're O types. What is it?"

"This lab of ours is pretty old. Twenty years old, and that's ancient for lab equipment."

"Come to the point; we don't have much time."

"I am… friends with a human that is also a scientist. The lab she works at is light years ahead of this one."

"Will this human let us use her facility?"

She smiled. "I'm sure she can be persuaded."

"How? Will she want money?"

"No, she'll want something entirely different."

"Like what?"

"She wants to be my girlfriend."

"Wait, a human woman wants to be girlfriends with a female vampire?"

"Yes, don't sound so homophobic, sir!"

Clayton sighed. "I don't care about your sexuality. I care about your friendship with a human. That can cause problems for us."

"It hasn't so far. I've known the human for three years. We went to school together."

"Sir, our surveillance cameras have picked up several vehicles speeding this way!" Jack said with fear.

"How far away are they?"

"About half an hour."

"What direction are they coming from?" Clayton demanded.

"From the north. And now we've picked up more vehicles coming from the south!"

"I'm sorry, I am at a loss as to what your name is," Clayton said to the woman in desperation.

"Cassidy, sir."

"Cassidy, what direction is your friend's lab?"

"East."

"How far east?"

"About two, maybe three hours."

"Let's go, all of you! Bring all the blood and whatever you think we'll need. I'll get the tote bag. Let's move! Use your vampire speed!"

"Sir, more cars are coming from the west and the east. They're going to surround us!"

"How far are they from the east where we have to go?"

"About an hour, sir."

"Everyone, you have one minute to get your things!" Clayton yelled as he grabbed the green tote bag and put it carefully over his shoulder.

In less than a minute, the thirteen scientists and Clayton packed their equipment into two vans.

"Let's move!" he yelled as he started up one of the two blue vans.

After fifteen minutes, Clayton felt a tinge of fear. While it was exhilarating and intoxicating, it unnerved him. He stole a glance at Jack, who managed to bring the laptop that was tracking the cameras, which in turn was tracking the O type vampires.

"Jack, how are we in relation to the vampires headed our way?"

"They are closing in. One thing we have going for us, and it's vice versa for the other vampires too, is we can't, and they can't, smell us in a closed place like the van."

"Let's take a different path! Let's go southeast to avoid them. They don't know we're in blue vans, do they?" Cassidy asked in a panic.

"I don't know if Desiree knew about the vans. I never took her to the garage, but she had plenty of free time to scope out the place," Clayton said with a heavy heart.

"Make a right at the next intersection, Clayton!" Cassidy said in desperation.

Clayton grabbed his phone. "Time to get our army prepared."

*****

Maryl sat quietly in her chair as she looked over the six scientists. She had them brought to her estate. They were in her spacious backyard on a large wooden deck with handrails surrounding the perimeter. A drop of over a hundred feet loomed close by. She was sipping some O negative blood from a wine glass while thinking.

It was pointless tieing them up. The A and B vampires would break free of any known bonds. Instead, each A and B vampires were held at bay by four vampires of her type, who had just fed and were at full strength.

Two men and a woman entered the large deck through sliding glass doors. They brought two trays of human food.

"You will eat human food, so it suppresses your vampire strength," Maryl said firmly.

"And if we don't?" a scientist asked with arrogance.

Maryl smirked. "The six of you vampires are scientists and not warriors. Give it a rest. Just be happy your types of blood allow you to consume human food."

The vampire guards forced them to the tables. The trays were put in front of them.

"Eat!" demanded Maryl.

"I don't like buttered toast," one of the scientists remarked.

"Oh, you don't like buttered toast? Is that right?" a vampire named Ray asked as he walked to the vampire.

"No, I don't. I am a very picky eater."

Ray chuckled. "Did you hear that, Maryl? He's a picky eater!" Ray nodded to two guards and grabbed the toast from the tray. He forced the vampire's mouth open and stuffed the toast inside. He held the man's nose, forcing him to chew and then swallow.

"How long does the depowering take once they eat human food?" Ray asked Maryl.

"I don't know. Several centuries ago, I recalled Eli telling us he attacked Clayton's village after they had eaten human food for two weeks."

"Two weeks? We can't wait that long, Maryl!"

Maryl threw her hands up in the air. "I know. What do you suggest, Ray?"

He pointed at the six prisoners. "This treatment of the criminals is way too soft for my liking."

"I'm too nice? Is that what you're implying, Ray?" Maryl demanded.

"Yes, you always have been to the other kinds of vampires too."

Maryl walked to Ray, who outweighed her by fifty pounds. "Are you purposely trying to offend me, Ray?"

"No, Maryl! I apologize!" Ray said as he backed away.

"That's what I thought. Tell you what; I'll let you think of a way of extracting information from them, how about that?"

"Yes, finally!" Ray said as he strolled to the prisoners.

Desiree walked outside and sat beside Maryl. She sized up the situation fast. "Maryl, if I may, may I make a suggestion?"

Maryl put up a hand for Ray to stop. "What is it, dear?"

She looked at the vampires. "Do what you will with the enemy, but I can lead you straight to Clayton."

"How so?"

"I told you what he was going to do with the serum."

"Yes, you did. What of it, Desiree?"

"He'll need a lab to alter the serum. I know where his lab is located."

A smile formed on her lips. "Ray, fun time is over. Gather as many troops as you can in this sector, and I'll do the same." Maryl looked at Desiree. "You can ride with me!"

Ray pointed to the prisoners. "What about them?"

Maryl thought briefly. "Before we go, Desiree, I want you to give them the gray mist, and make sure to film it."

Ray laughed. "How someone of your stature can be kind, and then in a split second, become the opposite is truly a spectacle to behold!"

"It has its perks," Maryl said as she opened the sliding glass door. "By the way, Ray. You stay here with some of your troops in case we're ambushed." Maryl started to walk inside.

"I have things to do, Maryl. I must leave and take my minions with me. You have enough vampires on your property."

Maryl appeared outside. "That's fine. I will confer with you later. Be available!"

Several minutes later, the tires spun as Desiree pushed the accelerator. "We will be there in half an hour, Maryl."

"Good. I want to see the look on Clayton's face when we get there."

"If it's not too late," Desiree remarked.

"Why would it be too late?"

"Like our blood types, they have listening posts, monitors, cameras… so they would probably know we're headed to their lab shortly. I am unfamiliar with the actual range of their surveillance."

"Then, I suggest you triple our speed to get there."

"Yes, Madame Rosser." Desiree pushed the car to the top speed while looking at Maryl and her soft features. A thought came to her mind. "May I ask you something?"

"Yes."

"How come Ray and *even* Clayton, fear you? You are an O negative. You can only take blood from one source of humans."

"And that fact makes me weaker than the other blood types?" Maryl said with a hint of anger in her voice.

"No, but there has to be a reason."

"Clayton does not fear me; he doesn't understand me. And Ray puts on a brave front, but underneath he is a pussycat that likes to be ordered around."

Desiree bit her lower lip. "And Ray noticed something that I did as well. One moment you're joking around, and the next second you change into something feral like an abandoned animal."

"Your point, Desiree?"

She looked at Maryl. "Nothing. Just making an observation. All I know is I am glad women vampires don't cycle every month because there would be a lot more wars with the amount of lifeblood I've witnessed from human women."

"Let's change the subject, shall we?"

Desiree looked out the window and did not speak the rest of the way to Clayton's laboratory.

She pulled up to the side of the structure. Both she and Maryl got out. Maryl scanned the perimeter and noticed dozens of cars parked carelessly.

Desiree walked to her and sniffed. "They are gone, Maryl," she said with disappointment.

Several vampires zoomed into the building and came out a minute later. "They are gone and took a great deal of lab equipment, which is odd," a tall vampire stated.

"How is that odd, Jerry?" asked Maryl.

"Because judging by the equipment they left behind, most, if not all, are outdated. I would imagine what they took wasn't much newer."

"Why would Clayton have them take equipment they can't use?" Maryl wondered aloud.

Desiree looked around and then stomped her feet. "It's a ruse! Clayton wanted us to think he took the items he needed to alter the serum!"

"What's his game plan, Desiree?" Maryl asked.

"He will need a state of the art laboratory," she said confidently.

"How many are there in a one-hundred-mile radius? That's the next neutral zone from here where some of his A and B blood types could give him refuge," Maryl said with a touch of annoyance.

Desiree took out her phone, typed in a query, looked up, and walked around.

"What are you doing?" Ray asked.

"Smart. Clayton and his tribes still have a jamming device running somewhere on the property. I can't get a signal." She put the phone in her front pocket and walked to the car. "I don't know the range of the jamming frequency. We'll have to drive until we get a signal."

They piled into the car, and several miles out, Desiree took out her phone. "We have a signal!"

"You're not supposed to use your phone and drive, Desiree," Maryl said with a suppressed smile.

"And vampires aren't supposed to exist," Desiree said with a warm smile. She typed in several strokes on the small keyboard and waited a few seconds. "It says there are three labs that meet the requirement for what Clayton needs, with two more where he could *possibly* perform the alteration."

"Possibly?" asked Maryl.

"Based on their websites, they don't do immunology, but they do gene splicing and DNA sequencing."

"I am not about to ask what the difference is, Desiree. I trust you and your instinct. Which one did you want to stop at first?"

"The closest one, which is about an hour away."

"Proceed."

Desiree grasped the steering wheel and bent it with her hands. She looked straight ahead and slammed on the gas.

"Oh Clayton, I can't wait until I get my hands around your throat," Desiree said to herself.

Chapter Eleven
Doctor Hayworth's Lab
Present Day July 13th

Cassidy pointed straight ahead. "There it is! There's the building my friend works at!"

"Let's park in the parking garage and find the closest spot," Clayton suggested.

Cassidy drove to the other side of the building, entered the parking garage, and grabbed a ticket from the machine. The long bar rose to allow them access.

Cassidy looked both ways, looking for a darkened corner to park with an elevator nearby. She found one three levels up.

"Are you sure it's safe?" Clayton asked as he got out of the vehicle.

Cassidy rushed in front of Clayton and put her hand out. "I am positive, but I can't let anyone come in with me yet."

"Why not?" Clayton asked suspiciously.

"Look around you! Would you want someone coming to your place of business with fourteen Strangers?"

"No, I would not. Go in, scope the place out, but be quick! We have no idea where any of the O types are!"

"Yes, sir," Cassidy said as she sped toward a glass door across the parking lot where the elevator was located.

"What about your army, Clayton?" Jack asked with nervousness. Clayton noticed Jack was chewing on his fingernails and spitting them on the concrete floor.

"Despite being told repeatedly over the centuries that the other A and B blood types had my back when the time came, and it really mattered, they will not be helping us."

"So, we're on our own?" Jack said as he hugged himself.

"Pull yourself together, Jack! You're an AB positive vampire! Show some backbone."

"I will show backbone until our enemies remove it."

Clayton ignored Jack's comment.

"After we're allowed to go inside, I think it best if we take a unit of blood and consume it. I want everyone at full power in case Maryl and Ray's troop of vampires should arrive," Clayton said as he addressed his scientists.

"Good idea. That way, it will take them five minutes instead of one minute to rip my backbone out," Jack said as he leaned against the blue van. "I mean, we're only outnumbered by maybe a few thousand to one. What could possibly go wrong?"

"Are you done complaining?" Clayton said harshly.

"No, but I don't think you're giving me the option to continue to whine."

"No, I'm not! Be quiet, or I will rip your tongue out!"

For the next several minutes, the tension mounted. Clayton was pacing around the van. He was getting worried that something happened to Cassidy. Were Maryl and Ray already inside? Would they be walking into an ambush? No, he didn't smell any other blood types other than the two women inside the building.

He would wait five more minutes, and then he would go in and see if anything was wrong. He mentally clicked off the minutes. When he couldn't take it any longer, he decided to start walking toward the door that led to the elevator, despite not knowing Cassidy's friend's name or what floor she worked on.

The elevator opened, and Cassidy walked out the door to the van. She was walking barefoot while her shoes were dangling in her hand. Her hair was rumpled, and her mascara had dripped on her face.

"What happened to you? Were you in a fight, Cassidy?" Clayton asked with concern.

"No, nothing like that," she said with an easy smile.

"Then why do you look so… messy?"

Jack looked at Cassidy and let out a chuckle.

"What's so funny, Jack?" demanded Clayton.

"She looks messy because she was playing catch me if you can. It looks like you were caught, Cassidy," Jack said jokingly.

Clayton was within inches of her face. "Do you mean to tell me you *tangled* while we were out here in mortal peril?"

"Do you need the use of this lab?" Cassidy shot back.

"Yes!"

"My friend would not allow us entry unless we were together."

Clayton sighed. "Fine. Are we allowed in?"

"Yes, grab your gear and let's go."

Clayton turned to the scientists. "Only one trip. Take only essentials. Let's move!"

They hauled everything except the outdated lab equipment. Clayton hoped by taking them along; it would fool Maryl. However, he doubted it. Desiree, if she was with her, was extremely bright. She would see through the deception.

The elevator door opened. Only two people with their instruments could fit in at a time.

"How did they manage to bring in all of their massive desks, shelving units, and equipment up this small elevator?" Clayton complained.

"They used the service elevator and had to haul it around the building to this section. This elevator is the closest one to her laboratory."

"And what is your friend's name?" Clayton asked.

"Andree Hayworth. Doctor Hayworth."

After a few trips, all of the equipment was brought into the lab.

Doctor Hayworth met them as the last of the equipment was inside the lab. Andree Hayworth was slightly taller than Cassidy and had light brown skin with green eyes. Her lab coat fit snug and accentuated her outfit with her white blouse and dark brown slacks.

"Andree, this is Clayton Cole, the one in charge," Cassidy said as the two shook hands.

"You have a strong grip, Mister Cole."

"I work out, thanks," Clayton said as he sniffed the air without Andree noticing. Interesting. An O negative, just as he sniffed her type outside. Why, he wondered, was Cassidy friends with a different blood type?

"I would be interested in learning what you plan on doing in the lab," Andree said with a touch of anxiety.

Clayton looked at Cassidy. "She did not tell you?"

"No. We didn't have time. We were busy catching up."
Andree looked at Cassidy and smiled. "I haven't seen her
for a while."

"Let's skip the formalities and get right to work. I'm
afraid we're pressed for time," Jack said as he pointed to
his fellow scientists.

"Of course. What work are you planning on doing
here?"

"Gene splicing and DNA sequencing using modified
enzymes," Jack said as he led the group to the nearest
station.

"I take it you have the altered enzyme?" Andree
inquired.

"Yes, we do," Jack stated simply.

"Huh, heavy hitters, I see," Andree said as she looked
at Cassidy with a raised eyebrow.

They walked down a few more rows of equipment as
Andree continued to talk.

"Since you already have the enzyme to help you, you
probably won't need *restriction* enzymes, correct?"

"No, we won't, Doctor Hayworth. We don't need the
restriction enzyme to cut the DNA at a specific location,"
Jack assured her. (5)

"Restriction enzymes are usually chosen after the
microorganisms from where they were separated. Where
did your enzymes come from?" (6)

"These are specialized enzymes produced to function
differently than most," Jack said as he took the green tote
bag from Clayton.

"Oh? Is this process ethical? Cassidy, what's going on here?" Andree said as she looked to Cassidy with concern.

"The enzymes Jack is taking out of the bag are specially designed to shred the sugars from the AB's, the A's and the B's blood. That will ensure everyone who gets the compound will have the ability to receive blood because the modified blood will be universal," Clayton said as he saw Andree's reaction.

"Incredible!" Doctor Hayworth's face went from surprise to somber. "But if the enzyme is already reworked to help people, what do you need the lab for?"

"Because it needs to be tweaked for optimal assimilation," Clayton said, hoping she wouldn't ask any more questions.

"Ah, I see. You need to know if it can be ingested, absorbed, or administered by a shot. And if it's the latter one, how many shots would it take to complete the transformation," Doctor Hayworth said as she marveled at the serum being spread across several desks.

"Exactly!" Jack exclaimed.

"Okay, well, I will let you guys do your thing. Do you know how long the process will take? My boss won't be back until next week, so you do have a few days."

"We hope to have preliminary results within that time span. Thank you for everything, Doctor Hayworth," Jack said pleasantly.

Andree Hayworth walked several aisles and turned right.

When Andree knew she was alone, she checked her watch.

"I knew they were vampires!" she said under her breath. She took out her phone and dialed a number. Since no one answered, she waited until she got the voicemail.

"Maryl! Clayton Cole is here with your enzymes! Tell me what to do!" She hung up and peered over her shoulder. She couldn't believe she had slept with Cassidy, a vampire!

Cassidy walked to the enzymes. "Let's get started," she said as she pulled up her sleeves.

"Cassidy, I don't think we will be done by next week," Clayton said.

"Why not?"

"Either the O types will get here before then, or if by some miracle they don't, I don't see the process completed by then. It will take a lot longer," Clayton said.

Cassidy looked at him. "What aren't you telling me, Clayton?"

"I sort of misled you."

"Sort of? What do you mean?"

"Everything we told you and Doctor Hayworth was a lie." Clayton looked at the other scientists and then back at Cassidy. "While we have known each other for a long time, your ethics can sometimes get in the way."

"What do moral principles have to do with anything? And equally disturbing is you made me sleep with a human being for nothing?"

"I didn't tell you to sleep with her. I only wanted the use of the lab! Don't pin that one on me! And what does that have anything to do with the fact that I lied to you?"

"I have known you for a long time, as you've stated, Clayton. I expect deception from you."

"You don't understand the consequences of that serum, Cassidy."

"Yes, I do. I am a scientist, and you are not." She picked up one of the vials. "What are we doing here with a ton of the serum, Clayton?" She looked at him and couldn't read his face. "With that serum administered worldwide, we won't have to worry anymore about what blood type is nourishable or not. It would usher in a new era. No more vampire wars or turfs. You don't seem to be on board with that."

"That's where the lie takes place. You see, you're looking at it the wrong way, Cassidy."

"Please, enlighten me, Clayton, because I fail to see any downside."

"This serum is an *abomination*! It's a disgrace to the A and B blood types!" Clayton seethed.

"How?" Cassidy asked sincerely.

"Because it will dilute our species! We are much stronger when we feed upon our own blood types! Can't you see that?"

Cassidy looked at the plethora of vials of serum. "What do you intend to do with the serum? You're not throwing it away, or we wouldn't have gone to this much trouble."

"Now, we come to the crux of why we are here, Cassidy." Clayton walked around the desk and picked up one of the vials. He watched as the other scientists were checking out the equipment and microscopes and turning them on. He cleared his throat. "I need everyone to use the blood that we brought here and using the serum, find a way

pg. 151

to reverse the stripping of the antigens off the top of the red blood cells."

"What on earth for?" Cassidy said in puzzlement. "It took Shelly Leadstone more than a decade to perfect that serum, and you want it to be changed by next week? And modified how?"

"The time frame isn't realistic, I know. I will have to improvise as we go along. However, the serum can change any type of blood to *just* the O types. I need you and the others to convert the enzyme to produce *just* A and B and AB blood types."

The implication staggered Cassidy. "But, the O blood type vampires won't be able to feed at all if you are successful! You are talking about wiping out two of the eight blood type vampires around the planet!"

"Collateral damage," Clayton said noncommittally.

"You seek to convert over forty percent of the human blood type just to get rid of the O negative and O positive vampires?"

"More like forty-four percent, but yes," Clayton said without remorse.

"I don't know if I can do this, Clayton. It's morally wrong and unethical. While I am a vampire, I am an ethical scientist as well."

Clayton grabbed Cassidy by her throat. "Look around you, Cassidy! Each one of these scientists believes strongly in my vision of the future of my blood types. I will not allow you to get in my way!"

"You're hurting me!" Cassidy said in-between ragged breaths.

He released his vice-like grip. "Are you going to abide by my vision, Cassidy?"

Cassidy massaged her throat. "Yes."

"I don't believe you. I can hear your heartbeat. It's beating at one hundred and seventy-seven beats per minute. You have no intention of helping us."

Cassidy tried to speed away, but Clayton quickly caught her. "Jack! Come here, please."

"What's up?"

"Cassidy doesn't believe in our vision of our future."

"I see," Jack said as he rubbed his stubbly chin. "What do you need from me?"

"I want you to drain her blood so we can add it to our stockpile. Can you do that?"

"Yes, but her B positive blood makes her strong. I won't be able to spare anyone to hold her down. No matter how we bound her, she will get loose."

With sudden ferociousness, Clayton seized Cassidy, found her jugular vein, and sucked her blood until she passed out.

"How about now? Can you restrain her and drain the rest?" Clayton said as blood dripped from his mouth.

"Can do," Jack said as he took hold of her arms and dragged her away.

Clayton heard the light tapping of rain hit the large window nearby. Then the rain turned from a light pattering to a torrential downpour. As he gazed out the window, he wondered where Maryl and Ray were.

The lightning crackled and branched out in all directions. Rain dove down to the ground in sheets. He liked to study mother nature and the power it bestowed upon the earth. After a moment, he turned around and leaned against a nearby desk.

Clayton hoped they had some progress before they were found. He walked back to the scientists. Jack had Cassidy strung up by a cord that was from a piece of equipment no one was using. She was still unconscious as Jack put an IV into her wrist. The deep and dark fluid was being drained into a bag and was filling up quickly.

"There are approximately eight to twelve units of blood in an average human and vampire," Jack stated as he attached another unit to the IV. "We will have plenty to nourish ourselves should this alteration of the serum take longer. At least, I hope."

Clayton nodded and took a seat. While he was concerned about the location of Maryl and Ray, he didn't understand his newfound feeling concerning Desiree. She was both a traitor and a friend. He confided in her, he had trusted her, and then in a split second, he found out she was a spy for Maryl for the last few hundred years. If his anger was so profoundly visible in his soul, if indeed he did possess one, then why could he not find it in himself to kill her? Was he falling for her?

He knew the risks of a relationship between an AB positive and an O negative blood type. They could never have children. Other types had tried, and not one vampire baby went full term. That was almost a thousand years ago, and the marriage between the O's, A's, B's, and AB's was strictly forbidden. Since his blood type had difficulty in reproducing children, it was an added complication. And he did not know if Desiree felt the same for him. He was much older, twice her age. With vampires, that fact wasn't as crucial because age wasn't too much of a factor.

"You seem lost in thought, Clayton," Jack said as he untied Cassidy and let her drop to the floor.

Clayton smiled briefly. "You might say that. I was thinking about Maryl and her ultimate plan." He lied.

"Gotcha. Speaking of plan," Jack said as he looked at the body of Cassidy, "What do you want me to do with her?"

"Get rid of her," Clayton said while returning to his thoughts.

"Okay," Jack said as he roughly hoisted Cassidy from the floor and put her over his shoulder. He walked to the window overlooking a field of trees, opened the window with his free hand, and threw her out the window, and closed it.

Clayton caught the tail end of Jack's actions. He swiftly rose from his chair but was too late to catch Cassidy.

"Why the hell did you throw her out of the window?"

Jack looked confused. "You told me to get rid of her!"

"A vampire should have a proper burial!"

"That's not what you implied! Besides, I threw her where the trees are. No one except the animals will find her."

Clayton took several deep breaths. "Okay. I will take care of it tomorrow."

Jack threw up his hands. "Next time tell me in no uncertain terms what you want!"

"Fine!" Clayton said as he realized Jack had no concept between speaking something figuratively or literally. He shook his head in frustration while sitting down.

He heard Jack mumbling under his breath about saying exactly what you mean. Clayton looked over, and Jack's friends nodded in agreement.

Clayton couldn't bear to listen to Jack's ranting. He got up and zipped to Andree's desk to see if he could learn anything else about her. Luckily, he heard her in the restroom several aisles down. She was listening to music and singing along with the tune.

He went to her desk and rummaged through her desk drawers. He opened one and found a junk drawer. Intrigued, he looked inside. He knew a junk drawer revealed what kind of person they were. He found an assortment of different styles of pens, markers, thumbtacks, safety pins, and something that could prove useful—a USB stick.

Hope gripped him as he inserted the thumb drive into her desktop. His smile faded when he saw there was only one folder. The name was unfamiliar to him.

"What does Bank clouds mean?" he said to himself out loud.

He clicked on the file, but it was password protected. He sifted through every drawer, searching for the password and found nothing.

Clayton drummed his fingers on the desk in thought. He tried her blood type, her name and other items on her desk, but was unsuccessful.

Then he remembered Andree was an O negative. Was she in the Fellowship of the Fangs? He tried all of the words of the organization. He was unsuccessful. Then Clayton tried each word individually. When he typed the name Fangs in the long rectangular box, it had worked!

His joy turned to anguish when he saw the files. And then he knew what the folder's name meant.

"Oh, no!" Clayton said as he scrolled down the list of every single A's, B's, and AB's bank records, including account numbers, what banks, and where they were located in the United States.

"How did someone on the low end of Maryl's group get access to the information? And why would Andree possess them?" he said out loud.

He was about to search the file with his name on it when he noticed a timer on the top right corner of the screen. It was a countdown from five seconds to insert a new password. He used his vampire speed to access the data. He got to see only one bank account of his that had been depleted when the time was up.

He wondered how many of his bank accounts had Maryl accessed and depleted? And why did she need all that money?

Unfortunately, the files and the folder were quickly deleted. No matter what Clayton did, he could not retrieve the folder. "Damn!"

Chapter Twelve
En Route To Laboratory
Present Day July 13th

The rain cascaded down as Desiree put the windshield wiper blades on full blast. It did little to see clearer despite having hyper eyesight. Nor did it help ease the built-up anger she was feeling. She had been duped. In three hundred years, Clayton had never had reason not to trust her. If she had not told Clayton about the functions of the stupid watch only humans from the Fellowship of the Fangs wore, she would be in a better place with Maryl!

Of all the secrets she had gleaned over the three centuries, the one she was most proud of was the knowledge, and subsequent whispering in Maryl's ear was helping, she prayed, offset the extermination of her beloved O blood types.

The watch wasn't the only recent blunder Desiree thought as she took a napkin from the side drawer and wiped her side of the window inside. It helped her see a tad bit better.

No, it was not as bad, but still a mistake in her eyes. She should have told Maryl about Stephen, and his meetings with the mysterious Max, who was Clayton. She knew the risk by not relating Maryl to the news. In her defense, she thought silently; she wanted to see how it played out. Killing Stephen Ward had to be done despite his grandfather starting the Fellowship of the Fangs. She was deep uncover and couldn't afford Stephen to learn anything about her role with Maryl, which was ironic because it was Maryl who brought the Fellowship of the Fang to its present-day powerhouse secret society.

"Are you with us, Desiree? You seemed lost," Maryl said softly as she stroked Desiree's hair.

"Yes, sorry. Thinking about the past is all."

"The past is gone. Pondering about the present and stopping Clayton and his insane plan is what you should be focused on."

"I've been doing some contemplation about that too. We have been to two out of the three laboratories, and they haven't been there. I am hoping the third one is the charm. We need to stop the extinction of our blood types."

"Do you think they will be able to convert the enzyme into the other six blood types?"

Desiree stopped at the light and looked at Maryl and her soft features. She smiled. "The good news is that it took Doctor Shelly Leadstone years and years to perfect her serum. To return that enzyme back to its original state and then change it again, I surmise it will take much longer."

The light turned green. They weren't far from the last laboratory on their list.

"Unless they can find a different enzyme to work with, which would prolong the process, thereby increasing the time frame," Desiree said while turning right.

"Basically, we have no clue. We still need to have a sense of urgency about this, Desiree."

Desiree swerved hard right, narrowly avoided a deer. The car veered toward an embankment. Desiree managed to pull the vehicle away at the last second.

"Streets are slippery; you might want to slow down," Maryl said with a tight smile.

"Every second we waste time slowing down, the more they are ahead of the game."

Maryl pointed ahead. "Here is the third one on our list."

They pulled into a long gravel driveway. Desiree noticed the dull gray paint of the building matched the mood she was in from the downpour.

They got out and took a look. "The windows are dark."

"Meaning the lights are off and no one is inside? Or meaning they are hiding inside?" Maryl asked to no one in particular.

"I can't smell them, Maryl. There would be a residual smell we should be able to pick up."

Maryl took her fist and smashed the back bumper of the car. "Damn! Where are they?"

Desiree leaned against the wet car, but because of her invulnerable skin did not feel her soaked clothes. She took out her phone and plugged in the other two laboratories. The nearest one was at a university about twenty miles from their present location.

"Maryl, another laboratory is at a university about forty minutes from here. Want to check it out?"

Maryl threw her hands in the air. "Why not? Might as well do something!" She got in and slammed the passenger car door so hard, Desiree thought the door hinges would separate from the frame.

Desiree put her phone in the holder and inserted the address.

"Head southeast and turn left on Hanson street."

"How am I supposed to know where southeast is?" Desiree complained out loud as she got in the vehicle.

"Just drive. The English woman will reroute you."

Desiree turned on the radio, and Maryl turned it off. "I prefer silence or listening to the pitter-patter of the rain beating against the window," Maryl said softly. She turned to Desiree. "Unless you want to engage in an intelligent conversation."

"No, I'm fine."

After a few moments of silence, Maryl asked, "What is the University's name?"

"It's not a top-notch university like MIT, but they do seem to get grants for the top of the line medical equipment. It is called the University of Indianapolis."

"I am acquainted with that school. They don't have a large laboratory. But they do have a large research lab led by Doctor Andree Hayworth. I am friends with her."

"Give her a call, Maryl. It could save us a trip."

Maryl took out her phone. "Look at that. Andree left a voicemail!"

Andree was at her desk, sipping coffee and eating a roast beef sandwich. She was listening to music on her iPhone. She pushed back her long blond hair as she belted out an old song.

"Telll meeee wwhhyyy I'm dreaamming of yyoouuu; I want the world to know..."

Andree almost jumped out of her chair when her phone ringtone interrupted her song.

"Hello?"

"Andree?"

"Yes, who's speaking?"

"It's Maryl. Maryl Rosser!"

Andree jumped up and spilled her coffee all over her lab coat. "Uh, hi, Maryl! How are you?"

"I'm doing wonderful! Are you putting the endowment I gave you to good use?"

She looked around her lab. All of the latest equipment was because of Maryl Rosser. "Yes! I sure am! I also downloaded the folder you gave me, but..."

"Good. Good. I have a question for you, an important one.'"

"Okay."

"You said Clayton and other people were there?"

"Yes. Clayton and his vampire friends! They wanted the use of my lab."

"Are they still there?"

"Yeah. They have your serum they're trying to tweak."

"How many of them are there?"

"Fourteen. Thirteen scientists and Clayton Cole."

"Excellent! Now, can you do me a favor, Andree?"

"Anything to get rid of the vile bunch," Andree said vehemently.

"No matter what, keep them there. I want to surprise them and then kill them."

"I will do my best."

"But you must not, under any circumstances, tell them I am coming. Are we clear?"

"Yes. How long until you get here?"

"We're about forty minutes out."

"Okay."

"Remember to keep them there, Andree, and you will be rewarded."

Andree was beside herself. "Will I get another blood droplet on my wrist?"

"Yes, I will make sure of it," Maryl promised.

"Okay, but I have to tell you something! Someone here that knows computers went on my computer and found the folder you had sent me."

Silence.

"Did you send it to the people I told you too?"

"Yes!"

"And the second password notification. Was the information obtained?"

"The second notification was used, and the folder and files were deleted. If someone managed to glean what was on those files, I do not know."

"Okay. I'm glad you still have it in your email attachment. We'll be there shortly."

"Bye!" Andree hung up and sprinted to action. The place was a mess. She spilled coffee on her keyboard, and her roast beef fell on the floor. She looked around for a towel. The kitchen! She walked swiftly around the corner and almost ran into Clayton.

"Sorry! I spilled my coffee and dropped my roast beef sandwich. Have to be tidy!"

"No problem. Need any help?"

"No," Andree said too quickly.

Clayton looked at her but did not move out of her way.

"Okay. Excuse me." Andree tried to step away, but Clayton moved in her direction.

"What are you doing?"

"I am wondering about something."

"Like what?" She tried to move away, but Clayton matched her move.

"We all heard you singing, badly, by the way. And then, poof! All of a sudden, you stopped. You were whispering."

"Of course, I was whispering. I just dropped coffee on myself."

"I would imagine you would yell if coffee fell on your lab coat," Clayton said as he pointed to her white jacket splattered with coffee stains.

She shrugged. "Some people yell, some people whisper. I whisper."

He moved away from her. "Sure. My apologies."

Andree muttered under her breath and walked away.

Clayton sped to her desk and found what he was looking for. Andree's phone. He could have sworn she was talking with someone. He picked it up and tried to see if anyone had called her, but he needed her four-digit pin. He tried numerous combinations. None worked. He knew she was coming back; he could hear her. Clayton decided to stay. He put the phone down.

"What are you doing?" Andree asked suspiciously.

"I told you I wanted to help you clean up the mess."

Andree tried to push Clayton. He didn't move. "And I told you I didn't need any help! You are abusing my hospitality, mister!"

Clayton decided it was time to switch tactics. "I know you were on the phone, Andree. Our work here is very private. I need to know who you spoke to."

"I told you I did not speak to anyone! Leave me alone!"

She brushed past him, but Clayton took hold of her arm. "I am not done with you."

"Let go of me!"

"*Who was on the phone?* I won't let you go until you tell me."

"Cassidy! Cassidy! Tell your idiot friend here to let me go!"

"Cassidy is no longer here, Andree. She left."

"You liar! Cassidy!"

"I have had enough, Andree" He grabbed Andree by the scruff of her neck and threw her across the room. He raced to her before she got up.

Andree felt the side of her head. Her hand came back bloody.

"Tell me who was on the phone, or I will continue to hurt you. I don't want to, but trust me, I will."

He knelt to Andree, who shrank in the corner like a scared puppy. She whimpered and started to cry. "I only wanted it to be a surprise!"

"What are you talking about?"

"The phone call! A mutual friend of ours made me swear not to tell you she was on her way."

Clayton's eyes creased. "*Who called you?* Tell me! Was it Maryl Rosser? I know you're an O negative like her!"

"Yes! It was Maryl Rosser, and she's coming for you!"
She stood up. "You don't know who you're up against! She
will tear you limb from limb!"

Andree went from a meek person to a tiger in seconds.

"How much time before she arrives?"

"She's almost here!" spit came from her mouth as she
yelled.

He didn't want to hurt Andree after she helped them
get situated here. However, he couldn't let her talk to Maryl
anymore. Typically he didn't mind taking people out if they
deserved it. With a heavy heart, he went behind Andree and
took a firm hold of her throat. The pulsating rhythm of the
blood beating energized Clayton, which made his fangs
appear. He had to control himself. He could take her blood;
he could take anyone's blood if he wanted to. But he did
not want to take hers.

"Scared to take my blood? Is it because of my blood
type? Are you that high and mighty you deem me unfit?
Perhaps my blood is unworthy?" Andree taunted.

"How long until Maryl comes?"

"You can go suck…"

Clayton's anger rose from her refusal to give him an
approximate time until Maryl got there and now her almost
eager willingness to die. He released his fangs and pierced
her skin.

As Clayton withdrew from sucking Andree's blood, he
felt no nourishment, no sudden energy beating through his
veins. He took out his fangs from her throat, turned her
around, and looked at her.

"Why am I not gaining nourishment from your blood, Andree?"

Andree smiled mischievously. "I have *Saccharum sanguine.*"

Clayton looked at her. "I know it's Latin you've spoken. The last word means blood. What does the first word mean?"

"It means I have synthetic blood." (7)

"Synthetic blood? Where? How? I did not think technology had come that far."

"It was synthesized with the A and B's in mind. It mimics blood, but you won't gain any nutrients. I make sure I have some every day in case I ever meet your blood types. That was what I was doing in the bathroom earlier!"

No wonder she didn't care if he sucked her blood! "Let me guess. Maryl Rosser?"

"Yes, and she has stuff coming down the pipeline that will make you want to consider turning human!"

Clayton looked at Andree's smug face. Her arrogance infuriated him. With a swift motion, he took his finger and sliced her throat from side to side. He made sure he did not cut too deep to prolong her death.

After Andree fell to the floor, he took off her stained lab coat and pulled up her left sleeve. Yup, just like he thought. She was part of the fellowship of the fangs. He wondered how many of the other fellowship humans had the same type of *Saccharum sanguine*; he thought as he took note that Andree had three red blood droplets on one side and none on the other. Still, she wasn't high in rank, but she wasn't the lowest minion.

Clayton noticed her watch now but hadn't seen one earlier. Damn!

He ran to his scientists. "We have to leave now! Unfortunately, we were discovered. Maryl is on her way, and I have no idea when she'll arrive. Pack your stuff, now! And don't take what you don't need. I'd like to leave without having to make eight trips." He grabbed the tote bag. "And leave the lights on, that old trick never fails."

They rushed to the vans and left without looking back in four trips.

Thirty minutes later, Desiree pulled up to the university and pointed upward. "The lights are on. Hopefully, they are still there."

"I see they have a parking garage around the corner. Let's go in there and get as close as we can," Maryl said while she pointed.

They drove slowly. The gravel and the rain made their progression slow.

Maryl aimed her finger at the ground. "Tire tracks."

The car screeched to a halt on the first floor in the parking garage.

"I don't see an entrance to the building on this floor," Maryl stated.

"There are stairs we can climb," Desiree suggested.

"No, I don't smell them. Go another level up."

They drove to the second floor. "Same stairs are leading up."

"Drive to the next level," Maryl commanded.

On the third level, they saw the elevator. They got out and sniffed the air.

"They are either here, or recently left," Desiree yelled.

"Go! Take the elevator, Desiree! Seek your revenge!"

Desiree's eyes grew darker, and when she smiled, fangs were protruding out. "Gladly!"

She and other vampires rushed to the elevator. They banged on the door impatiently, waiting for their floor so the door would open.

Maryl spoke to several vampires hanging out outside their cars. "Go and take the stairs from the floors! See if they are hiding there!"

Most of them left at once. Some stayed behind to protect Maryl. She still had close to two dozen O negative vampires at her disposal in case they came through an exit she wasn't expecting.

Several minutes later, Desiree came out of the elevator with the other vampires.

"They are gone."

"Let me talk to Andree. She was supposed to keep them here!" Maryl said in utter disappointment.

"I'm afraid she is dead, Maryl. Her neck was sliced from side to side, and her left wrist was exposed. They also drained the blood from one of their own scientists."

"What's gotten into Clayton?"

"He's desperate, which makes him dangerous, Maryl." Desiree said evenly.

"Why is he so hellbent on destroying our types? He can consume any human he wants, while we can't!"

"He's delusional. If he didn't know about the stupid serum, we wouldn't be in this predicament," Desiree said in agitation.

Maryl rushed to Desiree and grabbed her by the neck. "Are you saying that somehow this is all *my* fault? Who was the one that didn't tell me about Stephen visiting and *giving* the serum to Clayton?"

Desiree gasped for breath. She was losing consciousness. "I'm... sorry, I wanted to see how it played out," she said as Maryl released her sturdy grip. Desiree fell to the wet ground.

"Get up! I have work to do!" Maryl admonished.

Desiree grabbed the door handle for support as she slowly raised to a standing position.

"I favored you, Desiree, but don't think that off-handed remark won't go unpunished! Do we understand each other?" Maryl tilted her head. A few of the vampires sped to her. "Watch her. She is no longer trustworthy!"

Desiree held her throat and traced Maryl's fingertips along the neck. Her breath felt constricted as she sucked in air. She coughed so that she could expel air.

The vampires returned from the stairs. "No one was hiding, Maryl. We would have smelled them and heard them."

Maryl looked up to the rainy night and yelled, "Where are you, Clayton Cole?"

Chapter Thirteen
Indiana, Along Interstate 70
Present Day, July 15th

"We have been traveling for two days, Clayton! We need to find a research facility soon, or I'm going to go nuts," Jack lamented.

Clayton looked at the multitude of coolers. "Do we have enough ice?"

"For now, yes. Ice on blood will only last seven hours. We'll need some by tonight."

"Once we find a facility with large coolers, how long does blood last?" Clayton asked curiously.

Jack was driving and reading the phone map. "Thirty-five days from the time the blood was taken," Jack said as he looked up. "I've done an exhaustive search. We probably have to head eastward toward the east coast to find a facility that meets our needs."

"I'd prefer somewhere in the Midwest. I have more choices for safehouses here."

Jack turned right at the next exit. He slowed his speed at the exit ramp. "Right or left?"

"I always turn right," Clayton said.

Jack found a large shopping plaza with hardly any cars.

Clayton glanced around. Just outside the periphery of the stores lurked a myriad of trees that gave it a secluded look. "Forget something, Jack?"

Jack parked near the other cars. The other blue van pulled in beside her.

"What are we doing here?" Clayton asked.

"We need to talk," Jack said with seriousness.

"Okay, talk."

"Outside, please."

Clayton left the van. All of the scientists followed him.

"What's up, Jack?"

"We were talking amongst ourselves, and we decided we have had enough. We want out."

Clayton looked at all of them. "Is this a mutiny, Jack?"

"Of sorts. No, consider it an ultimatum."

"I'm listening."

"We need to know *definitively* by tonight, where we are going to work, or we're going to return to our old lives."

"Why?"

"Because we are not fighters or warriors. We are the peaceful bunch of the A and B blood types. We don't wage war with other vampires; we wage war on bacteria and viruses that could affect our blood type."

"That's what we're doing!" Clayton said in exasperation.

"If Maryl and Ray's merry vampire band weren't pursuing us, I would agree with you."

"Okay, let's talk about where we can go," Clayton said to appease them.

"We've discussed countless places, and we've come up *empty*," Jack said with frustration.

Abruptly, an idea surfaced. "Empty? Did you just use the word empty?" asked Clayton.

"Yes, what about it?"

"Do me a favor, Jack?"

"Sure, what is it?"

"Look to see what happened to the Sequencing Enzymes Institute of Technology after we stole the serum."

"Sure." Jack took out his phone, played with the keyboard, and waited. "Well, well. It seemed big named investors invested several billion into Doctor Leadstone's serum. When the enzymes were stolen, and Doctor Leadstone was killed at the institute, the stockholders sold their shares, and the stocks soon tanked. The building is vacant." He touched more keys. His hands were a blur. "They aren't even listed on the Dow Jones, the New York Stock Exchange or the Nasdaq. In essence, they no longer exist."

"Do you think their equipment would still be there?"

"I don't know how long it would take to sell off the machines and vacate the premises. Some companies wouldn't bother and just take the loss."

"There you have it. No mutiny. We go get ice tonight and then break-in."

"What about electricity? Even if it is still on, which I doubt, people will notice."

"I am more than sure they have backup generators, and given its remote location, I doubt a few lights would be noticed," Clayton said with false confidence. "Perhaps we can turn off the lights during nighttime."

Jack looked around the other scientists. "What do you think? Should we give it a try one last time?"

The murmurs of their agreement were music to Clayton's ears.

"Isn't this the time when humans say, 'let's get something to eat?'" Jack joked.

Clayton pointed to the van. "We have some blood inside if anyone is hungry?"

"Let's eat and get a move on," Jack said with authority. "It will take a couple of hours to get there."

They gulped the blood, not knowing if it would be their last meal.

"I feel so energized, I could lift a building," Jack teased.

"Since you're so full of energy, take some vampires and get some ice."

"What are you going to do?"

"I need to think about what our next move is going to be."

When Jack and several of the vampires left, Clayton went inside the van. He put his hand underneath the seat and pulled a rug loose. He extracted a prepaid phone and keyed in a number.

"Hello?"

"Hi Maryl, this is Clayton."

"How are you, Clayton? So good to hear from my frenemy."

"I am fine in spite of your attempts at finding me. I know you're telling someone to trace this call, don't bother. I don't plan on being here long."

"What do you want?"

"I want you to listen and understand my side of the story."

"Your side? Are you kidding me, Clayton? You are trying to destroy two species of vampires, which does not warrant me listening to your side!"

"Take away your hatred for me and listen!"

"No, I don't think I will."

"Then, you will never understand!" Clayton said with resentment.

"What's to understand, Clayton? Just because you are stronger than my O blood types doesn't give you the right to obliterate our kind!"

"And making a gray mist powder to kill us? And let's not forget the serum *you* created! You claim it is to level the playing field, but I submit to you it would destroy the A and B, plus the AB blood types!" Clayton let that sink in for a second. He had to watch how much longer he was on the phone before they could trace his call. "If we seemed arrogant, it was out of fear."

"Fear? I created the serum so every vampire could be equal, so every one of us may gain nourishment without the fear of sucking blood from the wrong blood type and suffering the consequences! What is the fear of being equal?"

"Maryl, there are so many more O type vampires compared to us even though we comprise fifty-six percent of the vampire's blood type. And because of our thirteen-year gap of ascension, it made us paranoid. Do I want to eradicate the O types? No, but your methods of trying to destroy us by your so-called failsafe weaponry is what I am trying to stop."

"By killing forty-four percent of the vampire species? That is ridiculous!"

"I am done trying to explain my side of the story to you." Clayton hung up the phone.

He had one more phone call to make. The phone battery was at seven percent. Plenty of juice to get something off his chest. He dialed a number.

"Hello?"

"Platov."

"Clayton? What is it?"

"It seems your after name is correct."

"Meaning?"

"Meaning you're the Compromiser, and that you did."

"I don't need to talk to you, Clayton."

"No, but you will. I know you're not craven. No, I would never call you a coward, but you did *back down* and told me you would not give me troops when I needed your support. If I survive this ordeal, I am coming for you."

"It would be suicide for you to try," Platov said with menace. "You know what the most important word in the human dictionary is? '*If.*' If I would have done this, if I would have done that. If Platov would have helped me, and this is the best 'if' there is. Want to hear it?"

"I imagine you'll tell me regardless," Clayton said through clenched teeth.

"*If* you survive, but I doubt you will," Platov quipped.

"You gave me the word if; I will provide you with one as well. *Doubt.* Never doubt me and my intentions, never doubt my tenacity, and never, ever doubt that I will survive and tear you limb from limb!"

"You wouldn't dare try such a bold move, Clayton! Our treaty specifically states we cannot kill one of our own blood types, and that includes all of the A's and B's!"

"Don't you get it? Can't you see the bigger picture here, Platov? The pact is no more! The boundary map that we signed with our blood no longer exists! The treaties, *all of them* are now null and void!"

"How can that be?" Platov asked in astonishment.

"Have you not bore witness to the sins, the wrongdoings that Maryl Rosser laid upon us over the centuries?"

"Methinks you've become paranoid, Clayton. Everything is fine. There have been no wars, no boundary disputes, and no civil unrest even after your abrupt departure."

Clayton took several deep breaths. "Now would be a good time to attack Maryl and Ray's troops. They wouldn't be expecting the onslaught that would follow."

"Are you insane? They outnumber us! Not to mention that would wipe out treaties we've had with the O's for centuries!"

"Platov, are you daft and stupid? Have you not listened to anything I've just told you? There are no *alliances*, no *treaties*, just *treachery* from every corner! Furthermore, what's to stop Maryl and Ray from wiping us out while I am gone?"

"You place too much importance on yourself, Clayton. Everything is fine. Go and find a cure or whatever you're trying to do with the serum. Hell, ninety-nine percent of us either don't *care* or understand what it is that you're trying to do."

Clayton felt deflated like he had been punched in the stomach. No one understood the importance of his work. It was for the preservation of all A and B's vampires! Why couldn't anyone see that?

Clayton hung up. He put the phone back where it belonged. Clayton got out of the van and leaned against it. He tried to feel the coolness of the van through his jeans, but his invulnerable skin felt nothing.

Clayton looked at the ground in sadness. He believed he was fighting a war on several fronts, and it hurt his soul.

He rubbed his face and brushed his hair with his hands. He gazed at the full moon and the cloudless sky. A tear managed to escape his tear duct and fell silently. His hearing was so acute; he heard the water droplet slowly trickle down his face. He closed his eyes and drowned out all of the noise of the cars speeding past.

Clayton listened to deer running and brushing by the thicket of bushes and trees. He heard the crickets chirping, which displayed the temperature. Clayton learned many years ago if someone counted the number of chirps in fifteen seconds and then added thirty-seven, it would give a rough calculation of the outdoor temperature in Fahrenheit.

With all that beautiful noise, Clayton managed to focus on the wind that whispered to the tree leaves that swayed with feverish delight. Humanity didn't appreciate the intricacies of how powerful and yet how subtle nature truly was.

Clayton came out of his reverie when he heard the distinctive sound of the other blue van long before it turned into the parking lot. When the van parked, Clayton helped the others pour the ice over the blood.

"Any problems obtaining the ice, Jack?"

Jack shook his head. "Nah. We bought plenty of bags."

"Good."

Jack and several of the scientists surrounded Clayton.

"What's going on, Jack? Another mutiny?"

"You tell me, Clayton."

"What do you mean?"

"A couple of us stayed behind. One of my fellow scientists called me and said you made two phone calls. Mind telling me who you called?"

"When did you become the brave one, Jack? A few days ago, you were telling me how you're a scientist and not a warrior."

"Circumstances dictate who I am, Clayton."

"What does that even mean?"

"It means, Clayton, that we outnumber you. We can defeat you if we have to even though we aren't warriors of your caliber. All I asked was a simple question. Who did you speak to?"

Clayton had severely underestimated Jack and his cohort of scientists. He didn't want to kill them. Jack and the other researcher's knowledge of genetics and DNA splicing were invaluable. Not to mention they had a vast array of expertise in immunology.

Clayton put up his hands in surrender. "I spoke to Maryl and Platov."

"What? I could understand Platov, but Maryl Rosser, the Seeker? Why her? Isn't Maryl our sworn immortal enemy?"

"Yes, she is. I was calling her for you and the other scientist's benefit."

"I find that hard to believe, Clayton," Jack said with suspicion.

"It's true. I was attempting to defuse the hostility between the different blood types. That way, she wouldn't try to locate us and take our serum."

"Why would you do that?"

Clayton looked at Jack incredulously. "Jack, it was you who said you and your scientists could work better without Maryl and Ray going after us!"

Jack's face softened. "I recall saying that a few days ago. How did it go?"

"She recoiled at my suggestion of peace. She wants war, which is why I called Platov after Maryl. I tried to convince him the time was ripe for us to invade Maryl and Ray's troops."

"And what did Platov, the Compromiser, say to your request?"

"He did not heed my advice, I'm afraid. He refused to compromise."

Jack gave a slight nod to his brethren. They moved away from Clayton.

"Now, can we be on our way?" Clayton asked nicely, even though he wanted to rip Jack's head off his shoulders.

Jack stood motionless in front of Clayton. "We believe in your vision, your quest to sequence the serum so the A's and B's can dominate the lands. It's our inherent right! But to be clear forward, we have to trust each other. Can you solemnly swear you will be straightforward and not lie? We don't mind your visions of grandeur; we find it compels us to help. But when lying, or an omission like making phone calls without telling us, get in the way of truth, we will not accept that."

"Yes, I promise to be forthright and honest."

Jack smiled and punched Clayton on his shoulder. "Good boy, now let's roll!"

Clayton suppressed his anger. Jack was getting too confident. Clayton's compliance with Jack's demands was a means to an end. He was going to let all of them live after they converted all blood types to A's and B's, but with such displays of dominance, he knew they would have to die.

Clayton got into the van, put on his seatbelt, and seethed in anger.

Chapter Fourteen
Maryl Rosser's Struggle
Present Day, July 23rd

Maryl Rosser, the Seeker was a duality, and she knew it. The two traits of her personality consistently fought for control, and for the last two centuries, she had noticed the darker side was winning. Only Maryl knew why and in the thousand years she had been alive; she had never told anyone the reason until an hour ago. She had told a female vampire who she had trusted the truth about herself during a meal of fresh blood. She became giddy, almost drunklike, and revealed her secret. The woman threatened to tell all of the blood types unless she became number two in Maryl's hierarchy. That was a fatal mistake on her part.

Thinking back, her family knew her secret too, but they perished at the hands of Clayton's tribe over seven hundred years ago.

She thought about the conversation she had with Clayton several days ago. He was so obstinate, yet his stubbornness would be his undoing.

"I will find you, Clayton, I swear it! I will put an end to the foolishness you have bestowed upon me!" She blushed. She hadn't meant to mouth the words that unexpectedly sprung from her.

Maryl was outside sitting in her favorite chair, overlooking the steep hilly landscape, trying to relax on her porch. Her attempt at relaxing had mixed results. She needed to be alone, yet she understood the need for bodyguards that surrounded her.

Maryl knew Clayton would not come for her at her estate. He was too busy setting up shop somewhere in an attempt to wipe out tens upon tens of thousands of her vampire kind. No, she needn't worry about him. She worried about his allies and his alliances. So far, none have attacked her or any of her business interests. That bothered her and comforted her, hence her duality. In one regard, she was comforted she had not been attacked. So far, peace reigned. That begged the question; Why hadn't she or Ray been attacked? Were there fractures in the once-solid A and B tribes? If so, were they scared of her? Sure, she had threatened them with death, but given their past transgressions, they would've taken that with a grain of salt.

Upon further reflection, since the demise of the neutral barriers, Maryl and Ray's O's have trampled upon the other blood types land with immunity, freedom, and without incident. Sure, they were very small incursions. She wanted to see if they reacted. And they hadn't called or complained to her.

A sudden thought occurred to Maryl, which made her spring up in her chair. Perhaps in all the madness, she had overlooked one crucial element. Maybe, just maybe, there *were* cracks and divisions among the other blood types because they disagreed with Clayton and his foolish scheme? That would explain why the O negatives and O positive vampires hadn't been assaulted.

Maryl tapped her lips with her finger, deep in contemplation.

She rose with elegance and straightened her dress and looked at her bodyguards. "You, Alexa, get Ray on the line for me. I need to speak to him immediately!"

A tall rail-thin woman bowed and then sped away. She came back seconds later and handed Maryl the phone.

Maryl put a hand over the phone. "Alexa, drink some blood! We have plenty. You're too thin. I need you in fighting condition."

"All my family for countless generations has been tall and lean, eager to do your bidding, Maryl Rosser!"

Maryl nodded absently as she put the phone to her ear. "Ray, I have an idea that you might be interested in hearing."

"I'm listening, Maryl."

"Before I lay out my plan, I have a question. Have you or any of your businesses been provoked or attacked since Clayton went awol?"

"What does awol mean?"

Maryl sighed to herself. "Absent without leave; it's a military term. He went missing without telling any of his subordinates."

"No, the O positives properties have not been breached, nor have we been hit. Now that I think about it, that is strange. What do you think?"

"I think there are deep cracks in the foundation of *all* of Clayton's tribes, which leads me to my question."

"Yes?"

"Do you think, as I do, it's the opportune time to attack Clayton tribes? We could amass such a force it would be written in the chronicles of the Vampire history books!"

"Aye, I believe the time is right as well, Maryl Rosser. I will set up an emergency meeting right away. I suggest you do the same."

"There is no time for a meeting, emergent or not! That would take days! Weeks! No, I want you to gather as many vampires as you can within twenty-four hours, and I will do the same."

"Will that be enough vampires? The other blood types are much stronger than we are."

"At first, yes, it should be enough troops. We will pick a place where there are the fewest of Clayton's blood types and target that location. Once we attack and defeat our enemies, the other O's will hear about our victory and will join our battle!"

"Maryl, you just made my day! No, you just made my century! I can't wait until Clayton hears the news his precious vampires were crushed in defeat!"

"I want you and all of your O positives to meet me at my house tomorrow. I have more than adequate space for everyone."

"I will make it happen. See you tomorrow!"

Maryl hung up and walked to the edge of the wooden deck. She looked at the land that sprawled for miles.

"Alexa, please get me something to drink."

Alexa sped away and came back with a wine glass filled with dark crimson fluid.

She turned around and faced the table where she was sitting.

"Do you think it wise to attack Clayton's tribes, Desiree?"

Desiree was seated with three guards surrounding her. "Since I fell out of favor, what does my opinion matter to you?"

Maryl smiled as she moved the glass of blood in circular motions. "It doesn't, but you must understand I need to make an example of vampires that failed in their orders."

"*Two mistakes* in three hundred years? And giving my opinion about the serum makes me untrustworthy?"

Maryl sat down beside her. "If your two mistakes occurred once every one hundred and fifty years, I would give you *some* leeway. But your mishaps happened in such a short period; I no longer trust you." Maryl looked at what was once her most trusted ally. "And your opinion of the serum wasn't an opinion; it was an accusation!"

Desiree knew better than to respond. She had to find a way back to Clayton to warn him of the peril his unsuspecting troops were about to encounter. She felt she owed him that much. Desiree felt a touch of something. Regret? Friendship? Something more? She didn't know.

"Alexa, I believe Desiree must be hungry by now. Give her the "special" food."

"I am not hungry, Maryl."

"Oh, I insist. Alexa, proceed."

Alexa zipped in the house and came back with a large platter of food. Human food.

Desiree sat up in her chair. "I'm not eating that garbage!"

"Garbage? I'll have you know humans love this meal! Steak and potatoes are a staple with humankind," Maryl exclaimed. "And I went into a grocery store just for you, Desiree. Show some gratitude."

"I don't care. I am not eating that food!" Desiree yelled as she pushed the platter away from her, nearly knocking it off the table.

"Desiree, is that how you treat your host? Manners seem to be a thing of the past." Maryl looked at Alexa sternly. "Alexa, you and Draven keep her at bay and force-feed her."

Draven's muscular frame had no trouble keeping Desiree securely in place while Alexa held Desiree's mouth wide open, took a handful of mashed potatoes, and shoved them inside. With one hand, Alexa closed Desiree's mouth and, with the other one, pinched her nose shut, which forced Desiree to swallow the mashed potatoes.

"I think Desiree needs more protein. Give her a mouthful of steak," Maryl said as she sat back in her chair, watching and sipping her life juice.

Desiree gagged several times. When her gagging subsided slightly, Alexa repeated the process, but this time, she shoved several pieces of steak inside her mouth.

The veins in Desiree's face popped to the surface. The veins bloated and threatened to explode. So weakened and allergic by the human food, her entire body of veins and arteries swelled in protest.

"I think she's going into shock. Alexa, be a dear and take Desiree to the wooden railing nearby that overlooks the cliff. I think she's going to throw-up or her veins are going to burst. And I will not be the one to clean the mess up."

In a blur, Alexa took Desiree and sped her to the end of the deck. Desiree leaned over and vomited for a couple of minutes. Alexa escorted her back to her chair and observed her, making sure she didn't try to escape. If Desiree escaped while Alexa was watching her, the same thing would happen to her.

"You look kind of pale, Desiree. Do you require some water?" Maryl nodded to Alexa. Upon her return with a large glass of water, Alexa said to Desiree, "Drink up, traitor!"

"Get that water away from me! Can't you see the food already weakened me? I am not about to try anything stupid!"

Alexa ignored her while Draven held Desiree at bay. She forced all of the water down Desiree's throat and kept her mouth closed. Desiree was attempting to throw up, but couldn't.

After several seconds Maryl said, "Okay, that's enough. Let her throw up over the side again."

Instead of speeding to the handrail, Alexa walked Desiree slowly. She could barely contain herself when she reached the edge.

While Desiree was forcing the water from her system, Maryl downed the last of the blood from her wine glass and then asked, "Now, where were we?"

"You were discussing invading Clayton's smaller tribes of the A and B's," Draven remarked.

"Thank you, Draven." She turned around. "Alexa, you have twenty-four hours to get as many of your most trusted vampires together. Make sure to scout the lands for troops willing to do battle against the A's and B's. Explain to them we're taking the smallest groups we have been monitoring, and it won't be a full assault. We will take them piece by piece! Do you think you can handle the assignment?"

A smile formed on Alexa's lips. "It will be my honor!" Alexa said before she zipped away.

"So I take it Alexa has become your new adoring disciple?" Desiree said in-between gagging.

"No need to be jealous. Alexa knows how honorable it is to be my devotee."

Desiree turned away from the handrail and faced Maryl. She spread her arms out and leaned them against the wooden guardrail. "Disciple. Devotee. How about a minion or a pawn?"

With rage coursing through her blood, Maryl zipped to Desiree, picked her upright, and hung her upside down just beyond the wooden railing of the porch.
"It's a long way down, Desiree, and you're looking a little pale. Overeat on human food and drank too much water, perhaps?" Maryl looked down the deep slope hillside and then looked at Desiree. "Don't worry, Desiree. Even our kind would not survive the fall."

"We're immortal… with thick skin and bone density… many times thicker than… humans! Let me go… I will survive…"

Maryl let Desiree dangle while she spoke. "Oh child, you believe us to be immortal? We're close but don't, for a second, believe the lies our ancestors have maintained over the centuries. If I were to throw you off this cliff, you would surely perish, especially eating human food. I know because I have thrown plenty of vampires down there using the same technique I used on you. As a matter of fact, I threw a traitorous vampire over the railing a little more than an hour ago."

Desiree held her stomach. She felt nauseous. "Why? What did… he do to you?"

"It was a female vampire. She was rising rapidly in my ranks, and as a reward, I allowed her to have fresh O negative blood with me instead of the units of blood that can be days old. As you may or may not know, if you drink a lot of fresh blood in a short duration, you can get drunk, similar to what humans feel when they drink too much alcohol." Mary looked at Desiree. "Am I boring you?"

"No, I'm… intoxicated with your story."

"I like your pun, Desiree. Anyway, after we drank in excess, I was feeling pretty good and made a grievous error. I told the woman my most private secret! Can you believe it?"

"And… Is she down there now? How… can you be sure?"

"Because I myself threw her down there. And in the past, I have climbed down the steep hill to witness firsthand the deaths of our kind!"

Desiree coughed, and dry heaved. "You… you lie! And even if it were true, it's illegal to kill… your own blood types!"

"That decree is only for the A's and B's. There is nothing in our laws or bylaws that state the same thing. I should know, I rewrote them after my family died in battle several centuries ago!"

Desiree looked at Maryl upside down. "I would live if you threw me down!"

"Do you have a death wish, Desiree? It's as if you *want* me to throw you down! You wish to prove me wrong and that you might live?"

Desiree spit and hit Maryl in her eye. She took her free hand and wiped it off.

"So be it," she said. Maryl was about to let her go but hoisted her back up and let her down on her feet.

Maryl looked at Desiree and laughed. "I was only joking, Desiree. I wasn't going to drop you."

Desiree took a few deep breaths and smiled. "For a second there, Maryl, I thought you were really going to throw me over."

"Don't be silly. Now stand straight up and let me straighten your beautiful, messy hair," Maryl said as she put her hands through Desiree's long black curly hair. "There, is that better?"

"Yes, thank you," Desiree said warmly.

With a swift undetectable motion, Maryl grabbed Desiree by her hair, tilted her head up, and sliced a thin long line across her throat.

"I wasn't going to throw you over the railing without giving you human food and draining your blood like all the other vampires I threw down. Don't worry; I didn't slice you too deep. I want you to take a long time to perish."

Desiree's eyes bulged in fear as Maryl held her in a tight grip.

"Yes, I see your lifeblood slowly draining your existence. How exquisite!"

Desiree's eyes were going in the back of her head when Maryl slapped her across the face.

"I'm not done talking with you! I have one thing left to say; then I will throw you down the cliff. If you were at full vampire power, you should survive the fall. I'm not sure because my other victims weren't at full strength either. Don't you see it, Desiree? That's how I ensure a zero survival rate and remain in control of my O negative vampires."

Maryl grabbed Desiree by her throat. Her blood slowly dripped onto Maryl's hand. "Goodbye, Desiree." She took her to the wooden rail guard, lifted Desiree in the air, and threw her over the side.

Maryl pointed to Draven as she licked Desiree's blood off her hands. "You! Wait until sunset, and retrieve Desiree's body. I want her death to be agonizing and slow in the hot sun. When her body is brought up to me, I want her corpse on display in my front yard before Ray's troops arrive. I want to show the vampires what it's like if they were to betray me!"

Maryl sat down and closed her eyes and started humming a tune.

Chapter Fifteen
Desiree's Predicament
Present Day July 23rd

By all accounts, Desiree Maholmes should have died falling down the steep terrain. However, luck had been on her side. Some may have called it fate.

Desiree frantically reached out with all of her dwindling strength and tried to latch onto anything within her grasp.

After several futile attempts at snatching loose tree limbs, her hope almost depleted, she reached out and felt something solid-like and immediately clamped down with her flailing hands.

The sudden stop of her falling at high speed from grasping the tree limb made her smash into the side of the hill. In such a weakened state, ribs had to be broken, she surmised. Desiree looked down with blurry eyes and saw her dress was covered with her blood. She knew she was still losing lifeblood and was close to death. Refusing to perish while clinging to a thick limb, Desiree saw that at least fifty feet below her were grasslands spread for miles with trees scattered over the expanse of the land. Further out, she could discern trails of some sort. There were two hikers, and they were walking on one of the paths.

"I will die whether I stay up here and lose all my blood, and I will surely die if I jumped the fifty feet to safety," Desiree grieved out loud.

Hanging on a tree limb and steadily losing blood, which made her lose her vampire strength, was too much to bear. Before losing her grip, she took one last look down. Not far from her position, she thought she saw several corpses piled on top of each other. She didn't know if it was a hallucination or if what Maryl had told her about the fallen vampires were correct, but if she were to descend, she needed to land on them to help cushion her fall!

With a colossal effort, Desiree bent her knees and, using the side of the hill as leverage, pushed outward while at the same time, let loose from the tree limb and fell.

Her life flashed in front of her as she descended at a quick pace. The rush of wind engulfed her body as memories of her hometown where she spent her vampire youth sprung up, only to be replaced with the memory of meeting Maryl for the first time at one of the battles Maryl had initiated. Still, more recollections soared up through her consciousness at a breathtaking speed until she felt a sudden thump.

When she landed on the pile of vampire corpses on her backside, she bounced a few times from the impact. Not soon afterward, she lost consciousness.

Desiree had no idea how long she had been unconscious when she woke up. She gazed upon the burning sun. She attempted to get up but fell back down.

With determination bordering on self-preservation, she struggled to sit up. When she rubbed the back of her head, she got lightheaded and woozy. She thought she might have what humans called a concussion. How, she wondered, if she had invulnerable skin and thicker bone density? Maybe in her weakened state, some of her invulnerability was lost?

"Damn, that was a long fall!" Desiree said after a moment of clarity.

"*Help me…*"

"What the hell?" Desiree cried as she found the strength to move away from the pile of vampire bodies.

"*Help me… please.*"

"Who… said that?" Desiree demanded as she struggled with delirium. She crawled back to the pile. "I said, …who said that?"

"*I did.*"

"Where are you?" Desiree asked as she stared at the stack of vampires.

"*I am on top of the heap. You fell on top of me,*" the voice said weakly.

Desiree found a woman with long blond hair that hid her face. She brushed the woman's greasy hair away. "How did you get down here?"

"*Please, my back… it's broken from the fall, and I can't move. Maryl force-fed me food and water, and then she slit my throat! Help me, and I will explain everything.*"

"I have a better… idea." Desiree slowly approached the woman and went down on her knees.

"*What are you doing? I have a secret about Maryl I will share with you if you help me!*"

"Sorry, … but down here, in the sweltering sun, … and with predatory animals… lurking until the sun goes down… it's survival of the fittest…"

"*No, let me explain! Maryl is…*"

"Normally, I… I *would* care who Maryl is… but… I am… at death's door… and I… hear the… knocking. It's imploring… no, begging me to… go inside. But… I'm not ready to die…"

"*No. Listen to me! Maryl is…*"

Desiree had no strength left in her as she crouched down. She fell on top of the woman. Desiree could tell her life was almost extinguished. She looked at the woman's tears flow, and Desiree knew why. If she were to die on top of her, the woman would die. If she were able to suck the blood from the woman, the woman would die.

Desiree's head fell back on the woman's chest and slowly, with death looming closer and closer, forced herself up inch by inch.

"*You don't have to do this! It's Maryl you want!*"

Desiree barely reached the woman's neck. Salvation was at her threshold! But Desiree could tell she had only a couple of breaths left before death would overtake her. On her last dying intake of air, one of Desiree's teeth managed to penetrate the woman's sweaty neck. A trickle of blood, no larger than the head of a pin, dripped on her tooth. The absorption was immediate. Suddenly a small surge of power flooded through her. Her body, instead of shutting down, found itself gradually awakening, and it wanted more!

"*Please don't do this! I can tell you a secret of why Maryl is…*" the woman said pleadingly.

But Desiree heard none of her meaningless words or their implications. Her body was being restored, and that's all that mattered. As life came back to her, clarity also reestablished itself. Her hunger was relentless and unceasing as the blood pumped out of the woman and into Desiree's eager mouth.

Not long afterward, Desiree stood up. She felt revitalized as she felt her ribs and the back of her head. They were slowly healing. Desiree felt as though she could take on Maryl Rosser and win. She got up and seriously considered climbing up the hill and launch a surprise attack.

Desiree went so far as to walk toward the hill when she stopped.

"No, that idea is insane," she said as she stared at the sky. The sun was starting its descent. Darkness would come sooner rather than later.

She had to leave. She had no interest in encountering coyotes, foxes, and whatever lifeforms prowled nocturnally. Besides, she thought, she couldn't take blood from them, but they could take hers if she were still in a deteriorated state.

Desiree turned around and sped away from the hillside. She ran a quarter of a mile when she stopped and noticed the trails she had seen earlier when she was perched over fifty feet in the air. Desiree could smell two hikers in the distance. One human was a B positive blood type, and the other one was an A negative, which was odd. This was Maryl's property. She would never allow different blood types here or anywhere on her land.

She peered at the human beings. It amazed her that the humans were probably good friends, hung out with other human friends, even have significant others, and perhaps children, but did not deem their blood type nearly as crucial as the vampire bloodlines.

Desiree considered them useless and was going to move on until she realized they had to have a means of transportation!

Desiree still had several hours until she needed to feed again. If she got hold of a vehicle, she had ample time to feed and try to find Clayton's location. The latter concerned her. Trying to find Clayton when even the resources of Maryl proved useless told her the enormity of her predicament. And how would Clayton react to her presence? Would he want to kill her on the spot or allow her to speak her mind based on three hundred years of friendship? She still did not know why she was going to warn Clayton, and that fact concerned her.

The hikers had set up camp and had started a fire, which was strange given the animals she could hear nearby.

Desiree zipped to the trail the humans were on and appeared at their base camp as the sun slowly veered over the horizon.

The two human men were sitting at the campfire. Both of them had shorts on with light jackets, zipped up.

One of the men had a full beard. He was the one that noticed Desiree first.

He was poking a stick in the fire when he looked up and saw her.

"What the hell happened to you?"

"What do you mean?" Desiree asked with confusion.

The other man, who was clean-shaven and had a hat on advertising a trucking company, spoke. "Your white dress has blood all over it, and it has rips and tears."

"Not to mention you have blood on your forehead, cheeks, mouth, throat... are you okay? Where did you come from? Were you attacked?" The bearded man asked.

"I was visiting my friend, who lives on top of the cliff." Desiree pointed to where she had come from.

"Did she throw you off?" the bearded man laughed as he jabbed his friend in the ribs with his elbow.

"Yes," Desiree said before she flew to the bearded man first and snapped his neck.

The clean-shaven man backtracked several feet with his hands up in the air. "I don't want no trouble, lady."

"You won't get any if you give me your keys and your wallet."

He reached into his pocket and took out a set of keys. "Here you go."

"Where is your car?"

"Just over the small hill about a quarter of a mile from the trail."

"Throw the keys to me," Desiree said as she put out her hands.

The human chucked the keys to her, and she grabbed them. "Now, your wallet."

"Why do you need my wallet?"

"If you must know, I need gas money."

"It has a full tank."

Desiree put her hands on her hips. "I have trust issues. Throw me your wallet."

The man took out his wallet from his back pocket and threw it to her, but it fell short. Desiree walked a couple of feet and bent down to pick the wallet up. The man rushed to her. He put his arm around her neck and had his other arm around her waist.

"A pretty lady like yourself shouldn't be roaming trails by her lonesome, asking for keys and money without some sort of compensation," he whispered in her ear.

Desiree could smell alcohol on his breath. "Typical macho human response," Desiree replied. She took hold of the man's arm and twisted it until the man fell, withering in pain. She let go of him and forced him to stand. She punched him in the chest that hurled him several yards. Desiree raced to him before he could flee.

"What are you that makes you so fast?"

"A vampire," she said as she snapped his neck. And for being a jerk, she sliced his throat too.

Desiree raced to the car. She didn't want to see the coyotes consume the human hikers. Desiree had heard them sneaking dangerously close to the campsite. She smelled two of them nearby and more, moving quickly toward the campground and their next meal. She was sure they would eat the dead vampires that were piling up half a mile toward Maryl's.

She climbed a small hill and came to a clearing. She found two pickup trucks parked in a small makeshift parking area off to the side of the road. Taking the keys, she pressed the unlock button to see which car she would have to drive. She dared not go back to the campsite and get the other set of keys. It was a feeding frenzy; she could hear them snarl and growl at each other. She heard vicious fights break out over who was going to feast upon the humans first.

Fortunately, the newer blue pickup truck's lights light up and unlocked. Desiree saw the truck had an extended cab and opened it. On the seat were a few packs of cigarettes with several books of matches. The clean-shaven man would more than likely have returned to his truck sooner or later to retrieve them.

Right past the cigarettes and matches, Desiree found a huge brown duffle bag and opened it. She smelled inside to make sure the clothes within were cleaner than the ones the humans were wearing at the fire. Desiree took out a flannel shirt and shook it in case bugs had crawled inside. The shirt was too large for her, but it would do.

She reached in and found a pair of shorts that were too big for her. And underneath the shorts was some rope with some spelunking equipment. She scanned the terrain. There were no caves that she knew about around here, so why the equipment?

At that point, it didn't matter. What mattered was getting out of the bloody dress. Desiree used her hyper hearing to make sure no cars were in the vicinity. Satisfied, she took off her dress and put on the shorts. Desiree grabbed the rope and looped it around to make a belt. She snapped the excess with ease and tied a bow to tighten the shorts.

She grabbed the flannel shirt, buttoned the buttons and tied the bottom of the shirt in a knot. "Now comes the hard part," Desiree remarked as she took her bloody and torn dress, grabbed a book of matches and lit it on fire. "I loved that dress," Desiree said as she got in the car and headed east.

She looked at the gas gauge. "Huh, the human was telling the truth. He did have a full tank of gas."

Chapter Sixteen
Maryl Rosser's Estate
Present Day July 24th

Twenty-four hours later, Maryl stood on her front porch and leaned against the lattice while looking at all of the O negative troops amassed across the expanse of her large estate. She was pleased her underlings had assembled such a large gathering of unity and strength in such a short time. Thousands of her blood type were mingling and laughing, perhaps catching up and reliving memories. Still, some stood solid, brooding, waiting for the imminent battle.

While Maryl was gratified with the turnout, she was not happy that Ray's troops were nearby, and Draven had not brought Desiree's body back. What was taking him so long?

She was about to tell Alexa to fetch Draven when someone came crashing through her front door and fell behind her. She turned around to see Draven get on his knees. His hair was disheveled, his green shirt and jeans were caked with dried mud. Standing beside Draven was Alexa, who had open contempt on her face.

"What is the meaning of this intrusion?" Maryl asked politely.

Alexa kicked Draven's back. He fell forward and almost hit Maryl's legs.

"Go ahead, tell her, Draven, the craven!"

"I am not a coward!" He seethed through gritted teeth.

"Yes, Draven, tell me. I see you," she said as she looked around. "But I don't see Desiree. Why is that?"

Draven went back to a kneeling position. "Madame Rosser, please hear me out before you kill me!"

Maryl's face softened as she leaned down. "Of course. Stand up. It doesn't make you look good groveling in front of our blood types."

Draven stood up. His eyes were downcast.

"Draven, look me in the eyes while you recount your riveting story. I want to see if you're lying to me."

He looked at her and nodded. "At the appointed time, I scaled down the back porch to get Desiree as you commanded."

"Yes, I'm sure you did. Please skip forward to the part as to why you came back empty-handed."

"She... she wasn't there!"

Maryl's eyes lit up. Her eyebrows arched. "Excuse me? Did you just tell me she wasn't there?"

"I swear it! She was not there!"

"That's impossible, Draven," Maryl said as she started walking around the porch, thinking back. "I gave her human food and water to weaken her and then drained her blood before I threw her over." Maryl stopped and looked at Draven. "No one in that condition can survive that fall. No one."

"Maybe the coyotes got her? I saw a pile of vampire corpses that were torn to shreds when I went looking for Draven," Alexa suggested.

"Did you, while you were searching for Desiree, find her body among the eaten corpses?" Maryl asked.

"Um… no. I checked thoroughly, Madame Rosser!" Draven said in a whimper.

Alexa grabbed Draven by the back of his neck. Maryl shook her head, and Alexa released her death grip.

"Go ahead, Draven. Tell our great leader what else you told me!" Alexa hissed.

Maryl zipped to Draven and stood inches from him. She tilted his head to face her. "There's more? This story is just getting better and better."

"When I could not find Desiree, I searched the perimeter, and you're not going to like what I'm about to tell you. Please take pity on me, and hear me out!"

"Draven, tell me what happened, and I promise you, I will not erase your existence," Maryl said softly.

Draven brushed away the few tears that escaped. "About… about a half-mile from the decomposing remains of the treacherous vampires that deserved to be thrown over, I came to a campsite. Two men were there, but there wasn't much left of them after the coyotes got hold of them."

"And how is that relevant to Desiree's disappearance?" Maryl asked as she slowly walked around Draven's trembling body.

"Because, my liege, they died *before* the beasts devoured them."

"And you know this: how?" Maryl asked as she stopped walking and faced Draven.

"I examined the skeletal remains of the two humans and then their campsite. A few things I noticed were important…"

"*I* will determine if they are important, Draven. Please, proceed."

Draven nodded. "Of course, Madame Rosser. The two human necks were snapped. Of that, I have no doubt. That *could* mean, at some point, Desiree encountered them. I have no proof since I did not smell any other humans or vampires in the vicinity. However, another thing I saw in both of their tents; they had extensive spelunking equipment."

Maryl's anxiety became apparent. "Did you say spelunking as in equipment to go cave diving?"

"Yes."

She swallowed and took a moment to regain her composure. "Anything else?"

"Yes. I could *not* smell what blood type the humans were! How is that possible? In my two hundred and twelve years of existence, I have always been able to smell our means of nourishment!"

"That's impossible!" Alexa said in anger. "Please let me kill this lying piece of shit!"

Maryl looked at Alexa and shook her head. "No."

"Then please let me go to the campsite and verify what he is saying."

"No, this is too important. I will go after we come back from launching our next attack." Maryl looked at Draven. "Proceed."

Draven licked his dry, cracked lips before resuming. "The human's clothing was close by. One of the humans still had his car keys and wallet in his pants pockets. The other one was missing both."

"So, it would seem, Desiree did indeed live," Maryl said softly. "There goes my zero survival rate."

"What are we going to do about Desiree, Maryl? And more importantly, what did you want me to do with Draven?" Alexa asked. "Can I suck his blood dry?"

Maryl was lost in thought. Desiree could pose a problem. Would she be stupid enough to try to find Clayton and expose her plan?

"Maryl? Can I *please* kill Draven?"

Maryl came out of her trance. "No. I gave Draven my word I would leave him be if he told me the truth. He did his part, and I will do mine."

"May I ask why?"

"I have this duality about me. The other side kicked in and decided to show him mercy."

Alexa knew better than to ask her what she was talking about. She turned around in time to see Ray the Conqueror approach with a staggering deployment of O positive vampires coming out of their cars, trucks, vans, and even three dozen semi tractor-trailers, it was a sight unlike she had ever borne witness to before.

"Um, Maryl? Take a look behind you," Alexa said in a mixture of awe and fear.

Maryl walked to the edge of the porch and looked over the landscape. "I knew they were here. I smelled them a few minutes ago."

Alexa observed Maryl. She wanted to see if Maryl displayed any signs of trepidation, fear, anything. Instead, surprisingly, Maryl smiled and waved to Ray as if they were best friends.

Ray saw her wave and waved back with a smile.

Alexa was confused. Maryl didn't seem afraid of Ray and his more massive and formidable army than theirs, but she showed unease about cave diving equipment?

Maryl walked down the stairs and strode toward Ray. Vampires of both blood types moved back to allow them room.

"Ray! Thank you for coming so soon," she said as she gave him a warm hug.

"Anything for my sister's blood type!"

Maryl did not like how he phrased her kind but opted to remain quiet. His troops were essential if her plan were to be executed.

"With all of the cars and semi's, did you have any trouble getting here with the local, state, and federal authorities?"

Ray pointed to the first row of vampires. "You see them? They *are* the local, state, and federal authorities."

Maryl smiled. "Come, let's dine on some red wine!" Maryl said as she put her arm inside Ray's and led him to her porch arm in arm to display unity.

"Do you have O positive blood? I am stronger with my own type of blood!" Ray commented lightly.

Maryl stopped, grabbed Ray by the arm, and squeezed tightly.

"Oww! That hurts, Maryl! What do you think you're doing? You're embarrassing me in front of my troops!"

"I invite you to my abode, and you have already made two insulting remarks! Who is embarrassing who?" Maryl hissed.

"What? What did I say?" Ray asked as Maryl let go of him.

"You referred me as *your other blood type* in a condescending manner, and then you wanted your own blood type to drink at *my* place? Frankly, I'm insulted!"

"My humble apologies! I am excited to proceed with our takeover, that's all."

Maryl smiled. "Apology accepted. Now, let's drink some blood, make some toasts, and not bicker over the type of blood since I can only have my kind, and you can have both yours and my blood type."

Maryl and Ray sat at the table on the porch. Alexa came and put a red table cloth on top of the table, and poured their life juice into two wine glasses.

"Fancy," Ray said as he gulped down the red fluid.

Maryl sipped her red liquid slowly. She put the glass down. "Do you want to hear my plan?"

"Your plan? I thought we were going to an A or B community and wreak havoc?"

"We can do that after they are caught off guard."

Ray looked puzzled. "How can we catch them off guard if they can smell us from far away?"

Maryl nodded to Alexa and Draven, who were close by. They sped away and came back, each holding a shoulder-fired missile.

"A shoulder-fired missile, Maryl? Really? A lot of good that simple weapon would do!" he said with sarcasm. "The artillery won't pierce their thick skin. We tried in previous skirmishes twenty years ago."

"Ah, but this shoulder-fired missile is special!" Maryl said with excitement.

Ray took one from Draven's hand and studied it. He turned it entirely around before saying anything. "No offense, Maryl, but it's just a shoulder-fired missile. They can't go further than 300 meters, which is less than two-tenths of a mile." He handed it back to Draven.

"My engineers were able to modify and enhance the range to two thousand meters."

"Say I believe you, which I don't necessarily, it's still only one and a quarter miles."

"Alexa, bring the prisoners from the chambers."

Alexa departed and came back a few minutes later, with a half dozen men and women vampires chained to each other.

Ray studied the vampires being led outside. "How are those vampires unable to break free of their chains?" He asked with intense curiosity.

"They are comprised of A's, B's, and one AB positive vampires. Since we don't have their blood type on my premises, they are in a weakened state, and we did not allow them to nourish themselves from my kind of blood. Even if I did have their blood types, I wouldn't give it to them. Nor did I give them any human food. A week ago, my guards found them lurking on my grounds and quickly surrounded them. We had a twelve to one ratio. Naturally, they surrendered without incident. I have kept them here for a demonstration, and your amusement."

"And that's where the shoulder-fired missile comes into play, I presume?"

"Yes." She sipped the last of the blood. "Alexa, you know what to do."

Alexa pushed the prisoner that was in the back of the line, which forced the others to move forward.

"When Clayton hears of your treachery, Maryl, he will make you pay!" one of the prisoners yelled.

"Oh, I doubt that," she said, as she licked a drop of blood that was on the outside of the glass. "Alexa, measure one and a quarter miles, and leave them there, please."

Alexa forced them out in the distance. She gave a slight nod to Maryl and sped back up the stairs.

"Draven, get me the two pouches, please."

He zipped inside and was back outside in seconds. He carried two closed pouches and put them on the table.

"No, don't tell me what I think is in there!" Ray remarked with a wicked grin.

"Yup, it's the gray powder I used nearly three hundred years ago."

He looked at the pouches. "Isn't two pouches overkill?"

"Not in my eyes," Maryl said sternly.

"And it will just target the A's and B's out there, right?" Ray asked with concern.

"Of course, Ray. *However*, I must warn you I've perfected the powder over the centuries. It has become so precise, it can target any blood type, whether it be A, B's, or even O's. And it won't matter if the blood types are negative or positive because I have powder for them as well."

Ray's smile turned upside down. "How is it, Maryl, that you possess technology far more advanced than the other blood type vampires, even Clayton's? What is your secret, because that fact worries me a great deal. I won't have any warning should you attack my blood," Ray cautioned. "Tell me you won't attack my troops, Maryl."

Maryl went to him. "I promise, on my life, I will not target your troops. We are blood family, Ray!"

"Okay," Ray said with a smile. "But you still haven't told me how you have so much technology at your disposal. Do you have an Einstein working for you?"

Maryl patted Ray's hands and grinned warmly. "It's my secret. If I told you, then I would have to force you to eat human food, then drain your blood, and lastly, throw you over the side of the steep hills that surround my estate."

Ray started to laugh until he noticed she was serious.

Maryl turned around. "Alexa, Draven! Untie the pouches, and then load the pouches into the shoulder-fired missiles as I showed you earlier!" Maryl commanded.

"Do I get to shoot one of them?" Draven asked with childish delight.

"No. That honor goes to Ray." She turned to him. "Would you like that, Ray?"

Ray quickly stood up. "Hell yeah!"

He took one of the loaded shoulder-fired missiles from Draven's saddened face, went to the lattice guardrail, and knelt. He raised the gun high in the air, took careful aim, and fired. The bag flew directly overhead the prisoners and released the powder, and fell harmlessly to the ground.

"Hand me the other one," Ray told Alexa.

He repeated the process.

The powder was so fine; it looked like a gray mist was raining down. The haze blanketed the helpless prisoners. Immediately, all of them were vomiting blood. In their weakened state, it did not take long for them to convulse and die.

The crowd was speechless at first; then, they erupted into a joyous chorus of cheers.

Maryl walked beside Ray, took his arm, and with her arm, raised both of them in solidarity.

The singing of praises was deafening.

Ray whispered so softly, not even the vampires in the vicinity could hear him. "You scare the hell out of me, Maryl Rosser."

"As you should be," she whispered back.

Maryl walked back to her chair and sat down. Ray followed.

"I have a troubling question for you, Maryl," Ray said as he looked at his fingernails.

"Really? What is it?"

He looked up and stared at Maryl before speaking. "If you have the gray powder, why do you need my troops and me?"

"This is war, Ray! Clayton's offensive scheme of converting everyone's blood type to his and his cousin's tribe, has to be stopped using all means necessary. You and your army are invaluable to help prevent his illusion of greatness. Besides, while I have a great deal of the gray mist in stock, I don't have enough to get rid of all of the treacherous A's and B's."

"When do you want to leave?" Ray asked.

"Now would be a good time."

"Alexa, bring me a whole bottle of your blood wine. I think I'm going to need it," Ray said as he stood up.

Alexa came back in seconds and gave Ray a green bottle with a long neck.

"Don't drink it too fast, Ray. You're liable to get drunk," Maryl warned him.

"The conflict we're about to engage in, my goal is to get drunk."

Maryl took the bottle from Ray before he was able to open it. "I will keep this to celebrate after we are victorious. I trust you have adequate provisions?"

"Aye, we have plenty of blood!"

"Then let's go!"

Ray got up and faced Maryl. "Yes, let's strike down our enemies!"

Both Maryl and Ray marched down the stairs and faced the enormous crowd.

"Prepare for battle!" Ray yelled as he raised his fist high in the air.

"One thing!" Maryl yelled to the enormous crowd. "They can smell just as good as we can! We want to take them by surprise, so keep all of your windows in your vehicles up!"

Ray looked at his group of blood types. "You heard the lady!"

Roars erupted as Ray's soldiers ran back into their respective vehicles.

"Ray, I want you to ride with me. Alexa will drive, and Draven will take the front passenger seat. I want to talk to you in the backseat." Maryl whistled a high piercing sound, and then yelled, "O negatives, get in your cars and follow me!"

A few miles from Maryl's property, Maryl looked out the back window. She saw vehicles of every shape, year, and size that stretched for miles.

She turned around and watched Ray as he studied the paperwork she had given him.

"If I understand this correctly, Maryl, Octavus the Brooder, who is A negative, is hosting a small party? And we're going to crash it?"

"That is correct."

"How far out do we have to be for them not to smell us?"

"If you read my report, you would know we need to be at least four miles from them, depending on the direction of the wind."

"Four miles it is then. I don't want any surprises. Run through our game plan one more time?'

Maryl sighed. Ray was a brute, didn't listen, and had clothes that smelled as if they had not been washed in weeks, but she wanted him here with her. "Sure, Ray," Maryl said with a false smile. "Since the missile launcher is only useful to one and a quarter mile at most, we have to take the risk and come in hot. At the appropriate time, you and I will have very little time to race outside and launch the pouches. Do you think you're up to the task?"

"Yes! I am of able mind, able spirit, and able-bodied!"

"Good! That's what I like to hear!"

"How many pouches did you bring?"

"About ten percent of my stock."

"That's a lot for a small party, don't you think?" Ray asked.

"I don't plan on using all of it, but I would rather have more on hand in case we need it."

Silence followed for the next several miles.

"How much further, Alexa?" Maryl asked.

"Six miles!" Alexa hollered as the stress of what they were going to do sunk in.

"Tell me when we're just outside of the four-mile mark."

Ray studied Maryl's soft and elegant features. "You don't seem too nervous, Maryl."

"What you see on the outside doesn't necessarily reflect what is going on in the inside," she said as she looked at Ray. "You, however, wear your emotions on your sleeve."

"What you see is what you get. You'll always know what I'm thinking. I'm just that transparent."

"We're at the four-mile range!" yelled Alexa.

Maryl took a few deep breaths. "Gun it!"

Alexa slammed on the accelerator. The sudden acceleration caused Maryl to fall back against the seat.

"Three miles!"

Ray opened the window and sniffed. "There is more than a small party here, Maryl," Ray said nervously.

"Idiot! Close the window! I told you it would prolong them from smelling us!"

Ray did what he was told when he saw Maryl's eyes darken.

"Two miles! They have to know we're here!" Alexa yelled uneasily.

"Keep going and don't stop until you get inside of one and a quarter mile!" Maryl yelled.

Alexa opened the window and then closed it, and sniffed. "They haven't smelled us yet!"

A few seconds later, Alexa slammed on the brakes and screeched to a halt.

"Let's move!" Maryl yelled.

Maryl and Ray jumped out, lifted the trunk, grabbed the launchers, and slammed the pouches inside.

"We don't have much time! Ray, fire just above where they're rushing to us like a bat out of hell," Maryl yelled.

Ray fired the pouch at the oncoming swarm of vampires, who immediately started to vomit.

"Reload, Ray! Hurry!"

Maryl shot higher and further and then reloaded and fired again.

"Alexa, get our troops and attack!" Yelled Maryl.

Ray fired another pouch much higher and further. Before he reloaded, he turned around and shouted, "Get your asses out there and fight for our blood types!"

Maryl marveled at the sight of thousands and thousands of O negative and O positive vampires banning together.

Maryl counted fifty-six pouches she and Ray had fired before she told him to stop.

"Ray, if there are any living A positive vampires left, I would be surprised. However, I need you to verify it. If there are any of them still breathing, I want you to finish them off."

"Why? My subordinates can handle it."

"Do you not want the glory that comes with a victory of this magnitude? *You*, Ray Greenwell, the Conqueror, will be written in both yours and my history books!"

Ray rubbed his unshaven chin. "When you put it that way, why not?"

"Go get them!" Maryl prodded him by gently pushing him forward.

Ray sped away. Maryl looked around and found no one was there except Alexa and Draven. Just the way she had planned.

"It's time for plan B!" she yelled at them. "Get the rocket launchers!"

Without wavering, Alexa and Draven took both rocket launchers.

"Wait a few seconds to give Ray and his army time to fight any stragglers, then take the green powder and fire at will. Take all of them!"

"Green powder?" Draven asked. "I thought we were using the gray powder?"

"Yes, I said the *green* powder. Do you have a problem with that?" Maryl asked Draven inches from his face.

"The gray powder kills the A's and B's. What does the green powder kill?" Draven asked.

"I would like to know the truth too, Maryl," Alexa said as she grabbed the launcher.

Maryl looked at both of them. Time was running out.

"Okay, but only a shortened version. I will tell you more later on. We have to hurry."

Draven took the other launcher.

"Okay. Octavus the Brooder did have a party. But it wasn't a small one like I told everyone. It was a massive party to celebrate his birthday with *thousands* of his blood type. His A positive blood accounts for thirty-five-point seven percent of the A and B blood types. With such a large congregation, it would be an ideal place to launch an assault. The less of them, the more we can live in peace."

"Okay, why did you lie to us about the party? That seems an insignificant piece of the pie."

"Because I didn't want to say this in front of Ray, but that's why I brought Ray in," Maryl said. "I knew he would bring in his horde of O positive vampires. If Ray knew his numbers would far outnumber the A positives, he would be more likely to amass as much of his troops as possible. I needed him to bring as many O positive vampires as he could. Ray prefers slaughters to an even fight. Trust me, I have known him for a few centuries."

"Why lie to Ray? What part does he serve in your plan?" Alexa inquired.

"You can't possibly understand my reasoning, but his O positive posse comprises a whopping thirty-seven-point four percent of all vampires among all the different blood types. If one day, he wanted to invade us or hurt our blood type, he could conceivably get his troops and kill as many O negative humans as possible. Think about it. It is *our only* source of the food supply. He could blackmail us because he can still drink O positive blood!"

"So… the green powder will kill only Ray's O positive blood?"

"Yes! Now hurry along! We don't have much time before they return!"

Alexa looked sternly at Draven. "We honor our O negative leader! I will do as she wishes!"

"As will I!"

"Come, Draven, let's gather all of the green powder and put forth Maryl's ingenious and live-saving plan!"

Seconds later, pouches and pouches that contained the green powder filled the sky and floated down. Many of the bags traveled more than a mile. While many were shot deliberately in-between a half-mile, and some were shot closer to their position.

Maryl hugged herself in delight while she counted the bags shot. She had brought one hundred and fifty-three bags. Using vampire speed to load and reload, Alexa and Draven fired all the sacks within fifteen minutes.

The gray and green powder had a one hundred percent rate of success; she knew that for certain. The two ingredients in the gray and green pouches were foolproof.

While the other vampires will be quite angry, she was sure no one would attack her, or she would use the powder on them.

"Go, and make sure everyone did not make it and bring our troops back," Maryl commanded.

Alexa and Draven sped toward the devastation they knew was waiting for them.

They stopped on the property. Alexa and Draven could tell it was once a celebration. All they saw were bodies lying on the ground, some twisted in awkward positions. None were still breathing in the immediate vicinity, except for the O negative troops. They were looking around in confusion.

Alexa and Draven scoured the grounds, indoors, in the woods, and a mile in all directions. They put down sixty-eight vampires who were still convulsing. They would have died eventually, but they put the poor bastards out of their unbearable misery.

Alexa and Draven sped back to their troops. "O negatives, come! Maryl Rosser's glorious mission has been accomplished!" Alexa yelled.

"But she killed our cousins!" one of them yelled.

"Kill or be killed!" Alexa shot back.

The vampire sped to Alexa. "I will not kill our cousins!"

"Okay," Alexa said before she took her hand and thrust it into his chest cavity and removed his heart.

"Any other whiners?" she shouted to the massive crowd of O negatives.

The mass of Maryl's troops returned to the car without any further complaint. They found Maryl leaning against the car with several vampires lying around her.

"Who are they?" Alexa asked.

"Loiterers of our own kind, who didn't like my vision." She stood up. "Let's go home and celebrate. I still have the bottle you gave Ray, Alexa."

"After that ordeal, it sounds wonderful!" Alexa said happily.

"By the way, how many less vile competitor vampires did we get rid of today?" Draven asked as he rubbed his hands together.

"By my count, eight thousand three hundred and ninety-five," Alexa stated with pride.

"And if you include the five you took down, Maryl, it was eight thousand four hundred," Draven boasted.

"All in all, it was a good day for the O negatives," Maryl said. She whistled loudly as a signal for the O negatives to get into their vehicles. Within ten minutes, they left Octavus the Brooder's compound.

Next on Maryl's agenda was to find Clayton. She had something special in store for him and the traitorous Desiree Maholmes.

Chapter Seventeen

Sequencing Enzymes Institute of Technology

S.E.I.T. Present Day August 17th

Jack and his fellow scientists were hunkered down with a Petri dish under their microscopes. Clayton was sitting on a chair next to Jack.

"How far along are you with sequencing the enzyme Doctor Shelly Leadstone created?" Clayton asked Jack while Jack was looking under the microscope.

"It's not that simple. I am getting negative results. More tests are needed."

"We're running out of blood, and we've been here for weeks."

Jack stopped what he was doing. "Clayton, let me explain something to you in a non-scientific way. Doctor Leadstone was a pioneer in this field. It took her over ten years to create the serum. And she was human!" He pointed to his colleagues. "We are not pioneers. We have to understand the process before we can even begin to make changes."

Clayton was perturbed at the lack of progress and Jack's blatant disrespect. He was frustrated.

"Maybe you're looking at this the wrong way, Jack," Clayton said lightly.

"Oh, so now you're a scientist?" Jack said sarcastically.

Clayton zipped to him and grabbed him by the throat and squeezed. "I am getting awfully tired of your disrespect, Jack. With a swift motion, I can snap your neck in either direction." He lifted Jack in the air and above his head. "From now on, when I talk to you, I expect a courteous answer, do you understand?"

Jack nodded feebly.

Clayton put him down and released his iron grip. "Now, as I was saying... maybe we're looking at this the wrong way." He looked to Jack in case another insult was forthcoming.

"What would that be?" Jack said while rubbing his neck.

"I now think the serum is useless," Clayton remarked with sadness.

"What? What do you mean?"

"Hear me out. The serum's job is to strip the antigen off the red blood cells, and it does that. Introducing our blood types into the serum renders them all O types. So, without changing the DNA structure of the serum itself, it won't matter what blood type is introduced."

"We know that, Clayton. We have known that from the beginning. No offense, but we have been trying to change the genetic code of the serum and then introduce our blood. We can't find the right combination to *create* antigens that would produce and then reproduce our blood types."

"So, you're no closer than when we started weeks ago?"

"I'm afraid not."

The silence that followed was deafening. It was broken by the sound of a vehicle pulling in the parking lot.

"We have a visitor. I will see who it is. Continue your work," Clayton said as he sped away.

He rushed down the steps and came to the large foyer. He zipped to a window, and even with his hyper eyesight, the grime from the window not being cleaned for so long, he was barely able to see outside.

A person came out of the car. It was a woman, and she wasn't trying to hide who she was.

Upon closer inspection, Clayton was shocked to discover it was Desiree.

He met her at the door but did not attempt to open it for her.

"You have a lot of nerve showing up here," Clayton said as he folded his arms across his chest.

Desiree did not attempt to move. She stood there like a statue.

"Well, aren't you going to say anything?" Clayton demanded.

Desiree said nothing.

Clayton turned around and started to walk away. He heard banging on the door but continued walking away when the banging resumed. The sound was not her fists pounding on the window. Curious, he went back to the door.

Desiree had her phone up against the window and was pointing at it to Clayton.

Clayton watched in horror as he witnessed the genocide of a large scale being filmed.

"*Maryl did this*? She killed Octavus the Brooder and his friends?" Clayton demanded.

Desiree nodded. "It was a birthday party. *Thousands* attended. None survived. Not only that, but she killed Ray Greenwell, the Conqueror, and a few thousand of his army!"

"What? How did you get hold of this?" he demanded.

"Let me in, and I will tell you."

"I don't exactly have much confidence in you, Desiree," Clayton admonished.

"I need you to listen to me, it's vital!"

"No, I don't think I will."

"Then, your blood types will surely perish."

"I don't believe you."

"Maryl has more than one type of powder, Clayton. She has been genetically modifying it for all the blood types!"

If blood could drain from vampires without being bitten or impaled by the hands of other vampires, Clayton would be pale. He looked at her for a moment, carefully weighing and calculating the risks.

Reluctantly, he opened the door and allowed her access.

"Don't think for one minute this means I trust you, Desiree. It was your treachery and deception that started all this!"

"That is open to debate, Clayton. Maybe some other time. Right now, we have more important stuff to talk about!"

He walked to a chair in the lobby. Desiree sat beside him.

"How did you find me, and how did you get the video?"

"It took some deduction. I took a map of the United States, looked at all of the places where the top of the line DNA facilities was located. I zoomed in on the Midwest, specifically Indiana since you're a resident. I didn't think you'd travel too far."

"And?"

"I ruled them all out because you would be noticed. After that, it was a simple analysis. You had to go somewhere where you could hide in plain sight. What better place than an abandoned building that, according to my research, still had their equipment housed inside? And voila! Here I am."

Clayton was impressed. He folded his arms again. "Okay. What about the video?"

"That would be a longer story. Do you want to hear the story before Maryl forced me to eat human food to weaken me, slit my throat, and threw me down a canyon because she erroneously thought I betrayed her?"

"The traitorous part sounds familiar," Clayton retorted.

"Funny, but I am not done. When I fell, I fell on top of a pile of other vampires she had done the same thing too. Or did you want me to start my hellish story after that?"

"The after story. Since you found me, Maryl won't be too far behind."

"I was on death's door when a vampire on top of the pile was still alive. With my dying breath, I sucked her blood so her death would bring me life."

"What does that captivating story have to do with the video?"

"Because by me being alive, I brought you the video. Had I died down in the canyon, you wouldn't know about Maryl's spiral into madness."

Clayton prodded her with his hands. "And?"

"After I found where you were hiding, I planned my revenge on Maryl. I trailed her beyond her sharp sight until recently."

"What happened after you trailed her? What did you see?"

She remained quiet for a moment. "From a distance, I saw her have a meeting with Ray and thousands of his cronies. I figured it prudent to film her actions after that."

"That's impossible, Desiree. I don't know of any camera that can zoom in and take pictures from four miles away."

Desiree peered at Clayton intensely. "I re-entered the compound. After all, I would just smell like another O negative. I… I have more videos for you to view, but there is something you need to know."

"What would that be?" Clayton said while shifting positions in his chair.

"I followed Maryl and Rays' army, keeping a safe distance. When her and Ray's soldiers stopped, I parked nearby, took cover, and continued to film." Desiree took a few deep breaths before resuming. "While she still does have the gray powder, which she used to wipe out thousands of Octavus the Brooder's tribes, I was able to discern that she had another color of the powder. It was green, which she betrayed Ray and the O positives by launching the green powder and killing Ray and several thousand of his troops too."

Clayton straightened up in his chair. "Wait, you're saying Maryl can target certain blood types? Like a doomsday device?"

"Yes, that's precisely what I am saying."

"How does she possess the know-how to create such powerful weaponry?"

"I don't know, but the vampire I drank her blood from told me if I saved her, she would tell me a secret about Maryl."

"And what was the secret?"

"I don't know. I was dying and needed nourishment, and her back was broken. She couldn't move, and I couldn't give her my blood to help her because I was practically devoid of it myself."

"I need to know what her secret is now more than ever with her new powder."

"I think it goes further than that, Clayton."

"How so?"

"If I would give an educated guess, if she had green powder to remove the O positives, might she have different colors for just the A positives, the A negatives, and so on? Even specifically targeting your blood type, the most powerful."

Clayton let that news sink in before responding. "Any other news I might not enjoy?"

"Just a hypothesis."

"Let's hear it," Clayton said with a heavy heart.

"Maryl succeeded in wiping out a significant portion of the A positive and O positives in the Midwest. If she continues her mad quest, her blood type will be the dominant species of vampires in the United States within two to five years. And in five to ten years? She may be able to control the feeding population of the world, especially if she gets her hands on the serum you stole."

Clayton pondered Desiree's theory. "Maryl has always sought to control the playing field. Her actions of late suggest you may be correct. Perhaps it's because she can only consume her own blood type, whereas I can feed off any human?"

Desiree interjected. "I don't think it is derived from jealousy if that is what you're suggesting. I think it stems from self-preservation." She looked at Clayton. "How's the transformation of the serum coming along? Figured it out yet?"

Clayton leaned forward in his chair and interlocked his fingers. "No, and I'm afraid we won't be able to. We don't have anyone on my science team that comes close to Doctor Leadstone's knowledge. Even her laptop provided no clues."

"Then, in my eyes, you only have two options if you can't reconstitute the serum where it would only accept the A's and B's."

"Why are you trying to help me? If I produced the serum, you would not survive."

"At this point, I no longer care. I do not want to be in the crosshairs of your feud."

Clayton looked at her carefully. He still didn't fully trust her. "And what would those two choices be?"

"The first one is obvious. Destroy the enzymes." She put up her hands. "I know what you're thinking. Why would I want you to destroy the serum when it would benefit me as well."

"That thought did cross my mind."

"Maryl is trying to play god. And you are too by trying to reconstruct the enzymes conducive to your blood types. I want no part of either scenario! Vampire wars were fought over lesser things."

Clayton smiled as he put his fingers to his lips. "And the second possibility?"

"Keep the serum as a bargaining chip with Maryl."

Clayton was horror struck. "That would be suicide if I traded something for the serum!"

Desiree put up a finger for emphasis. "Not if you *slightly* alter the sequence where it renders it ineffective."

"Slightly? Huh, that does hold merit! But what does Maryl possess that I would want for the serum? I have never been to her estate or any other properties she owns."

Desiree rolled her eyes. "Don't be so materialistic. It doesn't have to be a thing. It could be knowledge or something that isn't tangible."

"I will take what you said into consideration."

"And I will not," Jack said as he walked down the stairs and entered the large lobby. He sat across from Clayton.

"And what say do you have in this matter?" Desiree asked in confusion.

"I am the head scientist here, an AB positive like Clayton. I can smell your O negative lies!"

"You have another plan, *head scientist*?" Desiree asked cynically.

"Yes. We continue on course, with no swerves or deviations, by seeking advice from you!" Jack said in a tiff.

Desiree stood up and handed Clayton a piece of paper.

"Leaving so soon?" Clayton asked.

"Yes. Here's my phone number in case you come to your senses and don't listen to the jerk head scientist."

Clayton took the piece of paper, folded it, and put it in his front pocket.

Desiree zipped away.

"I never trust two things, Clayton."

"What are they?" he asked as he saw Desiree's truck speeding away.

"A pretty woman and the two O blood types. And she fits in both categories."

Chapter Eighteen
Trevor the Giant's Compound
August 24th

"Where the hell is Clayton, The Archetype? And why hasn't he responded to the provocation by Maryl Rosser?" Trevor, the Giant, yelled at his most trusted second in command, Joshua.

Joshua got up, and swatted flies off his finished meal. "Beats me, Trevor. Personally, I think he and Maryl have gone off the deep end."

Trevor rose his six-foot eleven-inch frame and stood next to Joshua, who was five foot nine. "I need answers and not opinions! Find him!"

Joshua looked to the ceiling and sighed. "Trevor, all the blood types are looking for him and all for different reasons."

Trevor put up a large finger. "Ray is no longer looking for him since Maryl broke their alliance and killed him!"

"She also took care of Octavus the Brooder along with a large portion of his A positive vampires."

Trevor looked at his phone and replayed one of the videos a private number had sent him. How they got his number was a mystery. The videos were disturbing. "With Maryl's gray, and now green powder, we dare not attack her lest she destroys all of our B negative brothers and sisters!"

Joshua looked at him in amazement. "Um, Trevor, I think she will attack us whether or not we seek justice or vengeance, depending on your perspective."

Trevor was going to respond when his phone vibrated in his hand. He looked at Joshua. "Another message from our friend, the private caller."

"What does it say?" Joshua asked as he looked in Trevor's fridge for more blood.

Trevor's eyes lit up. "Come, Joshua! Our mystery caller just gave us Clayton's location! We need answers! I am tired of the feud between Clayton and Maryl! Bring as many men with us as you can find!" Trevor said as he flew out of the dining room to the outside.

Trevor and six dozen vampires crammed into several cars, with Joshua driving the lead car and Trevor in the passenger's seat.

"Why is this person sending you videos of Maryl's crimes, and now provide us with Clayton's location?" Joshua asked as he peeled out of the long gravel driveway.

Trevor's arm leaned on the outside of the car. "I don't know. Maybe someone that they loved was killed in the raid? Maybe they have a beef with Maryl?"

"Maybe."

"Can't you speed up any, Joshua?"

"I have my foot to the floor."

"How long is it to Clayton's location?"

"They are in central Indiana. From our present location, the map app says it's a five and a half-hour drive," Joshua responded immediately.

Trevor blew out air in frustration. "Okay. We have no choice but to proceed."

"Trevor, do we need to call any of our blood type cousins to ask permission to cross their boundaries?"

He didn't answer right away. He was gazing at cornfields on one side of the road and soybeans on the other that stretched for miles. Beyond that, dairy farms that churned out milk and butter nestled beside cattle and pig farms. He marveled at humans that planted crops and raised farm animals. They planted crops and butchered animals to eat so they can stay alive, and that in turn made Trevor and the other blood types able to consume them to stay alive. It was like a symbiotic mutually beneficial relationship.

He came out of his philosophical thoughts. "Ask permission? Are you nuts? I would be surprised if the boundaries are still in effect. No, don't call anyone. If the mysterious caller called us, I suspect they have called the others too."

Four hours later, Joshua had endured four hours of Trevor snoring with his mouth wide open. The loud noise kept him awake. He didn't know if he could take another hour and a half of the relentless sound. He took a quick look at the others in the car. They seemed oblivious. Everyone but himself was asleep. Not that vampires required to sleep, but closing the eyes and resting the heartbeat was a great way of preserving their energy.

Joshua was about to wake Trevor to stop him from snoring when he stole a glance in the rearview mirror and noticed they were still being followed. It wasn't obvious, but the last few turns, several vehicles in the distance followed their route. Coincidence? He didn't think so.

He pushed Trevor's large frame, but Trevor didn't budge. He rechecked his rearview mirror. The cars had sped up and were closer. Much closer. This time he shoved Trevor. Trevor moved slightly, but his snoring continued.

Joshua leaned over and yelled in Trevor's ear and punched him in his thick arm. "Trevor!"

Trevor was instantly awake, but not alert. He grabbed Joshua by the throat. In a state of panic, Joshua tried to release Trevor's tremendous grip with one hand and steer with the other. His grip was so tight, Joshua was unable to talk and could barely breathe.

Panic overtook him as their car swerved right and left. He saw a cluster of trees to the right and decided to slam into it. It wouldn't hurt them, but it would fully wake Trevor up, and then they could deal with the multiple cars speeding toward them.

Joshua drove directly into the path of the trees and crashed the car in the middle of the engine. On impact, their bodies flew forward and then fell back.

"What the hell is wrong with you, Joshua?" Trevor demanded as he saw his car embedded in a tree. "Did you do this on purpose?"

Joshua tried to look at his colleague's vehicles in the rearview mirror, but the mirror had fallen off in the crash. Frantically, he looked in the side-view mirror. Gladly, the other cars had stopped and had come to make sure they were okay.

"We're being followed by several cars, and for the life of me, I could not wake you to tell you!"

"Let's see what they want," Trevor said as his massive frame exited the car.

The multitude of cars slammed into Trevor's vehicles. Several humans from each vehicle left, with more coming out of the trunks and started running away from them.

"Trevor, is it weird that the humans are running away from us with fists in the air?"

Trevor, Joshua, and the hordes of vampires raced after the humans. Trevor grabbed a human and turned her around. "Look at their left wrists, Joshua. They belong to the Fellowship of the Fangs."

Joshua didn't need to use his keen eyesight to see. "Why do they have blood droplets just below their fangs?"

Trevor sped to a few humans and dispatched them with ease. He saw Joshua up ahead. He raced to Joshua.

"The higher up they are in the organization, the more blood droplets they have tattooed on."

They were making mince-meat out of the humans as they spoke. More ran away, but Trevor and his vampires caught up with them.

"They must all be low-leveled members," Joshua stated.

"What makes you say that?" Trevor asked as he chased a human and put an end to his existence.

"Most of the ones we took care of had only one droplet. I don't see anyone with more than two droplets," Joshua remarked casually as he dispatched another human.

More ran with Trevor, Joshua, and the others pursuing them.

A sudden realization came to Trevor in midstride. The Fellowship of the Fang members were tactically forcing them away from their cars. So far away that, even at high speed, Trevor didn't think they would make it back in time. "Retreat! Everyone retreat back to the cars!"

"What? What on earth for?" Joshua said in disbelief.

"The Fellowship of the Fangs was a ruse to throw us off! We were set up for the real attack!"

The pouches descended from above seconds later. The orange mist was already hitting the ground when Trevor, Joshua, and the other B negative vampires approached their cars. They started to cough, and the vomiting started immediately. Blood trickled out their body cavities. They never made it inside the vehicle. Instead, the lifeless bodies sprawled in various positions. Trevor's' orange misted hand still grasped the car door handle while his body laid upon the ground with the orange mist covering his entire corpse.

Chapter Nineteen
Choices
Present Day September 9th

Clayton was sitting on the stoops outside the clinic, gazing at the sky. Night time had arrived, and the electricity had been turned off to make sure prying eyes wouldn't see the building's illumination.

Clayton enjoyed watching the clouds cloak the moon for brief seconds, and then a stream of moonlight would peek through that cast shadows of his surroundings. He absorbed the quietness, the absolute stillness of the night, which, by far, was his favorite part of the day.

Jack broke Clayton's quiet reverie by opening the door and sitting beside him.

"Choices, choices, and more choices," Jack whispered. His voice echoed against the vastness of the sparse surroundings.

"And what choices are you referring to, Jack?" Clayton asked with slight annoyance.

"We need to make our decision concerning the serum and our inability to coax an enzyme into reproducing our blood type and using it as leverage against Maryl."

Clayton turned to Jack. "I was under the distinct impression you vehemently opposed Desiree's options some time ago."

"I most assuredly did!"

"What made you change your mind?"

Jack threw up his hands. "We're not getting anywhere! The best-case scenario is to alter the serum to make it ineffective, but only marginally so as not to arouse suspicion."

"Again, that is what Desiree suggested."

Jack looked at Clayton. "Is there something going on between you and Desiree?"

"What? Of course not! And in the unlikely event there was, our blood types are incompatible for anything beyond... you know... *that*."

"Uh-huh."

"Let's get back on topic, shall we? How long will it take to modify the serum slightly?"

"I do have some good news in that regard. We've successfully modified it."

Clayton was stunned. "When?"

"A few hours ago. We had to run the test several times before I wanted to tell you," Jack said with no hint of sarcasm.

"How?"

"I extracted stem cells from one of the few bags of AB positive blood we have left. * I have never tried that before. I don't know why. Anyway, when I introduced the stem cells of our AB positive blood type into the serum, something happened," Jack said with excitement. "It didn't turn the serum into our blood type as I had hoped, but it did alter the DNA structure of the enzyme just enough to neutralize *one* of the vital components of the antigen, which renders Maryl's concoction useless. Under a general microscope without much magnification, the change isn't noticeable. When you put it under a powerful microscope such as an electron microscope, the change is more visible."

"Observable to the point of detection?" Clayton asked.

"It would depend on the scientist and their area of expertise."

"We have to take the chance. How long will the process take to do that to all of the samples we have?"

"Several days."

"Does that mean during the day and not the night?"

"Yes."

"Start first thing in the morning!"

Jack stood up. "Was planning on it," he said as he walked up the steps and entered the vast lobby.

Clayton watched him go inside. As soon as Jack had finished his job, he would call Maryl. She was clever. He had to come up with some good reasons to give her back the tainted serum.

He stayed outside a little while longer to view the skyline. He knew the wind had picked up from the tree leaves swaying while their attached limbs bent in protest. He couldn't feel the wind. No vampire could, with their invulnerable skin. His hair would blow with the direction of the wind, but he did not feel it.

Sometimes, in rare instances, he wanted to feel something physically, be it a partner's touch, hunkering down in front of the fireplace, or feel the snow in the palm of his hands. But that was not to be.

Clayton walked toward the bevy of trees when he heard Jack rush down the stair, past the lobby, and went outside.

"Clayton! Where are you going?"

"I was going to take a walk. Why?"

"Come inside and come upstairs with me and the others. We have to show you something!"

Clayton and Jack rushed upstairs. The other scientists were looking at a laptop, and their expressions were a mixture of stunned merged with horror.

"What's going on?" Clayton asked.

"Tiberius! Rewind the video so Clayton can see it!"

Tiberius's thin nimble fingers went to work as Jack led Clayton to the front of the monitor.

"Watch, but prepare yourself!" Jack hissed.

Tiberius pressed play. The screen was divided into two vertical halves with one side that had a news reporter standing by with a microphone in her hand. On the other side, another newswoman was ready to report the news with a microphone in her hand.

The camera panned to the news anchor in the studio. Even sitting down, the man was tall. His crisp white shirt with a red tie gave him an air of allure and superiority. He looked at the camera and nodded.

"This is Glenn Stuart with CVB news live in Indianapolis. There have been two separate reports of gruesome and hideous attacks. We have Cheryl Otterman, and Sarah Picks at the crime scenes. Describe to me what is going on where you are, Cheryl."

There was a slight pause until Cheryl heard Glenn through her earpiece. Her long blond hair whipped in the wind, causing her to brush back her hair with her free hand.

"*Glenn, I can tell you this. I spoke to detective Jay Washburn with the Indianapolis police a while ago. A huge celebratory gathering took place sometime yesterday afternoon on Lynhurst Drive. The owner of the place, which we have since learned was Octavus Brooder, was celebrating his birthday with a large congregation of friends and family…*"

"What the?" Clayton said as he leaned further inward.

"*Mister Brooder was a respected businessman who employed several hundred workers at his four vineyards spread across Indiana. His wine shops would attract thousands of people yearly for a sampling of his brands.*"

"What happened to him?" Clayton asked impatiently.

"She's coming to the part that we should be concerned with," Tiberius said in a deep voice.

"*The scene was incredible, Glenn. At last count, over four thousand bodies have been discovered, and they're still working the crime scene.*"

The camera went to Glenn. "*Cheryl, do we know the cause of death?*"

Cheryl's side came back. "*No, and that's what's so unusual about the crime scene, Glenn. All the police are willing to tell us is there was gray powder spread over a mile radius of Mister Brooder's property, including the powder that covered the deceased people. Police are taking samples to the lab as we speak.*"

Glenn came back. *"Disturbing! Okay, thank you, Cheryl Ottoman, from CVB news. We now go live with Sarah Picks. Sarah? What do you have for us?"*

Sarah's hair was in a tight ponytail. She wore glasses and had a green blouse with a white scarf around her neck. *"Thank you, Glenn. Just a hundred miles south of the Brooder estate murders, police discovered another grisly scene. A police spokesperson told me nearly two hundred people, many with their necks snapped, were brutally murdered. Just as many perished with the same type of powder covered the dead bodies. The powder was not gray as the other sickening scene, but orange. There are no suspects yet in these two bizarre mass killings. One of the victims was identified as Ray Greenwell Conqueror, who owned a chain of popular restaurants called Conqueror's Steak House and Grill. Other bodies are waiting to be identified. Back to you, Glenn..."*

Tiberius hit the pause button.

"She is systematically taking out her competition, including her sister's blood type!" Jack said as he slammed the desk. "This can not go unpunished, Clayton!"

"I know, Jack. I know," Clayton said as he sat down. "We can't do anything until you're done with the serum."

"Hopefully, it won't be much longer," Jack said in frustration. He glanced at the paused video, shook his head, and returned to his chair. "And it's nighttime, so we can't do anything until tomorrow at sunrise."

"We will get our revenge, Jack. That I solemnly swear!"

"You'll have to make it soon, or we're going to run out of vampires!" Jack said in protest.

"Jack, I can't do anything until all of the serum is slightly altered."

"I know, but seeing our family and cousins dying is tearing me apart, Clayton," Jack said with profound sadness.

Clayton patted Jack on his back. "We'll make this right, I promise."

Chapter Twenty
Show Time
Present Day September 19ᵗʰ

Clayton and the scientists took turns hunting humans to remain healthy. After Clayton came back from a hunt, he stepped into the lab and went to see Jack.

"Jack, I need to talk to you."

Jack's head peered up from the microscope. "What's up?"

Clayton pointed outside the building. "I discovered over thirty-five discarded humans within a few miles of the Institute."

Jack shrugged his shoulders. "And? They're just humans. Food. They are meaningless. Their sole job is to provide us with nourishment for our continued existence."

"I understand that, but that's not my point."

Jack looked at him in confusion. "Then what is your point, Clayton?"

"You can't leave dead bodies lying around! If one of their families is looking for them, or if someone stumbles upon them, that will bring in the police, and then they will know our location."

"Huh, we hadn't thought about that. What did you do with them?"

"I buried all of them so there wouldn't be any trace." Clayton looked at Jack. "How do you hunt where you used to work?"

"Hunt? We never hunted until recently with you."

"How did you obtain your nourishment?" Clayton asked with uncertainty.

"Our blood was given to us in units like the ones you see at hospitals."

Clayton smiled. "They sure spoiled you."

"You own the company, so you're the one that spoiled us!" Jack grinned, and then grew serious. "I have some news. The serum is done. It's ready. All you need to do is call Maryl, but you left your phone in the car."

Clayton smirked. "The one in the car is a prepaid phone. I have my other one in my pocket."

"I suggest you call her as soon as possible," Jack said with seriousness that bordered on terror.

Clayton took a few deep gulps of air before he called Maryl's number.

Jack looked at Clayton, who was looking at his phone. "Nervous? I know I am, and I'm not the one that is going to talk to her."

"I'm not usually, but this is an unusual circumstance."

He dialed, and after the second ring, he heard her familiar voice.

"Hello?"

"Maryl?"

"Clayton? What a pleasant surprise! How are you?"

"Fine. Listen, I need to talk to you."

"I am all ears."

"I have to be honest with you, Maryl."

"About what?"

"You know what, Maryl. I have been unable to alter your serum."

"I want my serum back, Clayton. That's all I ever wanted."

"And in retaliation, you are slowly getting rid of your competition?" Clayton said with bitterness.

"That is a matter we can discuss at another time, don't you agree?"

"What do you propose?"

"Bring my serum to my estate, and we can discuss what you desire."

"I want the serum destroyed," Clayton said with firmness.

There was silence for a moment. "Then why didn't you just discard it? I'm confused."

"I want to have a bargaining chip," Clayton said honestly.

"Clayton, you do realize if you give the serum back to me, I will still go ahead with my plan to find a way to assimilate it into humans?"

"I was hoping I could talk you out of it."

Laughter erupted in Clayton's ear. "You still have your sense of humor! I'm delighted!"

"Will you listen to my request?"

"Yes, of course! Come alone tomorrow evening to my place with the serum."

"And go into the lion's den alone? Give me more credit. I will bring a brigade of soldiers."

"Okay, why not for old times sake."

"Maryl, why are you killing off my tribes?"

"Because you were going to kill off my bloodline."

Clayton looked at the ground for a few seconds. "You've changed in the past few months, and I can't fathom why."

"Clayton, all your answers will be revealed tomorrow."

"Revealed to me? Before I die or as I am dying?"

"Whatever the mood I'm in at the time, Clayton."

"I will see you tomorrow, Maryl."

"One question before I hang up," Maryl said with a trace of humor.

"Shoot."

"Do you even have a brigade of soldiers left?" she hung up before Clayton could reply.

Jack overheard the conversation. "Humbug! Maryl does have a point. We don't have that many vampires left in Indiana."

Clayton smirked. "Or in the tri-state area. I will call Platov and see if he can spare any soldiers." He took the phone and dialed.

"Hello?"

"Platov? This is Clayton."

"Clayton! Where have you been? Have you seen the news?"

"Yes, and that's why I'm calling. I know we've had our differences recently, but I really need your help, buddy. I desperately need some vampires if you can spare any."

"Sorry, Clayton. After Ray and Octavus's death by Maryl, many of my blood types fled."

"Fled? Where?" Clayton asked in bafflement.

"Scattered about, I'm afraid. No idea."

"I understand. Normally there would be strength in numbers, but Maryl seeks all of us together. It makes it easier for her to spill her poison down from the tainted sky."

"True. And don't bother calling Salvatore the Great or Silvia the Hopeful if you haven't yet, both of them bolted after hearing the news."

"Damn! Thanks, Platov. Be careful."

"I will. And stay away from Maryl!"

"Will do."

Clayton hung up, pointed, and looked at the scientists. "I'm afraid it's just me and all of you."

"Woah now, Clayton! Don't look at us! We're science people, not warriors. Unfortunately, you're on your own." Jack got up, and his colleagues followed. "We're done with our mission. Going after Maryl Rosser was not part of the deal, regardless if we agreed with your vision." Jack pointed to the green tote bag. "We took the liberty of loading the serum in your bag." He started to walk away and then turned around. "We left you one unit of the blood of AB positive. Good luck."

"Why are you fleeing? You were the one telling me we need to get rid of Maryl! Furthermore, where will you go?"

"Far away from Maryl's influence," Tiberius said clearly scared.

"That's kind of vague, Jack. You do know she exerts vast influence around the globe, right?"

"We will take our chances. If we go with you, we will surely die. If we run away, we have a small chance," Jack said as one by one, they left.

Clayton remained in his chair, alone and afraid. He slightly trembled as he looked at the bag that contained the serum. Clayton briefly entertained the idea of torching the serum and leaving too. But Clayton knew he couldn't do that. He had to see it through regardless if he perished in the process!

He would feed on the one remaining bag of AB positive blood the scientists left for him, and then scout out Maryl's abode. Clayton got up with renewed determination.

He got to the blood, started to drink from the bag when it spilled down his shirt and pants. He wiped his clothes, which made the blood smear. He took out his handkerchief he always kept in his pants pocket. When he took it out, a piece of paper fell to the floor. Clayton had forgotten he had Desiree's number in his pocket. She was the only person he knew that he could talk to. He dialed quickly.

On the fourth ring, she answered. "Hello?"

"Hey, Desiree, it's me, Clayton…"

"Clayton! Thank goodness you called. I am driving and almost at the institute!"

"Why?"

"Maryl struck again. This time she targeted Silvia the Hopeful and several hundred of her tribe as they were entering her hotels! I think it's Platov and you that are left."

"There's Salvatore the Great that's left too. Who knows where he and the A negatives are now!" Clayton was silent for a second. "How did she get Silvia? I heard she had scattered like the others."

"Silvia did exactly what the others did. They thought if they were strong in numbers, it would dissuade Maryl from carrying out her plan. They were wrong. Silvia was bunkered up in her penthouse with over seven hundred members of her tribe in a few of the more lavish hotels she owned."

"How did they carry out their insidious plan?"

"The ventilation system," Desiree said simply.

"But Silvia and the others in the hotels would see the powder coming in through the vents."

"Maryl modified it to a fine white powder. By the time they became aware of the problem, it was far too late. It's odorless and tasteless, even for us."

"Damn! Well, I am going to meet Maryl tomorrow and give her the serum."

"What? You can't do that!" Desiree cried.

"I have to. But don't worry. The scientists were partially successful in altering the serum to render it useless."

"That's great news. But… once you give Maryl the enzymes, you're good as dead."

"I know, but I am not going to flee like the others. I have to make one last stand."

There was silence on the other end for a moment.

"I know I am going to regret this, but I will come with you," Desiree said with determination.

"I'm sure when she sees you, you will be on top of her list to eliminate, even topping me."

"I have no one, and neither do you. Let's take the last stand in unity, side by side, O negative by AB positive!"

"Okay, but I don't know why you would want to."

"I have my reasons. See you in a few minutes."

Clayton was outside sitting on the top stairs when Desiree's pick up screeched to a halt. She saw Clayton, waved, and zipped to the bottom step.

She leaned against the handrail and looked up at Clayton. "Gazing at the stars, I see."

"Yes, it makes me think."

"Think about what?" Desiree asked as she made the way up the stairs and sat beside Clayton.

"We are on the top of the food chain, yet when I stare upon the heavens, I often feel insignificant. There are trillions of galaxies that we are aware of, and within those trillions of galaxies, there are trillions of planets. We are but a speck in the universe."

Desiree put up a finger. "Ah, but *this* tiny speck we live on, we dominate. We are the center of the universe!"

Clayton looked at Desiree. "I'm surprised you want to sit so near to me. I am often told by your blood types that you cannot stand the smell of my blood."

"I'm getting used to it," she said with a smile.

They sat together in silence for several minutes.

"It's time to go, Desiree."

"I know. Do you even have a plan?"

"No, I'm afraid I do not."

Desiree got up. "I thought so. Come, let's go to our deaths."

Clayton got up. "A little melodramatic, aren't we?"

They strolled to Desiree's pick up truck.

"Perhaps, but I have been close to death. My statement may be exaggerated, but it's accurate," Desiree said as she looked at Clayton.

"In the thousand years I've been alive, I've been at death's door more than once as well."

"I know, I saved you from certain death during the purge over three hundred years ago."

Clayton stopped walking. "Only because Maryl had you save me so you could befriend me for three hundred years and extract secrets for her!"

"And you don't think that at some point, I became fond of you despite your blood type and the history of the animosity between our two tribes? You can trust me now, Clayton!"

Clayton got to the car and opened the passenger door. "If I didn't trust you, you would be dead by now. Get in and take us to Maryl's."

They drove in silence for a few minutes. Clayton looked around the inside. "Where did you get this pick up truck?"

"I stole it from one of the humans after I escaped Maryl's treachery."

For the rest of the way, each kept silent, each one taut with emotions, neither one could bring to the surface. The tension only increased as nighttime approached, and Maryl's estate loomed a few miles ahead.

"We need to be at least four miles outside of her sniffing zone, Desiree."

"I know. The problem lies with *you* and not me. Maryl and her O negative forces will, no doubt, smell you. They will think I would be one of the troops. Do you have any morsel, any kernel of an idea of how you can overcome your smell?"

"No." Clayton drummed his fingers on the dashboard, thinking. "I just wish there were a way I could get in undetected. How about I parachute myself from a helicopter?" Clayton joked.

Desiree slammed on her brakes and pulled over. "That's it!"

"What's it? Do you know someone with a helicopter?"

"No, something better!"

She got out of the truck with Clayton in tow. Desiree opened the extended cab and showed Clayton the spelunking equipment.

"You want to go cave diving? I am unaware of any caves in this region," Clayton said as he picked up a pair of socks. "The humans you told me about were serious about cave diving. These are neoprene socks. (8) The novice uses wool socks."

"And you would know this how?"

"I did some cave diving in my thousand years, Desiree."

Desiree picked up two helmets and two headlights and gave one of each to Clayton.

"We don't need their boots, wet suits, or under suits and over suits because of our thick skin. But we will need these waist belts for extra batteries if we do end up finding a cave, which is highly unlikely. We have great eyesight, but if there is a total void of light, we will need to use the headlights," Clayton said with authority.

Desiree looked at the rope that sprawled over the seat. "Will this be enough rope?"

"I don't know how far down we would have to descend. I hope so."

Desiree looked around the equipment. "Now, we need to find a cave."

"Can you show me the campsite where the humans were?"

"Yes. We're over the four-mile marker, but the human campsite is only two miles from Maryl's place."

"Okay, this is what you'll need to do, Desiree." He took the items she was holding and put it back in the backseat. "You won't need those. I need you to go to the campsite and look around, especially if their tent is still in one piece."

"What will I be looking for?"

"Maps. If the humanoids were on Maryl's terrain unannounced, they knew something no one else did."

"I don't understand why Maryl and the others didn't smell the two humans. Both of them did not have O negative blood."

"I don't know. You need to get going. While daylight is still several hours away, we still need to find a cave, go down, and come back out. I have no idea of how long we will be down there if a cavern even exists."

"Okay, the campsite isn't far. It's about two miles from here. You stay here while I check out the camping area."

Desiree drove as fast as she could. She found the spot from the last time she was there and pulled over. She took a second to marvel at the landscape below. There were plenty of hills, grasslands, and just over the horizon, she knew the tree that saved her life was perched unsteadily on a slope, eager to rescue someone else. Just over the first hill was where she needed to go. The trek down was difficult to navigate from the deep slope below.

It didn't take her long to find the grounds. The skeletal remains were still there. Both tents had been torn apart, possibly by the animals looking for food. Thankfully, the tents were still where they were initially located. She tore whatever was left of the first yellow tent and looked on the ground. She found a picture of the human's wife and three children, some books, glasses, but no map.

The other green canvas tent was thicker, and less ripped up as she tore a large hole in the side. She saw some of the cave diving equipment, a blow-up mattress, and some magazines. She did not find any map.

"I wonder what kind of magazines humans read," Desiree said as she picked up the stack. One by one, Desiree went through the magazines. She got disgusted with the humans and their frivolous ideas of what an idyllic lifestyle should be. She threw them to the ground.

"What the hell?" she said as she saw something protruding out from one of the publications. It was a map. She wasn't sure it was *the* map. She grabbed it but could not discern what it said.

It was then she heard the growling. She should have smelled the animals, Desiree thought as she turned and faced three coyotes. One was frothing from its mouth. They exposed their long sharp teeth as they tried to surround her.

She took a few hesitant steps backward. They matched steps with her. Unexpectedly, one of the feral animals lunged at her. Desiree ducked, and as the coyote was above her head, she took her fingernail and sliced the underside of the beast. It yelped as it fell to the ground, which alerted the other coyotes.

While the other two coyotes sniffed their brethren, Desiree raced to the truck.

When Desiree got to the place where she had left Clayton, Clayton was just getting off the phone. He did not seem happy.

"Why the grim look, Clayton?" she asked as she got out of the car with the map.

"Jack, one of the scientists just called me. It's all over the news. Platov and his entire regiment of AB negatives were killed. Maryl tracked all of them down and shot small traces of blue powder at each location. Platov's tribe accounted for less than one percent of the entire A and B tribes!"

"That's terrible!" She handed Clayton the map she found. "Do any of the A's and B's have families around the globe like Maryl?"

"Yes, I'm sure they're next."

"*No, you and I are next.*"

Clayton nodded as he scanned the map.

"Wow, there might be a cave on Maryl's property after all, not far from the campsite. I wonder who those humans were."

"How can you read that thing?"

"It's topographical, meaning it shows the landscape. See the small bumps on the map? They indicate hills." Clayton traced the hills eastward. "The men were only about three hundred feet from a section they highlighted in yellow marker. I would imagine that's where we need to start looking for the cave."

"Okay," she said as she looked at him. "We need to be careful. I just had a run-in with some coyotes. I killed one of them. I don't know how many more there are."

"Okay," Clayton said as he looked at the ground.

"Do you need a minute to gather your composure?"

"No. My anger is fueling me. Let's go."

"What about your sweet scent?"

"I am what I am. If Maryl sends troops, let's pray they don't overwhelm us."

"Okay, I'll drive to the location. It's not far from here," Desiree said as she got in the driving seat.

It didn't take them long when Desiree parked close to the metal railing.

She and Clayton took only as much as the cave diving equipment they needed. Clayton wrapped the thick rope across his shoulders and chest.

"Let's hurry. I want to find the cave before the O's come for us," Clayton said tensely.

"I want to hurry because of the coyotes!" Desiree said as she looked around. "I couldn't smell them. I only heard them at the last second, so be on the lookout."

"You couldn't smell them?"

"No, and I don't know why."

Clayton nodded as they climbed slowly down the embankment, trying to navigate the treacherous terrain before they could speed to the site. Every few seconds Clayton and Desiree would look toward Maryl's estate, ready to engage the enemy.

But as time went on, no vampires came down from the cliff, and they didn't see any coyotes.

"Why isn't anyone upon us?" Clayton asked out loud.

"Beats me," Desiree said before she sped away.

Clayton caught up to her at the campground. He looked over the scene and was going to say something when he looked up and sniffed. "Why can't I smell you?"

Desiree sniffed the air. "I don't know because I can't smell you either! I told you I couldn't smell the coyotes earlier!"

Thoughts surfaced inside Clayton. He looked at Desiree.

"How were you able to smell the blood types of humans if we can't now?"

"I smelled them a mile away. When I entered their campground, I wasn't thinking about if I could smell them or not. I was in survival mode."

"Okay, that makes sense. But if we can't smell each other, it's good odds no one at Maryl's can either," Clayton said with a hint of relief.

"That will help us," Desiree said with a sense of calm.

Clayton looked at the map and then at the ground beyond and pointed. "This way."

They continued to walk fast but didn't speed.

"We have to be careful."

"Why? They can't smell us," Desiree said.

"Yes, but if Maryl finds out about this anomaly, she will post guards so no intruders would come on her land," Clayton said as he became lost in thought.

"What is it, Clayton?"

"What unknown force is powerful enough to negate our sense of smell?"

"I wonder if it has affected any other things about us?" Desiree exclaimed as she smacked Clayton across the face.

"Ow!"

"Huh, I wonder if you felt that smack because we're losing our vampire power and can now feel things, or it's because vampires are the only thing that can hurt other vampires?" Desiree said, smiling.

"There's another way without hurting each other, Desiree!" Clayton said as he rubbed his face.

"Like what?"

"Our speed, our eyesight, yet you resorted to violence right away."

Desiree smiled and shrugged her shoulders. "We're vampires. It's what we do."

Clayton looked at the map. "Go run to the nearest tree, Desiree."

"Why me?"

"Because I asked you to," he said with exasperation.

"Fine." Desiree ran to the nearest tree and stopped.

"Looks like we still have our speed, for now," Clayton said happily.

Desiree gave a slight nod as she started to walk back. She glanced at her left and to her right. "Hey Clayton, come look at this," Desiree said as she pointed to the ground.

Clayton saw faint animal tracks and two sets of human footprints that were almost gone. They led to a large rock.

Clayton looked at Desiree. "The tracks stop at the rock. Go around the boulder to see if the animals and humans walked around it to continue onward, or they somehow stumbled upon the cave."

"Why am I doing all of the grunt work?" she asked as she sped around the large rock.

"Because you are just under five hundred years old, and I am a thousand. Have some respect for your elder vampires."

"I think you want me to exert my energy to see if I lose any."

"That's another reason too."

She nodded absently as she pointed to the rock. "The tracks end at the boulder, but they couldn't have gone through."

"Let's take a closer look at the large stone," Clayton said before he zipped toward it.

When he came to the boulder, he pressed his hands against it. "It feels solid." He punched it, and nothing happened.

"Let me try," Desiree said as she placed her hands delicately across the stone until she felt something peculiar. "There is a soft spot," she said as she pushed the spot in using her hands.

The rock slid open, and a small entryway appeared.

"How did you do that, Desiree?" Clayton asked with shock.

"I'm not quite sure, but if I had to hazard a guess, I would say it's because of my blood type being an O negative. Maybe it sensed me? I wonder what other treasures await us?"

"I think since you are the golden child on this property with your blood type, you should lead."

"What happened to the old saying age before beauty? Shouldn't you lead?"

"Funny. Who's the grunt now?"

Clayton was able to see down the narrow passage despite the little illumination the moonlight provided. He started walking and then turned to Desiree. "There seems to be a dead-end, but something seems off to me."

"Like what?"

"I feel a breeze. I think it's coming from below."

"Just use your hyper-sight."

"I think I am losing that ability as well," Clayton said as he moved a few more steps tentatively with Desiree close behind.

"Stop!" Clayton said as he put his hand up.

"What's going on, Clayton? You're making me nervous!"

"You should be. We're losing our vampire powers, and I almost fell through the large opening a couple of steps ahead of me."

"I'll turn on my headlight; I suggest you do the same," Desiree said as she turned hers on.

Clayton did the same and was astonished to see skeleton bones of varying types of species were laying on both sides of the gaping hole.

"I recognize animal bones, perhaps feral dogs and coyotes," Clayton said as he looked around. "And there! I see human remains."

Desiree walked to the opposite side and pointed around her. "These are definitely vampire remains. Their fangs are protruding." She looked around the dimly lit area. "What is going on here, Clayton?"

"I am unsure. Did you want to go down and find out?"

"How do you know the answer is down there and not up here?"

Clayton spread his hands as the headlight shown on her feet. "I don't. The sun will be coming up in a few hours. We need to descend to the core."

"I'm afraid what we'll find at the abyss."

"Nevertheless, we must proceed even though we don't have anything to tie the rope to."

Desiree looked at him. "Are you saying we jump? You can't be serious! With our continued power loss, would we live? We don't even know how far down it is!" Desiree looked down with her headlight. "I can't even see the bottom."

"I have to continue, Desiree. I would understand if you left now."

"I may have to, Clayton. I'm too young to lose power and die."

Clayton smiled warmly. "If I get out of here alive, I'll look you up."

"You must live, Clayton!" She went to him and gave him a prolonged hug.

She turned and walked toward the opening. She noticed the rock was sliding back, and the moonlight's light that shone on the dirt floor became more narrow. She rushed to the passage opening as the rock slid closed.

"Damn!"

Now the only light was from her headlight. She braced herself against the wall and went to the end of the tunnel. The fact that she couldn't feel the wall's temperature told her that her invulnerable skin was still resistant to cold and heat. She reached the end. She could sense the hole a few feet away from her.

"Clayton! I've come back to help you!" she yelled. Then softly to herself, she said, "I had no choice with the door closed, but I'm here…" She waited a few seconds. "Clayton!" No answer, which could only mean he jumped down. "Damn!"

Chapter Twenty-One
Into the Abyss!
Present Day

Clayton had no choice but to jump. He counted out loud, "One, two, three!" He leaped downward. As he plunged down, he could see a thin sliver of light below. As Clayton dropped further down, the walls became more constricted, which helped him slow his descent. He pushed out his arms and legs as the walls came closer to him. He slowed down considerably and only had to fall fifteen feet from the end of the hole to the floor where he landed on his feet. Clayton was thankful he retained his invulnerable skin, or he would have burns on his hands and legs from the friction of stopping his fall.

Desiree's departure saddened him. He felt an odd connection with her even though she had deceived him for three centuries. She had grown on him over the years. He also thought she was smitten with him. Yes, he thought, Desiree, was falling for him.

As that last thought rummaged through his mind, Desiree did not fall *for* him but fell *on* top of him as she dropped down from the hole.

Desiree was on top of him, face to face. "Desiree? I thought you had left."

She looked at him for a second and realized the position she was in and got up. Clayton followed. "I changed my mind. It seems we are destined to figure this out together," Desiree said as she retightened the rope on her shorts.

Desiree looked around the vast room. It was a humongous glass aquarium that seemed to stretch for miles on both sides of the walls. She peered closer as Clayton stood beside her.

"Are those what I think they are?" Desiree asked with dread.

"Yes," Clayton said with abject fear. "Come on! We need to see where the aquarium leads to so we can stop Maryl's evil and dangerous plan!"

"I agree. Good news, I can feel my vampire powers returning. I wonder what is up there that is negating them?" Desiree asked.

"We have more important things to worry about right now, Desiree!"

"Yes, you do," Maryl said as she appeared with a small army of O negative vampires.

"How did you find us?" Clayton asked.

"For some reason, the area directly above us inhibits most of our powers. I am at a loss as to why. For that reason, I started posting guards there. A little while ago, they reported to me they saw two beings enter where the two humans were killed on my land." Maryl looked at Desiree. "I surmised it was you who had found the entrance. Only one of our blood types may trigger the opening." Maryl looked at Clayton with scorn matched only with a hint of humor. "And you, Clayton? I see you couldn't wait until morning for our agreed-upon meeting. Tell me, do you still have the serum?"

"I do."

"Where is it?"

"In the pickup truck just over the ridge a couple of miles west of here."

Maryl glanced at someone in front of the line. "You, Samuel, go to the truck, grab the serum, and then destroy all of it."

"At once!" Samuel sped away.

"Wait! Why are you destroying the enzyme?" Clayton asked in shock.

Maryl snickered. "Oh, really, Clayton! Don't you think I wouldn't make more?"

Clayton was speechless. All that work for nothing! "But… but why did you tell me you wanted it back?"

"To lure you into my trap," Maryl said with excitement.

Clayton was stunned.

"The lack of a comeback tells me you were expecting another outcome?" Maryl said as she walked closer to Clayton. "Clayton, you disappoint me. With all of your A and B power you had at your disposal, you didn't harness the one thing that mattered." She pointed to her head. "You didn't further educate your mind! You didn't tap into your potential!"

"And that's what you did with all of your fancy watches? And the different color powders you have reworked over the centuries?"

"Yes and no."

"Explain!" Clayton shouted.

"You're in no position to make demands to *me*!" Maryl slapped Clayton across his face. "You sicken me!"

Clayton rubbed his cheek as several guards went to him and Desiree and surrounded them.

"Come with me; I have a few things to show you," Maryl said eagerly.

They were pushed forward as Maryl looked back at them. "I take it you are aware of what's in the aquarium?"

"Yes. Tell me, Maryl, what hellish plan are you preparing now?" Clayton said in a demanding tone.

Maryl looked at Desiree. "Surely, you know, don't you?"

Desiree looked at her in disgust. "I'm pretty sure."

"Well, I don't! Spit it out, Maryl!" Clayton commanded.

Maryl clapped her hands in delight and turned to the small group. "He doesn't understand!"

Their laughter echoed throughout the large chamber.

"Tell you what, Clayton. I will describe your worst-case scenario. Follow me."

The guards shoved Desiree and Clayton forward as Maryl spoke. "As you already know, the aquarium encompasses most of the layout down here. With our hyper-hearing, you were able to tell what I am keeping housed inside the glass."

"Yes, we know. There are a lot of mosquitos and animals. The animals are caged too so that the mosquitos can suck their blood," Desiree said in terror.

"Yes, millions upon millions of them. And the great thing about these mosquitos? They trudged through all the different powders too!"

The horror came to light. Clayton struggled to break free but was beaten back.

Maryl looked at him without concern. "Let's talk about some interesting facts about mosquitos, shall we?"

Desiree tried to break free, but she was hit in the back of her head and fell down. Clayton rushed to her and helped her stand up.

"Look at the two lovebirds. And to think I trusted you, Desiree." She shook her head and shrugged her shoulders. "Where were we? Oh yes! Mosquitos!"

Maryl walked to the glass and looked inside. "Did you know only the female mosquitos bite you? (9) They need blood for protein for nourishment, just like us."

"Fascinating," Clayton said with sarcasm.

Maryl tapped the glass before turning around and resuming. "Mosquitos are vectors, or carriers, of diseases. They are responsible for killing nearly a million humans a year."

"Yes, they are deadly to humans, what of it? They have been around millions of years. They're not going away anytime soon, Maryl," Clayton said as he gazed at the thick glass.

Maryl grinned. "I know, but why not use what nature provided?" She paused to collect her thoughts. "Another fact is they're attracted to sweat and Co_2, but because of our thicker skin, we don't sweat; the moisture gets reabsorbed. But our carbon dioxide? It seems they're not attracted to vampires."

"Any more riveting facts?" Clayton inquired.

"Yes! Mosquitos can drink three times their weight in blood, a feat that impressed even me. Unfortunately, they don't live long—only about three months. I simply do not want to devote the time to try to enhance their lifespan through genetic manipulation."

"That surprises me since the time it took you to develop your different powders and watches," Clayton remarked.

"Yes, I do have the time, but I am also trying to find a way for my O type families to age slower than your types."

"You seemed to have stopped your aging process," Desiree noted.

"Yes, to a point. I will show you what I mean later. But I digress! Any questions before I resume?"

"Yes. What is your aim in arming the mosquitos with your agent of death? The total annihilation of our species?" Clayton asked.

Maryl gave a warm, disarming smile. "Ah, there lies my dilemma!"

"How so?" asked Desiree.

"Because, as my research grew, I learned mosquitos are mostly attracted to O type blood, and then they like A types next. (10)" Maryl shrugged. "I can't have the mosquitos affecting humans with my blood type! Heavens, no! That would defeat the whole purpose."

Clayton realized Maryl's predicament. "Then your experiment failed because the mosquitos are primarily attracted to your O types, and the serum, which would make every human an O type, would make the mosquitos go after everyone!"

"Precisely. However, it's not a total failure, just a setback. I'll have to keep my insects on the back burner for now."

Maryl resumed walking with Clayton and Desiree being forced to move forward.

"You're insane, Maryl! Why go through all this trouble?" Clayton fumed.

Maryl suddenly stopped and zipped to Clayton. "Why?" She smacked Clayton across the face again. "Because of you!" She raised her arms in disgust. "You and your high almighty A and B blood types and your superiority complex!"

"Just because we're stronger than the O's doesn't mean I think we're superior!"

"That's where you're wrong, Clayton! I can provide example after example where you exercised your might in the name of self-defense!"

"And I can say the same about you too! O negatives and O positives comprise almost *half* the population of the eight blood types! You simply outnumber us in proportion."

"Semantics," Maryl said as she continued walking.

"I know it's all about the interpretation, that's my point, Maryl," Clayton said with mounting irritation.

"Enough talk! I want to show you and Desiree something which will make you quiver in fear and realize my O negatives will become the dominant species of vampires!"

Maryl and her ensemble came to a door on their left and opened it. The room was enormous, Clayton thought as he entered.

"I can see by the expression on your face you were not expecting what you see displayed on the tables," Maryl said with delight.

"Are these… weapons, Maryl?" Clayton asked in shock.

"Yes," Maryl said as she approached the nearest table.

Clayton quickly counted fifty feet long rectangular tables. On each table, there were weapons of all kinds. Some were simple, like a crossbow with arrows and guns. Others were more complicated. Then he looked at several towering canisters in the back.

"This is where you make the powder?" Clayton asked dumbfounded.

"Yes, the large containers in the back are where the powders are mixed with my secret ingredients, and then stored in the area to your right."

Clayton and Desiree turned to their right and saw over a half dozen different color pouches on pallets.

Clayton veered from the pallets and looked at Maryl. "And what are your secret ingredients? Why don't you tell us since I know you're planning on killing Desiree and me?"

Maryl tapped her finger on her lips for a few seconds. "Why not? Come with me. There's an anteroom beyond the huge cylinders that feed into it."

She led them to a wall behind the canisters.

"I don't see a door handle, Maryl," Clayton said with amusement.

"You don't need a door handle to have a door, Clayton," Maryl said as she pushed on the wall. An opening emerged.

When the group entered the door that led to a vast warehouse, all noise the employees made stopped several seconds before resuming.

"We'll stop right here," Maryl said with a slight hint of nervousness.

Desiree noticed a red tape going horizontal. "Why? Does it have to do with the red tape?" she asked.

"Yes. We don't go any further than right here. This area behind the red tape is the safety zone."

Clayton noticed there were over a hundred humans working at different sections. They were not wearing any protective gear. Some gulped for breath as they labored without complaint. Still, others had blood dripping down their bodies, but it was hard to tell where the blood had come from because a lot of it was caked on them.

Clayton couldn't do anything to save the humans. He couldn't even save himself or Desiree. He addressed Desiree's question. "The red tape is there because Desiree, Maryl is using humans to make the powders." He looked at Maryl. "I presume the pitiful humans here are of the Fellowship Of The Fangs?"

Maryl nodded, and Clayton continued. "Vampires can't get close, or they will start displaying symptoms," Clayton said with a tight frown. He looked around in puzzlement. "Maryl, I can understand why *I* can't go any further because of my blood type, but what about you, Desiree, and your security guards that are O negative? The powders shouldn't affect you, and there shouldn't be a safety zone that you seem to adhere to so strictly."

Maryl was quiet for a second. "Let's just say I have had to take certain precautions in case of an uprising within my ranks."

The implications were staggering. "*You… you are making powder for O negatives too?*" Clayton asked in genuine shock.

"Don't act surprised, Clayton. With significant responsibilities comes enormous sacrifices."

"You keep this up, Maryl, and you'll be the only vampire left on this planet," Desiree said in disgust.

"I don't expect you or Clayton to understand because you're not forward thinkers! Come, let's go," Maryl said as she reached for the wall.

"I thought you were going to tell me the secret ingredients?" Clayton said as he placed his hand on Maryl's shoulder.

The guards tackled Clayton to the ground. Clayton put up his hands in surrender. "For three hundred years, this location and your ingredients have been a closely guarded secret. I simply must know," Clayton said as he was dragged back on his feet.

"Fine!" She shouted. Maryl walked to the red line. "Do you see the conveyor belts that are transporting the clear boxes of gray powder?"

"Yes," Clayton said.

"That is the original powder."

"What is it a mixture of?" Clayton asked in bewilderment. To think that was the powder that killed his family three centuries ago, Clayton thought in anger.

"I had tried many different compounds for two hundred years before I perfected it and used it at the purge of 1751. But in the beginning, nothing could penetrate the invulnerable skin of all eight blood types. Then there were some major battles between my blood type and all the other types, except for Ray Greenwell and his O positives, who would often aid my side."

"Until you killed him too," Clayton remarked.

"Yes, a shame really because he was a great ally to have, but alas, he was power-hungry too." She thought a moment before continuing. "As a result of the conflicts, there were many dead vampires. As a sign of good faith, I told the other leaders of the blood types I would honor their warriors with ceremonial burials because I was chiefly responsible for starting the clashes."

"I remember. It was, at the time, a kind gesture. I take it you didn't?" Clayton asked.

"Hell no! After the last battle, I had a revelation! Here laid thousands and thousands of dead vampires, and the only thing that could kill a vampire of *any* blood type was another vampire."

Desiree looked at Maryl in confusion. "We all get that. So?"

"I buried all of the O negatives and O positives in a mass grave not far from here. As for the rest of your A's and B's? I took them down here, which was just a vast underground cave at the time. And crudely at first, had my type vampires help me with what would change vampire history."

Clayton gasped when he looked at the machine, and the consequences sunk in. "Noooo…"

"What is it, Clayton?" Desiree asked him with uneasiness.

Maryl looked at Clayton with a twisted smile. "Tell her."

Clayton staggered to the ground and pounded his fists against the concrete floor. Impressions of his knuckles were clearly visible. He looked up at Maryl with tears in his eyes. "Maryl… how could you do something so monstrous?"

Desiree grabbed him and hoisted him upright. She took Clayton by the shirt collar and forced him inches from her face. "Tell me what the hell is going on!"

"Look at the gray powder coming *out* of the machine," he said sadly.

Desiree looked. "I see it. So what?"

"Take… take a good look at what's going *inside* the cylinder!"

Desiree focused her uncanny vision across the expanse of the immense room. It was hard to see through the haze of the different colors when the powder was poured into the clear tubes and put on the conveyor belts. When she finally saw it, she stared at Maryl in shock. "Oh my god…"

Maryl looked at her nails. "I found the idea brilliant. The first part of the process is to take the skeletons of Clayton's different blood types and crush them into a fine powder, which that grinder does all too well." She allowed a moment of silence to let it sink in. "Now, since the bones are from your colleagues, they will easily be able to penetrate several of the orifices of your body. The nose, mouth, ears, and eyes are just a few places where the gray powder can enter."

"Clayton, I swear I never knew how the powder was able to bypass the vampire's impenetrable skin," Desiree said with profound sadness.

Maryl smiled amid the two grieving vampires. "Oh, it gets better!"

"What do you mean it gets better, Maryl?" Clayton said as his anger built.

"Well, think about it, Clayton. If it were just vampire powder, it wouldn't do anything to you if you inhaled it. No, I had to come up with a compound to blend it with. I must admit that was something I played with for quite some time."

"And what did you blend the powder with, Maryl?" Clayton asked.

"That's only part of the question you should be asking, Clayton," Desiree said.

"What's the other part?" Clayton said in confusion.

She looked down at the concrete floor before looking back at him. Sadness consumed her face. "If she took a lot of time to perfect the gray powder, how many vampires did she subject them too before she perfected it?"

"Desiree did bring up a good point, Clayton. I would have to say within the two hundred years, plus or minus a decade, we're talking in the thousands. But don't worry, their bones were recycled to make more powder."

Clayton had to put that disturbing thought aside; otherwise, he would try to kill Maryl. With so many guards protecting her, that was out of the question for now.

"What was the final compound?"

"Inorganic arsenic powder," Maryl said proudly.

"What's the difference between inorganic and organic arsenic?" (11) Clayton asked.

Maryl sighed. "Do I have to explain everything to you?"

"Yes, humor me," Clayton advised.

"Very well. Organic arsenic is usually found in low concentrations in foods like fish, shellfish, potatoes, and rice. Inorganic arsenic is from the soil, sediment, and contaminated water. Inorganic arsenic is highly toxic. In high doses, it can cause red blood cells to burst."

"Ah, so that's why we bleed from our orifices," Clayton said with sorrow as he remembered how his family suffered.

"And you mix this with the powder?" Clayton asked.

"Yes. We grind them together."

"Why the different colors of powders?" Desiree asked.

"Because each color powder represents a different blood type of a vampire that was killed and crushed."

"So, the gray powder has all the bones of every blood type vampire bones that were pulverized except yours and Ray's? And the other colors of powder are of only a single blood type, so it would only affect their blood?"

Maryl slapped Clayton on the back. "Now you're getting it." Maryl nodded to the guards, and they were pushed back out in the large warehouse. "Now, let's go back to the room where we came from, shall we?"

When they came to the area, Desiree looked at the table closest to them that had different types of guns. "Guns can't hurt us, Maryl."

Maryl grinned. "These can," she said as she took one of the guns off the table and aimed it at Clayton.

Clayton put his hands up in surrender. "Whoa, don't do anything stupid, Maryl!"

Maryl fired, and the bullet hit Clayton in his left shoulder. Searing pain rocketed Clayton as he fell to the ground holding his shoulder. Blood came through his clenched hand that held his shoulder.

Through wretched pain, Clayton asked, "How is a bullet able to hurt me?"

"Get him up," Maryl said forcibly.

Her troops forced Clayton upright as Maryl walked to him.

"This gun is for close-quarter combat. The bullets are made from the bones of vampires I've killed too. The vampire's bones are crushed, compressed, and molded for maximum efficiency. Don't worry, Clayton. This particular gun doesn't contain any inorganic arsenic. We have those at a different table."

"I... imagine the arrows are made from the bones of our ...comrades too?" Clayton asked in searing pain.

"Yes," she said as she waved her arm all around the room. "Everything in this room is made to incapacitate or kill vampires."

"How *human* of you," Desiree sneered.

Maryl chuckled. "Humans don't have the ingenuity for such devices because most of them don't know we even exist. Oh, there are small bands of humans besides the Fellowship of the Fangs that know of our existence. But the Fellowship ensures our survival because they serve my needs around the globe. And they are food for us too." She waved her hand in dismissal. "We give them vague and shallow promises of vampire-hood by adding more and more small red droplets of tattoos. Plus, as a bonus when they combat humans who hunt vampires, we promise them we will convert them to vampire hood, which was the primary reason I created the group in 1912 at Stanford after the lecture. Remember that, Clayton?"

"Yes… I left because I thought you were going to take care of Stanley Pearson and his assistant."

"Do the human hunters know of our weakness?" Desiree asked.

"Yes. The hunters were formed after disagreements within the ranks of the Fellowship of the Fangs."

Desiree now understood something she didn't earlier. "So, the humans at the campsite? They were hunters?"

"Exactly! Humans being humans… word spread. When the human being found out they had to have O negative blood to become a member of the Fellowship of the Fangs, dissension grew. How they knew of my cave is still a mystery to me."

Desiree looked at Clayton, who was slowly wobbling from side to side. "Can you do something for Clayton? He doesn't look good!" She asked in desperation.

"Your affinity for him disgusts me!" Maryl scolded.

"And your lack of compassion sickens me more!" Desiree yelled back.

Maryl snapped her fingers. "Draven, attend to Clayton!"

"Why? He's the leader of AB positive, the enemy!"

"Do not question me! I can't have him die before I show him the last piece of the puzzle!"

Draven zipped away and came back seconds later. "Hold him down while I take out the bullet. He'll recover quickly after the projectile is removed," Draven said to two nearby guards.

Once the bullet was taken out, Clayton felt better.

"What is the last piece of the mystery, Maryl?" Desiree asked, frightened.

Maryl waved them forward. "Come this way. It's through this room at the door at the end."

The group walked in silence as they passed table after table. When they got to the door, Maryl stopped, turned, and faced everyone.

"Brace yourself."

Maryl opened the double-wide door and flew it open.

Clayton and Desiree entered, and what they saw made them stop dead in their tracks.

Chapter Twenty-Two
Behold, The Stranger!

Clayton studied the tall female Stranger in the thick glass enclosure. Her reddish-brown matted and tangled hair almost entirely covered her warm, radiant face. Her big, round brown eyes were set low within their sockets, observing with those outside the cage. It seemed as though a sword had left a mark reaching from the top of her left cheek, first running toward her thick lips and ending on her forehead.

Clayton could hear the heavy humming of electricity emanating from the pen.

"What the hell?" whispered Clayton.

"My ultimate weapon, our *creator*." Maryl murmured back.

Clayton looked to the Stranger and then to Maryl. "How did you manage to capture her, and when?"

"The Stranger's emergence every hundred years was the key."

Clayton looked at Maryl in confusion. "How?"

"In 1920, when the Stranger was due to appear on May the fourth at seven-thirty three in the morning, I had the O positive, and the O negative scientists put out instruments over the globe the day before that could detect any strange energy signatures. While they are rudimentary by today's technological standards, they were sophisticated back then. They discovered an enormous energy field fifteen seconds before the Stranger appeared. It was as if she was using a vast amount of energy that took time before she could appear on earth. With each successive decade, we were able to make the instruments more precise in detecting *any* kind of energy discharge. We even anomalously gave human scientists warning about earthquakes before their arrival."

"You're helping out humans?" Desiree scoffed.

Maryl shrugged. "We need their nourishment. I had to protect my food source."

"How many minutes were you able to detect the Stranger's location before she appeared this year?" Clayton asked.

"The location of the Stranger's appearance was almost as important as when she would arrive. We detected the energy field a full three minutes with our newest advances in technology. Not only did we know when and where she would show up, but we carefully studied the readings for a century and determined the source of her energy. We couldn't duplicate it here, but we knew how to negate her energy once she arrived."

"And you had the cage ready for her when she emerged?" Clayton asked as he felt his left shoulder. The pain was almost gone, but he would need blood soon.

"Not only did we have it ready, we knew the exact location, so when she arrived, she *appeared* in the cage!"

"And brought her here? Interesting. Have you interrogated her yet?" Clayton asked as he continued to look at the cage.

"Yes, tortured too. She has given up nothing."

"Did you ask her why she comes back every hundred years?" Clayton wondered.

"No, I did not."

"Why not? Don't you want to know her purpose? Our purpose?"

"I care not how or why we were made, only that I must have her power for the O negatives to thrive!"

"That's a little self-centered, Maryl."

"I don't care for your tone, Clayton. Remember with whom you are speaking with!"

Clayton changed the subject. "How did you come about all the technology when the other seven blood types did not?"

"Because of my need to prosper and flourish because we are low on the totem pole of vampire power."

"That's not true," Clayton said with disdain.

"Oh, no?" Maryl's eyes blazed. "What would you have me do when seven of the eight types of vampires can thrive, consuming blood outside of their own? I relied on my intellect to even the playing field!"

"I know your ultimate goal is still to make humanity all O negative blood types, so you'll never run out of nourishment!" Clayton said coldly.

"Yes, hence the serum. That should've been obvious from the beginning, Clayton."

"But Maryl, there are over seven billion humans. At the rate of their reproducing ability, you would never have to worry about a lack of nourishing yourself and the others. There must be something deeper going on here."

Maryl's eyes glazed over. "There is, but that's none of your business."

"Why isn't it my business? Seven billion people is a lot of food."

"I have my reasons, Clayton. Leave it at that!"

He looked at Maryl Rosser. He knew he didn't want to push her. "Fine."

"There is something I want to share with you both before you die. You see, I have this duality about me…"

"Being around her, I can attest to that," Desiree stated.

Maryl ignored her outburst. "My duality is, in part, due to my vampirism. But my well-kept secret is… before my grandmother was bitten by the Stranger a couple of thousand years ago, my family were potent witches."

Clayton was stunned. "That is not possible! Witches were exterminated a thousand years ago. No lineage continued."

"It's the truth, Clayton. Witch blood and vampire blood course through me. I am a hybrid."

Clayton shook his head in disbelief. "My father led the witch hunt, which eliminated all of them. He told me he had removed all of the witches a few months before the Great Yeomen Purge of 1751."

Maryl chuckled. "You think the Purge was because of *land*? No, it was because I had King George the second under my spell to remove your farms, although it always amused me you thought the Purge was about taking your properties." She scoffed. "I didn't care one way or another."

"Then why kill most of my family?"

"Because your family killed mine! The Yeomen Purge was a disguise in retaliation from your blood types murdering my family of witches! I am the only living witch left, and thanks to the addition of being a vampire, I not only live longer and am stronger, but I still can practice witchcraft," Maryl yelled. "And because of my vampire blood, my children never received the witch gene. It's only me that's left!" she said with profound sadness.

"And the technology to make the watches that can discern your blood type?"

"That was good old fashion science," Maryl said dismissively.

Clayton glared at Maryl. "And now would be the time to kill Desiree and me because we know your secret?"

"Also, yes."

The Stranger smirked as she sat down and leaned her head against the glass wall.

Maryl walked within several yards of the cage. "And you find all of this funny? Do you want to get tortured in front of my subjects?"

"No, I sneered because all of you are missing the point here."

"What's the point?" Maryl asked.

"You see, but you are blind."

"I hate riddles. Maybe I should kill her now?" Maryl suggested as she looked at Clayton and Desiree.

"No, wait!" Clayton begged. "There are so many questions!"

Desiree walked to the cage. "What is your name, Stranger?"

"I am Esme."

"No last name or your role?"

Esme looked down at the cage floor. "My role? My role was once clear as day. Nowadays, being withered with age and decay makes my role obsolete."

"Was this hundredth year to be your last visit?" Clayton asked with sorrow.

"Yes, because of my advanced age," Esme said with her eyes closed.

Clayton looked at her in amazement. "Esme, you don't look over forty, forty-five years old tops. How are you withered with age and decay?"

"My appearance belies my age. I am two thousand years old and quite old for my race. I am dying, and with my death will come great suffering."

"Suffering? Of what kind?" Desiree asked in fear.

"Do not worry, my child; you will find out soon enough," Esme said nonchalantly.

"I am worried," Desiree said as she looked up at everyone.

"You're worried about an old woman who claims that pain and agony will happen when she dies? Really, Desiree! She should be the one that's worried about what I'm going to do to her!" Maryl remarked as she looked at Esme in contempt.

Clayton ignored the verbal exchange. "What is your heritage? Where do you hail from?" Clayton remarked with interest.

Maryl came upon Clayton. "I don't care about who she is and where she came from. It's time for you and Desiree to die." Maryl turned to Desiree. "And you will not survive this time!"

Clayton was riveted with the woman and her plight. "Maryl, if you take us now, you'll have the fight of your life on your hands. However, if you allow us to hear Esme's story, I will go willingly to my death. I so swear it."

Desiree smirked. "Clayton, look around you. I have more vampires, I have the guns with the boned bullets, and the powder within reach of me. And I recently learned that you are now aware of my financial secret by extracting money from all of your blood types so I can continue my science projects." She looked at Clayton with contempt. "You're in no position to make demands."

"Then, I implore you, Maryl. I beg you to let me listen to Esme's story. Please"

Maryl threw her arms up in the air. "Why are you so captivated? It will be just a story. You won't know if it's a lie or the truth."

"I sense her story will be lost if it is not told to our ears. Esme has been around a thousand more years than we have. Think of the stories she could tell us."

"Or stories she could weave like a spider's web," Maryl said in disgust.

"Why is her presence such an annoyance to you, Maryl?" Desiree asked.

"I have held Esme captive a hundred years, and in all those years, I have yet to extract the source of her power. It's maddening!"

"Maybe she doesn't have any power left? Or maybe she never had any?" Desiree asked out loud.

"That's preposterous! She made us!" Maryl bellowed.

"And kept making us century after century after century," Clayton reasoned. "And that's why she can't escape the cage. Or perhaps she doesn't want to. Maybe the power it took to get to earth, coupled with creating us, used all of her energy?"

Maryl looked to the ceiling while licking her lips. Her hands were on her hips. She looked back down and glared at Clayton. "Fine, Clayton. Extract information from her. Then you and Desiree will perish by my hands."

Clayton pointed to Esme. "And what of her?"

Maryl looked at Esme. "She's useless to me if she is devoid of energy. I will get rid of her too."

Clayton sat down and leaned against the outer wall of the glass cage. "Who are you?" he whispered.

"I am Esme."

"I know that. But who are you? Where do you come from? Why did you make us into vampires?"

Esme was quiet for a second. "Tell me, Clayton. Are you religious?"

"Yes and no," Clayton said carefully. "I tend to shy away from that topic."

Esme nodded slowly. Her eyes were still closed. "Have you ever heard of the Nephilim's?"

Clayton rummaged through his mind, trying to recall the term. "Yes, I have."

"Well, I haven't. So, tell me," Desiree said as she sat beside Clayton.

Their knees touched, and a small electrical current passed through them. Their eyes met, but neither one mentioned it.

"The Nephilim's were, depending upon your theological slant, a byproduct or a hybrid of an angel and a human woman. They were known as giants or titans. What about it? You're tall, but you're not as tall as a giant. And with their legendary strength, this cage wouldn't hold them," Clayton said with conviction.

"Which means you're not a Nephilim. Then why bring them up?" Desiree inquired.

Esme smiled. She opened her eyes, looked around her surroundings, and closed her eyes again. She sighed heavily. "You are correct. I am not a Nephilim. I am one of *their* offspring. The last survivor."

Clayton was confused. "Wait, did you say you were the *child* of a Nephilim?"

Esme opened her eyes and stared at Clayton. "Yes, that is what I'm telling you."

Maryl rolled her eyes. "Are you going to believe the nonsense that spews from her lips?"

Clayton looked up at Maryl. "Believe it? I don't know yet. I will tell you that I am intrigued."

"They spawned a new race?" Desiree asked incredulously.

"Yes," Esme said in a neutral tone.

Maryl grinned in disbelief. "Oh? And what were you referred to as?"

"We were called the Elioud." **

There was a moment of stunned silence. Each vampire looked at each other in awe and with some measure of trepidation.

"They are briefly mentioned in different religious affiliations, Esme," Clayton remarked. "But, you're all but forgotten in the human world, I'm afraid."

"I am aware of what happens when time passes and the disappearance of memories in human history."

"How did you manage to live as long as you have? I thought you had a lifespan of a thousand years. You're double that," Clayton said as he peered at the inert form.

"I lived longer than the rest of the Nephilims and the Eliouds because my hatred kept me going until time has eroded my soul."

"Hatred? Esme, what's your story?" Desiree said as she grew more concerned.

Esme put her head down between her arms for a few seconds. Her head suddenly came up with tears streaming down her face.

"I was the last born of my kind in my tiny village in Canaan, or what is now called Israel. We lived in the antediluvian (12) period."

"Excuse my historical ignorance, but what was the Antediluvian period?" Desiree asked shyly.

Esme wiped away her tears as she smiled and reminisced. "It was between the collapse of humanity and the great flood that lasted for forty days."

"I thought, and excuse my unfamiliarity with ancient culture, but didn't every last thing perish except what was on the ark?"

"Then, you would be incorrect. The fact that I am here disproves your assumption."

"Okay, say that we believe you and you survived the global catastrophe, what does that have to do with anything that led you to create us?" Clayton asked in exasperation.

Esme shook her head. "Your reasoning is one of misplaced impracticality and twisted idealism. You think the creation of vampires was the sole reason for my existence?" She slammed her fist against the inner wall. "Ignorant!"

"Umm, yes?" Desiree said. "Other than the oral history that has passed down, what other reference do we have?"

"I am an Elioud! I was able-bodied, abound with goodness, and unmatched energy, and that was my downfall. My father, the great Surot, was a Nephilim who was known as the greatest warrior in all the lands! He sought to teach me the ways of the soldier." Esme rocked her head back and forth as the tears streamed down again. "But time after time, being shown the ways of combat, I could not even grasp the simplest concepts."

"I bet that was frustrating," Clayton said.

"Frustrating? Frustrating for *whom*? Me, who could not follow in her father's footsteps? Who was a disgrace to the family? Whose father showed open contempt toward me? Or was it frustrating for my father, who sired a daughter that could not match his ferocity or his unparalleled skill set? Whose neighbors openly scoffed at us when I had to walk several feet behind him at the marketplace because I embarrassed him? *Define* frustrating!"

"Yes, Clayton, not everyone like you can eclipse their father," Maryl said sarcastically.

"So, your father was discouraged with your lack of prowess? So what? There should have been other things to compensate," Desiree said with sincerity.

Esme wiped off tears with the back of her hand. She took a deep breath and blew it out. "Do you know what happens to the Elioud, who doesn't have what it takes to become a warrior?"

"I can't even imagine," Clayton said with renewed respect.

A single tear escaped and slowly dripped down her wet face. "Before you get exiled, something far, far worse happens for my kind!" Esme smiled briefly and exhaled. "Even after a thousand years of training, in my last sparring session, I had made a futile attempt to avert my father's spear; it spliced my side. He got so angry that I wasn't able to deflect a simple swipe, he told me he was done training me for good."

"That was a good thing, right?" asked Desiree.

Esme looked down at the floor. "Far from it. The next morning, my father took me by the back of my hair from the kitchen table and forced me outside. During the night, he had made a large wooden table. He forced me on all fours with my back facing him. He pushed me onto the table and was careful to rip only the back of my nightgown off. My father took his spear and completely sheared my wings off. Then he took a heated iron and put them on my back, so I would never be able to have them again." She looked at the ceiling. "Ah, to fly again and see the wondrous landscapes of earth and other dimensional places." Esme's eyes dulled with sadness. She wiped her face again.

"You had wings?" Maryl asked in shock.

"Yes, and the process of having them removed was excruciatingly painful, but my father did not care. My Nephilim mother stopped caring for me after that. And that incident led to the creation of vampires."

"I see absolutely no connection between the shearing of your wings and the inception of my species," Clayton said in disbelief.

"My wings were taken away because of my lack of fighting ability and the good deeds I did for humans that upset both parents."

"We surmised as much, come to the point," Maryl said with impatience.

"I'm sorry, but I am purposely trying to delay the ending of my story."

"Why?" asked Clayton.

"Because I am dying and trying to hold on."

"Please try to continue, Esme!" begged Clayton.

Esme tried to gather her thoughts. "With my wings gone, for whatever reason, I fundamentally changed. The inner wickedness and warrior instinct my father could not produce within me in combat came out in other ways. From the point of my wing's being hacked off, I was exiled from my family and stole food from the marketplace. Instead of seeking forgiveness, I rebelled and sought out how to get back at my father when, through my travels, I came upon a village in southern England. By coincidence, I came upon your family, Maryl Rosser. I had heard rumors, whispers of an extremely powerful witch family that, for the right price, would provide any potion I needed."

"Wait, you visited my family first, yet you bit Clayton's family before mine?"

"Yes. I spoke with your great grandmother, who, at that time, was the supreme witch of that region. She sensed my inner agony and knew who I truly was. She bestowed upon me a spell that would bind and attach to me forever that enabled me to alter humans. The drawback to the potent enchantment was I could only infect eight people at one time and only once every hundred years. If I did it less than one hundred years, the binding spell would cease."

"Why did you pick Clayton's family? And why did you come back and bite mine?" Maryl said as she slapped the side of the cage.

"Your great grandmother's asking price was to avoid biting her family. And at first, I honored her request. That night I headed further south and found Clayton's grandfather and bit his pregnant wife."

"Then, why did you come back to my descendants?" Maryl asked in confusion.

"Because the more I thought about it, the more I realized your great grandmother was the only being on the planet that would be able to reverse the binding spell. I was too angry at my father and sought retribution, that the thought of your great-grandmother ruining my plan was unbearable. So, at first light the morning after biting Clayton's expectant grandmother, I snuck around your great grandmother's house when she was tending to her garden and getting herbs. I attacked her and slit her throat. Then I snuck in and bit your expectant grandma. The rest, you know."

"That's not possible," Maryl said.

"Why not?" asked Clayton.

"My great grandmother would've sensed you. Not to mention she would have protective spells so you could not enter her abode!"

"I understand your lack of faith in what I am telling you, Maryl Rosser, but believe me; I am telling you the truth."

"How were you able to get to my great grandmother?" Maryl demanded.

Esme closed her eyes. Blood trickled from her nose. "Because. Because the spell was so incredibly powerful, it left her drained of her lifeforce, her energy. She had not the power or energy to put up any protective wards, and I knew that."

Silence followed while the information sunk in.

"What did you do while waiting for the next hundred years?" Desiree asked.

"I was observing all of you through dimensional portals I had access to via my binding spell."

Desiree raised her hand. "How come you picked May fourth at seven thirty-three in the morning to come back every hundred years? That's a precise date."

"That was when the spell was cast, and I was attached or bound to it. It was my new birthdate."

"Why did you want to infect humans and turn them into vampires in the first place?"

"Because of my father! I wanted a species that would be as strong or stronger than the Nephilims and the Eliouds."

"Again, why?" Clayton asked.

"To kill both species and get even with my father. I hated him! And to have someone else be the alpha and omega race for once!"

"How did you know to bite the humans?" asked Desiree.

"In order to alter something, it must reside from within the body. I needed a way inward to change eight women. I asked the spell to be puncture wounds into the neck where the blood flowed the fastest."

"Why pregnant women?" Desiree asked in bafflement.

"Because your great grandmother told me the spell was so strong the initial alteration needed brewing time to change the human, roughly five to six months. Why not infect pregnant women? It was the perfect opportunity. What're a thousand years compared to nine months?" Esme finally noticed the blood dripping from her nose. After several futile attempts at stopping it, she let it slowly trickle down. She looked up at everyone. "Once the child was born, he or she was able to reproduce when old enough, have invulnerable skin, and all the other attributes that were needed to defeat my father and his ilk!"

"Except for the A's and B's, who needed thirteen years," Clayton offered.

"Yes, that came as a surprise. I wasn't certain of the effects the enchantment would have on anyone."

"Okay, what about the eight different blood types of vampires you created?"

Esme took a minute to catch her breath. She knew she wouldn't last much longer. "I thought if I created just one blood type vampire, I wouldn't be able to see much evolution or variation."

"You wanted a difference? Why?" asked Desiree.

Esme smiled with sadness. "You were my creation, my experiment. I wanted to see how far I could take it. And believe me, you took it to an extreme! All the different blood types far exceeded my expectations. You utterly defeated the Nephilims and the Eliouds, which thrilled me to no end."

"We didn't, but the vampires you created, later on, battled them with help from an unknown source. Even today, no one knows who helped us. That part is not in the history books of our species," Clayton said grudgingly.

"Why did you continue creating us, when your goal was to get rid of your father and the rest of his clan was completed?" Maryl asked in bewilderment.

Esme coughed, and the blood dripped from her nose at a faster pace. She absently wiped her nose with her hand and continued. "Because the division among the eight leaders, who forced their subordinates to their way of thinking, was astounding to watch! And another benefit to watch was how some vampires became stronger right away, and some couldn't ascend until puberty, which surprised even me! Still, others leveled the playing field with science, and others remained unchanged."

Silence followed. Everyone was lost in their thoughts.

Clayton thought of something. "So… if you only bit a pregnant woman every hundred years, you only produced one child of each blood type. And my bloodline had difficulty producing children. I would imagine you needed an army to defeat your father and his trained warriors pretty fast."

Esme was barely able to mutter, "You assume I only created vampires? You assume in my last thousand years I only went to one witch?"

"What? What do you mean by that?" Clayton demanded as he looked at Esme.

He noticed Esme was slumped to one side. Her hands were limp. He could hear her shallow breath. "Esme! Answer my question!" demanded Clayton.

It wouldn't be long until she was gone, and Clayton's answer would be forever lost!

Desiree noticed Esme slumped too as she stood up. "Esme! Are you all alright? Is there anything we can do for you?"

Esme coughed a few times. She did not have the energy to move. In a herculean effort, she managed to speak. "Know this, my time has come, and that means…," Esme couldn't finish her sentence. Gradually resolve came upon her face. "And with my death comes great suffering…"

"Yes, yes, you told us that already," Maryl said with irritation.

"Esme, what did you mean by your statement? Tell me!"

Esme smiled but did not answer him.

"What do you mean, Esme?" Clayton demanded. He refused to stop asking the question.

Esme coughed up more blood. Sweat dripped from her forehead down into her blouse. "I.. I must tell you something before I perish."

"How about the truth?" Clayton said.

"Enough, Clayton! She's not going to tell us. Let her finish what she has to say!" Desiree said in frustration.

Esme coughed several times. With each cough, blood gushed out from her nose and mouth. "With my dying breath, I must… tell you something. I… I made you with a binding spell. When I die, so does … the spell," she said weakly.

"What do you mean?" Desiree said in shock.

"The… spell was bound… attached *to me*. When I die… the spell dies too. That was part of the deal set forth two thousand years ago…"

"Will all of the vampires around the globe become human again?" Maryl asked in terror.

"Will we all die?" Desiree asked with dread.

"Yes," Esme whispered as she fell to the floor.

The first sign Clayton had turned human was the vampires that were the furthest away became blurry to him. Then the talking started, but it was difficult to hear what anyone was saying. It had been over a thousand years since he was human. He'd forgotten the frailties and shortcomings of being mortal.

A few seconds later, Maryl yelled, "What's happening to me?" She looked at her disappearing form and let out a blood-curdling scream.

Clayton saw that he was dematerializing too. He looked around the room. They were all slowly fading away.

Desiree looked at Clayton in utter terror as her lower body slowly vanished in front of their eyes.

Clayton looked at his fading form.

"Clayton! Help me! Do something!" she cried.

"Stay calm, Desiree. Stay calm," he said to try to reassure her that their end would be painless.

"I'm too young of a vampire to die! I have much more I want to accomplish!" Desiree said through tears.

Little by little, their forms became less and less visible.

"Goodbye, Desiree…" Clayton said with profound sadness.

"Goodbye, Clayton."

"I. I loved you."

"I know. I…"

Bibliography

*This part is only partially correct. You *can* extract stem cells from blood using a *peripheral blood stem cell collection technique*. The article below elaborates:

http://leukemiabmtprogram.org/patients_and_family/treatment/blood_and_marrow_transplant/transplant_basics/how_are_stem_cells_collected.html

** The Elioud were the children of the Nephilim. There are several references in various theological faiths. However, I have given them a creative license, and in my book, they in no way reflect what little was written about them. If you're interested, you can read this article:

http://www.fallenangels-ckquarterman.com/the-elioud-race/

(1) Blood Type Genetics and Compatibility. (No referenced date) retrieved from:

https://www.bswhealth.com/patient-tools/blood-center/Pages/blood-type-genetics-and-compatibility.aspx

(2) Blood-Type-Altering Enzyme Could Make Anyone a Universal Donor. (2015) retrieved from:

https://www.genengnews.com/news/blood-type-altering-enzyme-could-make-anyone-a-universal-donor/

(3) CT State Library. The 1752 calendar change. (No referenced date) Retrieved from:

https://libguides.ctstatelibrary.org/hg/colonialresearch/calendar#:~:text=Changes%20of%201752&text=The%20Julian%20Calendar%20was%20replaced,the%20month%20of%20September%201752.

(4) Humbug ~ Wikipedia

https://en.wikipedia.org/wiki/Humbug

(5)Vampire Myths Originated With a Real Blood Disorder. (7/5/2020) retrieved from: https://www.inverse.com/culture/vampire-myths-originated-with-a-real-blood-disorder

(6)What is used to cut DNA at a specific location for Splicing? https://sciencing.com/used-cut-dna-specific-location-splicing-2422.html

(7) While scientists have created synthetic blood, its purpose in my book differs from the article because, obviously, they're vampires. If you're interested in learning more about synthetic blood, please read the following article.

Synthetic red blood cells mimic natural ones, and have new abilities. (June 3rd, 2020) retrieved from: https://www.sciencedaily.com/releases/2020/06/200603122955.htm

(8) Essential Caving Gear and Equipment. (3/2019) retrieved from: https://www.liveabout.com/your-essential-caving-equipment-755632#:~:text=Waist%20Belt%20%2D%20Carry%20a%20small,if%20you%27re%20crawling%20around.

(9) Ten interesting facts about Mosquitos. 8/14/2017 retrieved from: https://www.westernexterminator.com/blog/10-interesting-facts-mosquitoes/

(10) Myth-busting Mosquitos. (No date referenced.) https://www.unitypoint.org/livewell/article.aspx?id=f4d37ba9-b3cb-465f-9043-

f2858cda74a7#:~:text=From%20the%20study%2C%20whe
n%20looking,the%20next%20preferred%20blood%20type.

(11)What is the difference between organic and
inorganic arsenic? (8/30/2018) retrieved from:

https://www.mcgill.ca/oss/article/health/what-difference-
between-organic-and-inorganic-arsenic

(12) Antediluvian. (No date referenced) Retrieved
from:

https://en.wikipedia.org/wiki/Antediluvian

Author's Note and disclaimer

There is a lot to know about blood. If I put all the research of the different blood types I learned into my story, it would stray from my intended storyline. Unless you are in the medical field and deal with the different blood types, getting too technical would burden the reader.

While I have checked and rechecked data and talked to people in the blood business, sometimes, I felt it prudent to alter some information and had to make things up to help the story move along. After all, it's a story about vampires too.

Certain information in the story is accurate with some alterations. At the time of this publication, scientists are working on an enzyme to shred the antigens off the top of the red blood cell, making everyone a universal donor. However, I made up the part where the enzyme changes the blood cells from A and B and AB to O type blood.

There is an assembly hall at Stanford University, but I don't know if the curtains were red. I made up the long pole to unlatch the locked windows in the scene too.

The University of Indianapolis does not possess a large medical laboratory. It seemed to fit the storyline.